THE UNIVERSE
BETWEEN US

Visit us at www.boldstrokesbooks.com

THE UNIVERSE BETWEEN US

by

Jane C. Esther

2018

THE UNIVERSE BETWEEN US

ISBN 13: 978-1-63555-106-8

This Trade Paperback Original Is Published By
Bold Strokes Books, Inc.
P.O. Box 249
Valley Falls, NY 12185

First Edition: January 2018

CREDITS
EDITOR: ASHLEY TILLMAN
PRODUCTION DESIGN: SUSAN RAMUNDO
COVER DESIGN BY TAMMY SEIDICK

Acknowledgments

I'm thrilled to be publishing my first novel with Bold Strokes Books. To the whole BSB family, you made me feel welcome immediately and have provided me with inspiration and motivation to create. Special thanks to my editor, Ash. You're really good at your job, and I appreciate that.

Thank you to many friends who have helped me write this, including Gemma for your brilliant feedback, Suzy for interrupting your tropical vacation to be a beta reader, and Zooey, for sitting with me during many long evenings of writing. Sandra, you take the best photos and are also wicked smaht. Thank you for using those two skills to my advantage.

Shout out to my sisters, who are awesome people. I'd be lonely without you. Mom and Dad, thanks for raising me to know that I can do anything I put my mind to, like write a book. Finally, to my wife, Gabi, you're the best brainstormer, reader, and editor that a girl can ask for. Without your encouragement and insight, I could not have written this book.

Dedication

For my two favorite people, Gabi and Zooey.

CHAPTER ONE

Jolie Dann stood in front of Singer University's digital bulletin board, Nova's chin resting on her shoulder, mesmerized by the scene unfolding before her. The din of the student union faded into the background, a steady stream of voices rising and falling over one another. Usually, Jolie would be among the students passing through the campus center, stopping to fill her mug with black coffee before heading to class, but today, she was on a mission.

She'd chosen the far right screen on the long wall labeled "Community," a place where students could find and post messages, roommate ads, and service flyers. The wall lit up with a swirling panoramic view of countryside as the drone-recorded virtual rental tour began. The camera panned around the property, pausing on an odd looking modular house attached to some kind of dome covered in solar cells, and an impressively large garden. Surrounding it was nothing but fields and trees, as far as Jolie could tell.

"Holy shit. You have got to check this place out. Looks like a crazy old inventor or something." Nova's chin dug into Jolie's shoulder with each syllable.

"It's not that bad. It looks…functional. And look, green space, and nobody around for miles." Jolie raised her eyebrows at her best friend. "And get your face off me. Your hair is tickling my cheek."

"I think you're being a little too kind. Look, there's a house that's obviously not even a quarter of a mile away," Nova exclaimed, pointing at the screen. She shook her head of curly hair against

Jolie's cheek, then moved to her side as Jolie elbowed her. "I can't believe you would rather live there than with your bestie and the girls."

"You know how that would go. Party all the time, hang out. I mean, really, when do you actually work for those grades you seem to get? And you've seen me drunk. Didn't that turn out spectacularly?"

"Oh, it was pretty spectacular," Nova said with a smirk. "The way you hit on almost everyone at that party was the highlight of my spring." She thought for a moment. "Maybe even my year. At least one person got something out of it, even if you claim you didn't."

"Whatever. I'm not living in the sorority house. I actually want some privacy and space, and you ladies have none of that. It's like a giant, continuous orgy over there." Jolie touched the screen to replay the tour.

"Please. Only, like, half the time. So dramatic. All I'm saying is that you would definitely get some, you'd be almost right on campus, and you'd get to live with your best lady." Nova hip-checked her gently. "Unless you're trying to drop me slowly. If that's the case, I can take a hint."

"Shut up, I'm trying to pay attention," Jolie said. She linked her arm in Nova's and pulled her close as they watched the remainder of the tour. A hologram of the interior walls revealed a series of small rooms along a hallway that connected to a large circular space containing the kitchen and dining areas.

"Super weird," Nova said. "Find out who listed it." She began to reach toward the screen to touch the box with further information about the owner, but Jolie batted her arm out of the way and touched the screen herself. A photograph of an attractive young woman appeared, her angular face twisted into a look of annoyance, as if she was just then figuring out that she'd need to pose for a picture. "Oh, she's cute," Nova said. "Deep brown eyes, dark brown hair, totally my type."

Jolie shot her a look. "Everyone's your type. Let's see. She's looking for someone to take care of the place because she'll be out of town a lot in the next few months, blah blah blah." Jolie skimmed. She touched the arrow to display even more information. "Rent.

Let's see. Rent. Oh, here it is. Wow, that's really cheap. It says that labor is part of the rent." She shook her head in confusion.

"What is the deal with this place?" Nova asked. "That's a billion times cheaper than anything I've seen around here. Even I'd get off my ass and do work for that price."

Jolie smiled and said, "Would you? I don't know."

Nova giggled. "I dare you to go meet this weirdo and try to be her roommate. Hopefully she doesn't murder you and chop you up and bury you somewhere in her giant field."

"Hilarious. And real nice. Now if I do get murdered, you're going to feel pretty bad for saying that." Jolie elbowed Nova in the side. "You know what? You're on. I'll accept your dare and I bet you'll eat your words."

"Okay, so do it," Nova said. "Reply right now." She thrust her chin toward the camera on the bottom of the screen.

"Not right here. I'll do it when I get back to my room, pinky swear."

"Hey, sexy ladies." Jolie and Nova both jumped at the squeaky voice behind them. "Not moving out on us, are you Nov?" Karlee, one of Nova's sorority sisters, pushed between them and put her arms over their shoulders.

"You couldn't get rid of me if you tried," Nova said. She proudly flashed her sorority ring, a band of rippled silver against her dark skin.

"And you, Jo-Jo. Are you looking? I know someone with a space in her bed just for you, in case you ever want to give that a spin again." She gave Jolie a full body once over.

Jolie rolled her eyes and extricated herself from under Karlee's arm. "I'll let you know if I'm ever that desperate," she said.

Karlee pouted, and Jolie had to admit that she wouldn't mind ending up in her bed for a second time, if she truly wanted mindless comfort. She just wished Karlee wouldn't make it so easy.

"I have to get to the studio. Got to keep that art scholarship. I'll call you later, Nova?" Jolie felt like a squeaky third wheel to their sorority bonding, and quickly moved away from the pair.

"You got it," Nova yelled. "Don't forget the dare." Jolie could hear them looking at the listing and giggling over the woman's picture.

Once she was safely outside, Jolie made her way to a bench surrounded by a mound of crisp leaves. She looked out over the quad, framed by a mixture of concrete monstrosities retrofitted with solar cells and rooftop gardens. On nice days, it seemed like half the campus took over the lawn, studying in small groups or reading alone. Jolie and Nova had made a tradition out of studying on the quad during finals, in the middle of December. It had been warm enough the last two years that they didn't even need jackets. She reached into her pocket and unfolded her screen, navigating to the listing. If nobody had snatched it up yet, she'd be able to save enough money to quit her job in the cafe and focus completely on her art. Even with the short commute, she'd save hours a week not working on someone else's schedule. She might even be able to hang out with her friends again without thinking she'd rather be in bed, catching up on much needed sleep.

Jolie set her screen to record, cleared her throat and finger-combed her long strawberry blond hair, then recorded her message. She replayed it and recorded again. Once she was satisfied with her tone and inflection, she hovered over the send button, pausing a moment to read about her potential roommate once more. Name: Ana Mitchell. Age: 26. She had a distinguished look, not exactly youthful, Jolie thought, more weathered, like she wasn't afraid of hard work. Jolie knew the type well, her father working himself into the ground every day with the farm. Ana would make an interesting subject for drawing, her sculpted shoulders hinting at an athletic body, and her expression indicating that she had something more important to do than sit for a rental drone's intrusive photo shoot.

Jolie wondered what distracted her, and it occurred to her that it might be a spammer listing. They weren't common anymore, but when virtual touring first became popular, there were some rogue drones that recorded houses unsolicited. Unsuspecting homeowners and landlords were flooded with messages, and listing companies had to scramble to clean up the mess they had created. Now, there was a law criminalizing the fraudulent listings, but they still popped up from time to time.

Jolie tilted her head back and squinted at the clear blue sky. A few drones buzzed overhead at various heights, no doubt filming or performing research for a class. She sighed. Part of her dreaded the moving process and the inevitable unease of spending so much time in a car, but the anxiety she felt since the accident that left her with a prosthetic leg was fading. Besides, her packed schedule left her exhausted, and something had to give. Money was tight, and anything she could save by living off campus at such a low price would be a help to her parents and the farm. She swallowed hard and flicked her finger to send the reply.

CHAPTER TWO

Ana Mitchell was scrubbing the dirt from her fingernails when she heard the chime over her speaker system. "Read," she said aloud.

Her personal assistant, Cassiopeia, replied in an almost-human voice, "Ana, you have one new reply to your roommate listing. It is from Jolie Dann, a student at Singer University." The voice paused.

"More."

"Here is Jolie Dann's personal information. She is majoring in studio art. She is twenty years old and was born in Lincoln, Nebraska. Mother: Iris. Father: William. Sister: Danielle. Hobbies: drawing, dancing, running."

"Picture," Ana said as she looked at the large, wall-integrated screen. She could activate any of her walls, but she preferred the one directly across from the kitchen because she could watch it while she cooked. A high resolution photograph of a smiling redhead in a green summer dress appeared on the screen. She dried her hands and walked closer, her heartbeat drumming in her throat. "Wow."

"I'm sorry, what did you say?" Cassiopeia was the closest she had to a real friend, aside from her six future crewmates, but sometimes she wished the droid would ignore some of her comments.

"Nothing." Ana shook her head as if that would slow her heartbeat. "Just thinking about how much trouble I'm getting myself into," she said under her breath. She closed her eyes, harnessing all of her brainpower to calm the flood of adrenaline. When she opened them again, she swiped the picture off screen and brought up the video message. Her chest pounded again with an unfamiliar nervousness as Jolie began speaking. Her voice was exactly how Ana imagined it would sound, melodic and bold.

"Hi, I'm really interested in meeting you to see if we would make good roommates. To be honest, I need to move off campus to save some money on room and board, so I was happy to see your place listed at such an affordable rate," she said, a brazen smile crossing her freckled face. "I'm fine with your work-for-rent requirement. I grew up on a farm, so I can do pretty much anything. Fix machinery, whatever." She shrugged, then smiled again. It was a radiant look for her, Ana thought. "Let me know. Hope to hear from you."

"Message complete. What would you like me to do, Ana?"

She thought for a moment. On the one hand, none of the candidates had seemed remotely interesting, except for Jolie. On the other, it would not be her most well-informed decision, judging from her immediate attraction. "Can you recall all of the replies to my ad?"

"Of course." Cassiopeia tiled the pictures and information for each prospective tenant on the screen.

"Get rid of one and four." Two pictures disappeared. "How old is two?"

"Forty-eight, divorced father of three."

"Get rid of him." If Ana didn't have a choice about who she'd be living with for the rest of her life, she sure as hell was going to exercise that freedom now. She looked at the calendar on her wall. Two more weeks until her mother, Dr. Deborah Mitchell, would be back from France. Two more weeks of a semblance of privacy. If she got herself a roommate now, it might be too late for her mother to raise objections by the time she returned. She pictured Dr. Mitchell's twisted face when she found out, and a flutter of panic resonated through her, followed by the burn of excitement. She figured she did what her mother wanted often enough to do something that she wanted every once in a while.

In truth, she didn't really need help with the property, or the small sum of money she'd advertised as rent. She just wanted the house to remain in good hands during her brief absences, and then once she was gone from this world. Dr. Mitchell had almost certainly planned for that, but Ana didn't trust her mother to make major decisions about a house she'd practically built herself. It was too precious to be left to some idiot assistant who wouldn't know what it could do or how to take care of it, and they'd probably sell it to someone who would tear it down. She needed someone she trusted to keep it the way she'd intended. Could that be the cute girl staring back at her from the wall?

"Reply to Jolie," Ana said. The nervousness crept back in as she recorded her message. She ended it with directions and a list of times when Jolie could come by to meet her. "Send."

"Good choice, Ana. She appears to be the most similar to you, and by my calculations, she's the most attractive choice."

"That was obvious," she muttered as her pulse began to return to normal. Since when had Cassiopeia started commenting on attractiveness? Had she picked up on the change in Ana's biomarkers? "Thanks, Cass. You may hibernate. I'm going to the terrarium." She said the last part to no one in particular, the house already tracking her every move, and grabbed a book off the table.

The sun seemed to stream through the small dome of the terrarium, illuminating Ana's hammock. She smiled as she pushed open the sealed glass door and stepped inside. They'd have three of these once the settlement was complete, for growing food and maintaining some kind of mental health for the seven colonists. Ana spent hours in her replica dome, experimenting or taking a break from her massive list of responsibilities. The dome was one of the only constants she'd have between this life and her future.

Ana needed to shake the nervous anticipation that was making her palms sweat at the thought of meeting Jolie. She had a difficult afternoon of exercise ahead, four miles of running, some weightlifting, and hours in her lab afterward. She'd figured out a long time ago that the only way she'd be able to accomplish everything she needed to was through an agile mind and careful manipulation of her emotions. Having a roommate, she reasoned, was a necessary shake up that would double as mission prep, testing her psychological stamina and ability to live in close quarters with another person. She only had a few months left to make absolute certain that she was prepared for her role, so it was now or never.

She couldn't turn back now. She had found herself a roommate, assuming it all worked out, and by the time Dr. Mitchell returned from Paris, there would be nothing her mother could do about it. Defiance settled uneasily in her bones. The dry terrarium air swirled around her, and she breathed in the overwhelming scent of rosemary. It smelled like Earth, sweet and musky, heavy and comforting. She'd pushed for some rosemary to be added to the seed bank, and it was one of the small concessions she was granted by the team.

She stepped over and around some genetically-enhanced kale and climbed into her hammock, supported by thin stakes on either end. It looked especially inviting today, as Ana had been up throughout the night checking on bacterial cultures. With all of the promise of robotics and artificial intelligence, it was a shame that nobody had developed a machine that would do her experiments for her, especially during the night. She yawned. Five minutes, she told herself. Five minutes to relax and get back on track. She opened the faded paperback to a dog-eared page, and after re-reading the same paragraph several times, gave in to a light and pleasant sleep.

CHAPTER THREE

K arlee likes you," Nova said, stuffing a couple of fries into her mouth.

"She tell you that after she visually undressed me last week?"

Nova ignored her. "You should give her a chance."

"Oh, please. I gave her one chance and that was enough. I don't think I could deal with her following me around all the time. She gets way too excited about nothing. Thank God you didn't adopt her attitude when you joined the sorority, or we wouldn't be sitting here today." Jolie kicked Nova's foot under the table.

"I just think you two would be so cute together. That's all I'm saying." Nova raised her palms in surrender.

"No way." Jolie laughed. "Easy to get is not my style."

"But—"

"Next topic, please," Jolie said in the least annoyed tone she could muster. The truth was that Nova had been by her side through thick and thin the last few years, but ever since her best friend had joined the sorority last spring, Jolie had felt a quiet distance wedging between them. It was especially obnoxious when Nova tried to set her up with her sorority sisters, and her main push lately was Karlee. She was fine being single, why couldn't Nova see that? She glanced at her friend, who had her thick eyebrows raised in a holier-than-thou expression.

"Fine," Nova said. "When are you meeting crazy inventor chick?"

"When are you going to stop being an asshole about it?" They looked at each other and broke into laughter.

"Okay, when are you going to be meeting your wonderful new roommate, who is sure to be normal and sane?" Nova asked again.

"Actually, this afternoon. I should go get ready in a few."

"I'm intrigued. She's not what you'd call unattractive." Nova smiled slyly and Jolie rolled her eyes. "Don't try to tell me you didn't check her out, Jo. I know your type." Jolie pursed her lips and glared. "Okay, okay." Nova became serious and put her hand on top of Jolie's. "Are you going to be okay getting over there? And making that trip every day?"

Jolie took a deep breath and sighed, imagining taking that ride every day, at least twice. "Yeah. I'll get used to it," was all she said. Her stomach tightened and she quickly changed the subject. "So, you think she's hot? From that picture?" Damn. Wrong subject.

"Didn't you see it?" Nova waved her off. "Trust me, girlfriend, I can tell a hot mama from a mile away. It's called animal magnetism."

"I don't think that's what that is."

"Doesn't matter. I have it, and I'm going to use it as long as I do," Nova said.

"Okay. Whatever you say." Jolie felt the uncomfortable tingle in her right knee that usually came on when she was anxious, and closed her eyes, envisioning the flat, agrarian landscape of home. In a moment, it passed. She was becoming more nervous about her upcoming meeting each time she thought about it. It wasn't just the car ride that gave her pause. That part would take some getting used to, but it was nothing she couldn't handle. Moving out here for school was the last major change she'd made. Aside from that, she coasted through life embracing the familiar, her days punctuated by habit and security. Did she really want to disrupt that?

"Your knee hurts again, doesn't it."

Jolie nodded, burying her face in her hands. "What am I doing? It's nice here. I like it. Maybe I should just live with you after all," she whined.

Nova took her hands and looked deeply into her eyes. "Woman. As much as I want to agree with you, you are going. You are going to impress her, and she will ask you to be her roommate, and you will say yes. Because I know, deep down, you want time for doing non-school and work things. Plus, I dared you," she said with a wink.

"I know. I miss home. Not even the people, really, but the open space. I would love to have that again, but what if it really isn't better? I'm so used to the noise here. What if it turns out I need that?"

Nova shook her head. "Just go and find out. And if you don't think she's cute, give her my number."

"You're incorrigible." Jolie felt a pang of jealousy at the thought of her best friend dating her future roommate.

"I'll help you get ready. Want to hang out on the quad first?"

Jolie nodded. "Sure. I have nothing better to do." She playfully punched Nova in the arm.

"I'm glad I'm your nothing-better-to-do friend."

They pushed their chairs out, squeaking them across the linoleum floor, and walked past the afternoon coffee crowd trickling into the campus center.

CHAPTER FOUR

Ana wiped her clammy hands on her jeans. She busied herself with tidying up the few items in her house that didn't have a designated storage space. Jolie was due in forty-five minutes and Ana had never felt so wretched.

"Cassiopeia, please conduct a health scan," she said, her cheeks on fire.

"Conducting scan. Stand in front of me." Ana moved in front of the wall monitor and waited. "It appears you are having an episode of acute anxiety. Blood pressure and heart rate are elevated. There is no indication of any illness. I believe you are nervous about your upcoming meeting."

"Are you kidding me? I'm supposed to be saving humanity and I can't even deal with meeting a potential roommate?" Ana silently cursed all of her carefully constructed socialization the last thirteen years. She had her mission crew, she talked to people, just not on her own terms. All of it was related to her work, though the lines between work and life blurred so heavily that she'd never been able to separate the two. She was prepared for so many different spacecraft and medical emergencies she'd likely never encounter, yet her mother had neglected to put something as simple as screening roommates into the training plan. Ana knew it was because that work had been done years ago for her. She closed her eyes and tried to center herself, but couldn't shake the jitters emanating from somewhere deep inside.

"Ana, please go meditate. I will alert you when Ms. Dann arrives." Cassiopeia dimmed the screen in a show of finality. Sometimes the droid was too intuitive for its own good.

Ana sighed heavily and smoothed her flannel shirt. If this was how she was going to feel until she got used to having a roommate, maybe she should forget the idea. "Mom, you'd like that, wouldn't you?" she mumbled. She turned to face the screen again and almost called on Cassiopeia to cancel the meeting, but a burn of defiance rippled through her and she strode out the side door instead.

Picking up a colander lying upside down in the dirt, she began to harvest the large cherry tomatoes that hung from her eight tomato plants. They'd stood up as best they could to the hail storms that came in late summer, and many of the fruits now displayed the familiar brown pockmarks. Ana hoped Jolie liked to snack on damaged tomatoes. She heard a rumbling and looked toward the sky, surprised to see that dark clouds were rolling in from the Northeast. They were as black as she'd seen them. She touched the bracelet on her wrist and brought up a weather report. She should have seen this by now, but she'd been thrown off all day nervously anticipating the meeting.

Ana jogged to her shed and pulled out some old sheets and a bag of stakes. Within a few minutes, she had covered her entire garden from the large hail and high winds of the advancing nor'easter. She stood back and looked at her work, the once white sheets billowing slightly with the wind. This was at least the tenth time this year that she'd had to do this, and there were even a few storms she had missed, when she was away or asleep. By far the worst year yet, according to Luke's research. The last report her fellow mission specialist had sent included a milestone for North America. Thirty straight years of steadily increasing storm numbers, rising temperatures, and elevated sea levels. Ana knew this wasn't even the worst place to be living these days. At least there was relative peace in the States.

She cursed the impending storm, wishing it would move out to the Midwest where the rain was sorely needed. But she couldn't will it away. All she could do was hope that her work with the mission would somehow make the future better. She'd known she would be a part of it her entire life, and now, as the time for launch drew near, the responsibility weighed heavily on her psyche. Unfailingly, she felt it most acutely each time it stormed.

As she walked back toward the house, the first few drops of rain fell. Soon, it was coming down in sheets. She watched from her living room window as it poured, and worried about Jolie traveling in this weather. By now it would be too late to reschedule. Besides, with a renewed sense of purpose and her mission before her, she realized that she really did need someone to take care of everything while she was gone. She couldn't leave it to chance, or her mother, who was competent beyond measure, but not compassionate. She wanted to know exactly what would become of the little plot of land she'd called home for over a decade. She'd miss it more than anything, and believing that it would be in good hands was some comfort.

"A vehicle is approaching with Ms. Dann inside," Cassiopeia chimed suddenly. Ana snapped to attention and moved to the kitchen to warm two mugs of water. She peered outside and watched Jolie step out of the driverless taxi, her clothes immediately soaking through in the drenching rain. Ana ran to the door and held it open, motioning her inside as the car backed down the gravel driveway.

"Oh, God, I'm so sorry," Jolie said as she reached the door. "I'm dripping everywhere." Her strawberry hair was matted to her head and her clothing clung in a way that made Ana draw a quick breath. She realized she was staring and a blush crept up her neck.

"Uh, hold on a second, let me get a towel." Ana dashed to a cabinet and grabbed two of them. "Here," she said as she pushed the towels toward Jolie. Their eyes met for a moment and Ana saw Jolie shiver.

"Thanks." Jolie took the towels. She smiled distractedly as she blotted her clothing and hair. "Not sure how much good this is going to do, but I appreciate the effort."

Ana silently chastised herself for not being able to work through this problem. Obviously she should offer her dry clothes and tea. Why couldn't she think? Her planning and problem solving skills were usually impeccable. She cleared her throat and put her hands on her hips. "Here, uh, wait here for a second and I'll get you something to wear." She fumbled the words like an idiot, and realized that she was acting like one as well. "I'll put your clothes in the dryer while we chat."

"Thanks, that would be great. Oh, by the way, I'm Jolie," she said, grinning widely. She stuck her trembling hand out toward Ana, who had begun to walk away. "It's really nice to meet you."

"Ana." She turned back sheepishly and shook Jolie's cool hand. "Guess the weather could have been better for your trip. I was going to reschedule, but by the time I realized how bad the storm was, it was too late."

"It's no problem. Just a little rain, right?" Jolie chuckled, but her eyebrows arched in a way that made it seem like the drive had indeed been precarious. They both listened for a moment as some hail started to pelt the windows.

"You might be stuck here for a bit," Ana said.

"Tornado warning?"

"Usually. Follow me," Ana said as she walked toward her room. She emerged with an armful of clothing and a thin blanket. "Just some sweatpants and a sweatshirt. Here's a heat blanket, too. Oh, and if you want to change in there," she pointed toward the spare room, "that would be your room." Ana opened a sealed door to reveal a bed pod inset into the wall with some shelves over it. A small desk fit into the corner next to a door that opened into a closet and some storage space.

Jolie glanced around the room and nodded. "This is cozy, and very white."

Ana suddenly realized that it must seem tiny and sterile to someone used to living in a Singer dorm room. When she had designed the house all those years ago, she wasn't expecting to share it with anyone, though she'd added the guest room just in case. An unexpected wave of panic rose in her as she realized what little space and privacy she had to offer a potential roommate.

"But, you know," Jolie continued, "it might be just what I'm looking for. Let me change and I'll let you know for sure."

Ana let out an audible sigh and realized she'd been holding her breath. "Okay. I'll just be on the couch. With the tea." Ana winced at her awkwardness as she walked out and shut the door. She put some tea powder in the mugs and sat down, tapping her foot on the floor. What was she doing inviting a stranger to live in her house? There were so many ways this could go wrong. She had only months to go before departure, and a lot of classified experiments to be running in that time. Hopefully, Jolie wouldn't have the science background to realize what was going on, but what if she figured it out? Ana heard the bedroom door open and snapped her head up.

Jolie emerged with a lightness that warmed the room. She was wearing the gray sweatshirt and matching pants, and toweling her hair. The sweats hung off of her slight frame, the shoulders drooping comically, but she seemed happy and the color was returning to her cheeks. Ana once again found herself staring. She would have a lot of weird behavior to think about tonight. Hoping Jolie wasn't put off by her awkwardness, Ana motioned her over to the couch.

The hail had changed to rain, and the light filtering into the living area was gray and dull. Ana handed a mug to Jolie, then lifted her own and blew on the hot tea. She moved her fingers over the corner of the coffee table and the light in the room changed to a late afternoon scape.

"So, what do you think?" Ana asked.

"This place is interesting. I like it. And it's definitely in my price range."

Ana laughed and pulled her dark hair over her shoulder. "Oh, that," she said. "I had to put an amount in there. Honestly, I don't need the money. I already own the house and I don't really have any expenses that need to be covered. If you're willing to help me out when I'm away, then just chip in for any extra food we buy. There's not much, since I grow almost everything here, anyway. Everything except meat."

"I don't eat meat. I mean, I would eat it, it's just usually out of my price range." Jolie shrugged.

"I haven't had meat in years," Ana said. "I do like the occasional bag of roasted crickets, but now that I think about it, it's been a while for those, too."

Jolie crinkled her nose. "Never understood the appeal, honestly."

Ana leaned in and said, "You know what's really disgusting? Those frozen caterpillars that are supposed to be some kind of replacement for sausage. I can tell you definitively that they are not at all like sausage."

Laughing, Jolie held her stomach. "You have to stop. I'm going to throw up. I guess I'm lucky I grew up in the middle of nowhere without all the selection you had. We had some chickens for a while, but I think wild animals got them and we just never got more."

"Speaking of food, I was thinking we could try to share, if you want," Ana said. "I mean, I like to cook, so I'm happy to share meals. But no pressure," she added quickly.

"I'm okay with that, yeah. I cook, too, and it's been a while since I've been in a real kitchen. I have a weird schedule, though, so I don't know if we'll be home at the same times."

"Trust me." Ana laughed. "It can't be weirder than mine. I'm at Singer a few days a week to teach biochem courses, and I do some of my research there. And sometimes I'm up in the middle of the night working on…things." Ana caught herself before she gave away more than she should. She saw Jolie's eyes widen in interest, or perhaps admiration.

"Wow, so you're a professor? Will it be weird living with a student?" Jolie shifted slightly with discomfort.

"God, no. I'm only a lecturer, and that's not my real job anyway," Ana said, dismissing the idea with a wave of her hand. She wondered at how it was so easy to play down her role as liaison between the biochemistry department and their biggest donor, the Hammer Corporation. That part wasn't entirely secret. Usually, she had to use her clout to convince the corporation stakeholders of their investment's worth.

A low bell startled the women. "Ana, Martine would like to speak with you. Would you like me to take a message?" Cassiopeia's voice reminded Ana that there was, and would always be, a third person in the room, watching.

"I'll call her back later, Cass." Ana turned away from the wall displaying a picture of Martine, dressed to the nines in Paris.

"She's really pretty. Who is she?" Jolie asked.

"One of my best friends in the world." Ana smiled. Martine was gorgeous and brilliant, and if she hadn't already found her soul mate in Liv, the mission specialist from Antarctica, Ana may have been interested. "Anyway, back to us." Ana cringed at her suggestion that they were an "us."

"Do you still keep in touch with your old roommates?" Jolie asked.

Ana looked down at her hands. Would Jolie think it was weird that she hadn't lived with anybody in thirteen years, didn't even have friends who came over, and really just wanted a roommate to spite her mother, among other things? If she were in a meeting with stakeholders, or talking to her mother, she would have simply evaded the question. But as Jolie sat intimately next to her, upsetting her equilibrium in what seemed to be a pleasant way, the truth tumbled out without censorship.

"I've never had a roommate. I've never lived with anyone besides my mother, and I've been alone here for over a decade." She looked carefully at Jolie to gauge her reaction. When she was met with curiosity, she continued. "Actually, the reason that I want one now is that I need someone to take care of the place when I'm not here. I'm going to be gone a lot over the next few months, and then I'll be gone permanently."

Before she could continue, a horrified Jolie grabbed her wrist and whispered, "Oh my God, are you dying?"

"What? No, I'm just leaving."

"Just…leaving?" Jolie asked, confused.

"I can't actually say much more about it, but that's the basics. I probably won't ever come back here, even if I technically could someday." Ana felt a surge of sadness saying it aloud, but quickly steeled her emotions as she had been practicing for years. "It's not that nobody will know where I'm going. I just can't say more about it now."

Jolie looked at her, still puzzled, and glanced back at the wall where Martine's picture had been. "Okay, well, it's cute, the price is right, and you seem nice enough. I'm in, even with all the weird secretive stuff."

As Jolie's declaration sank in, Ana sobered. Jolie's hand still rested on her arm, and the sensation was distracting. She shifted uncomfortably and Jolie seemed to realize where her hand was, quickly drawing it away. Ana was sorry she did.

Maybe having a roommate was a bad idea after all. Ana was sure she wanted to get to know Jolie, but she worried that her training and preparation might suffer from the distraction. It was no wonder that Dr. Mitchell kept her isolated. If having friends of her own, friends she saw on a regular basis, friends who casually touched her arm, was going to be like this, there was no chance that she'd be able to invest all of her attention in the mission. When she flicked her eyes back in front of her, she noticed a hint of amusement play across Jolie's lips, and it made her insides crumble. For someone who had so carefully planned out her life, the uncontrollable magnetism of the woman across from her was strangely irresistible.

"Okay," Ana said. "You're hired. As my new roommate."

Jolie beamed. "That's wonderful. Anyway, I feel like I'm already halfway moved in, wearing your clothes and all. Speaking of which, I left mine on the floor in the—my room, I guess. Where's your dryer?"

"I'll take care of it," Ana said. She needed a moment to catch her breath. She'd committed, fully, to the unexpectedly enchanting woman sitting on her couch. In the room, she bent to pick up Jolie's clothing, holding it carefully in her hands for a moment as she imagined the room occupied, for once. It was an odd thought. For thirteen years, she'd walked by the door, almost never going in except to clean. There was so much she'd have to get used to, but especially the closeness of another body. She looked down at the damp clothing, very aware of how it had spent the earlier part of the day covering Jolie's fair skin.

As she brought the clothes to the dryer in the hallway, she glanced into the main room. Jolie had picked up her creased and faded paperback and was reading a passage with amusement. Ten or so years ago, Ana had sat on that very couch, cheap romance novel in hand, engrossed in some erotic passage, when her mother came over to check on her. Cassiopeia must have been installed the year afterward because there was nobody to alert her to her visitor. She was reclined while one hand lazily stroked the skin just below her belly button. Before she even registered what was happening, the book was snatched out of her hands. She shivered as she remembered standing, fists clenched, not quite comprehending her mother's anger. It had been so out of the ordinary to have her mother in the same room that it seemed as if she watched her mother yell at her from afar.

"This is what you read in your free time? I'm disappointed, Ana. I thought you were better than this. The world will be watching and you'll have more important things to worry about, like survival." Ana had simply nodded as her mother continued her tirade. "Besides, it doesn't work like that. Nobody can keep up with you, and it will distract you from your work. Don't even think about having a relationship until you are settled in your new home, or at least on board the ship." Up until that point, Ana hadn't really thought much about relationships or romance as anything other than abstract activities that other people participated in. They had never really fit into her life, and frankly, she hadn't seen how they could. Ten years later, her mother's words still rang in her head like a warning.

Standing there, absentmindedly feeding the clothes into the dryer, she regarded Jolie, and knew her mother was right. It would be a distraction, a huge one. But if it felt even a little like the adrenaline rush she was getting thinking about sharing a space with Jolie, she wanted more. Besides, what was a little harmless flirting, as long as she kept her emotions in check?

She returned to the main room just as Jolie was hailing a taxi with her bracelet.

"Are you sure it's okay to drive in this?" Ana nodded toward the window, which framed an ongoing torrent of rain.

"Technically, a computer's driving, so I would probably leave that decision to It."

Ana ran her fingers through her shoulder length chestnut hair and chuckled. "Okay, well do you want to ride in this?" She hoped she didn't sound too desperate to get Jolie to stay.

"Depends. I'm getting hungry. Are you making dinner?" Jolie asked with a gleam in her eye.

"Only if you're staying for it," Ana said.

"I'm starving."

"Well, okay then. Dinner coming up." Ana busied herself in the kitchenette, while Jolie sat patiently on the couch, reading the paperback. So far, so good. They seemed to be able to exist in the same space with ease. She'd never been so immediately comfortable with anyone, certainly not the rest of the crew. Their first meeting had been strange, a group of awkward teenagers sitting around a boardroom table, weighing their choices to commit the rest of their lives to a plan that wouldn't be realized for years. Dr. Mitchell had said to them, "This is your family. You will learn to love each other, work together, and you will carry out the second greatest mission of this century as a cohesive, mentally fit unit. We're doing it right this time." Ana had signed the contract as a formality, since she didn't have a choice. As the daughter of the mission director, she'd been born into this role.

"What are you cooking?" Jolie asked.

Ana jumped, pulled from her thoughts. She hadn't noticed Jolie settling herself on her elbows on the other side of the island. Jolie was effortlessly attractive, her hair just beginning to dry, a mixture of dark orange clumps framed by wild, wiry strands that danced with static. Ana felt the urge to smooth them and thank her for suddenly making her life more interesting. Her pulse raced as she caught the gingery scent of Jolie's perfume, or maybe her shampoo. Unexpected heat rose in her cheeks and she dropped her knife in the pile of red pepper she was dicing.

"I, uh—will you excuse me for a minute?" She wiped her hands on her jeans and walked quickly to her room, gently shutting the door behind her. After a few deep, meditative breaths, Ana felt like she might be able to continue making dinner without imagining touching Jolie. But she'd have to send her far, far away from the island.

She returned to the kitchen, avoiding Jolie's questioning gaze. "Sorry, I just needed a minute. Really weird. Got dizzy for a second."

"Okay." Jolie looked concerned. "Are you sure you want me to stay? I can definitely just eat when I'm back, if you don't feel like cooking."

Ana shook her head. "No, no need." The thought of Jolie leaving so soon was worse than her inability to stay focused and the creeping nervousness that churned her stomach. "Besides, I've already cut way too many vegetables just for myself, and I'd hate to have to eat the same thing twice in a row." It was a lie, since she often cooked in large batches to save time. She forced a smile at Jolie, who settled contentedly on the couch with the book, snacking on the cherry tomatoes Ana had left out.

Ana finished cooking and brought the food over to the couch. Jolie's eyes lit up with the first bite. "This food is amazing, Ana," she said. "It's been such a long time since I've eaten a meal without any synthetics."

"Thanks." Ana blushed. "I'm happy to have someone to cook for. It gets pretty boring cooking for one all the time."

Jolie breathed in the scent of the food on her plate. "Is that rosemary? It smells incredible."

"Oh, yeah, it's my favorite. I put it in practically everything, which I'm sure would be frowned upon in culinary circles."

"Well, I'm not a culinary circle, so you're safe." Jolie smirked. "So, you grew all of this?"

Ana's heart swelled with pride. "All of it. I've got the garden outside, and a terrarium that I'll show you some other time. Lots of it comes from there, and I store a lot of the extras in my cold storage." She gestured toward the island.

"That's a kitchen island," Jolie said, confused.

"Almost everything in here is more than it seems." Ana smiled and glanced around the room.

Jolie didn't miss a beat. Her eyes pierced Ana's as a devilish grin spread across her face. "I get that impression," she said. Ana almost choked on a piece of lettuce.

The storm blew over as soon as they'd finished. Ana didn't realize she was having so much fun until Jolie stood to retrieve her own clothes. She felt a hint of regret as the taxi crept up her gravel driveway.

"So, I'll be here Thursday to move in. Let me know if something changes and I'll come another day," Jolie said as she moved toward the door.

"Thursday is fine." Ana thought for a moment. "Actually, I'm going to be teaching a class in the morning, so if you need help getting your stuff together after that, give me a call." She found herself willing to make any excuse to spend time with Jolie, the sooner the better.

"That would actually be great, if you don't mind. I don't have much stuff, so it won't take long. My best friend, Nova, will probably be there helping, and I know she wants to meet you."

Ana blushed. "I didn't realize I was so famous," she said.

"She dared me—I mean, she wanted me to come out here and look at this place. She saw your ad, too."

"Wow, I've never been a dare before," Ana said, amused at Jolie's attempt to cover up her words.

Jolie winced. "Sorry, that's not what I meant to say."

"It's okay, I don't mind. I understand that the whole thing is a little weird." Ana shrugged. "Anyway, I'll be there. Send me the details."

"You got it. Better go. These storms don't like to wait too long for you before they start up again," Jolie said almost apologetically as she gestured toward the driveway. They both walked to the door and stood facing each other. "Well, bye. Really, really nice to meet you, Ana. Thanks for everything."

"Of course," Ana said.

Jolie stuck out her hand and Ana melted as their fingers touched. Before she knew it, Jolie was out the door.

"Cassiopeia," she said a few moments after the door closed. "What the hell just happened?"

"I believe you know what just happened, Ana."

She covered her face and groaned in frustration, then flopped down on the couch with a ridiculous smile and replayed the afternoon in her mind.

CHAPTER FIVE

I can't believe I've barely said two words to you this whole week." Jolie threw a pile of shirts into an open box and tucked in the flaps. They'd been packing her room for ten minutes, and she was already over it.

"Sorry, girl, I've barely said two words to myself. Pledging all week. And all next week. I can't believe how busy I've been." Nova sighed heavily as she dumped the contents of a drawer into another box.

"See? This is why I can't be in your sorority." Jolie emptied the rest of her clothing in a third box. "No me time. I already have no time to go to the studio, then you add pledging, all the parties."

"Understood, understood. So? Are you going to tell me about crazy inventor chick?" Nova yawned and sat on the bed in a patch of sunshine.

Jolie gave up packing and joined her, running her hands over the colorful quilt that her mother had made her as a high school graduation present. "You'd better start calling her Ana, or else she'll think we've been talking about her."

"Well, we have. And sure, if I ever meet her, I'll use her given name. So, was she as hot in person as she was in that photo?"

"Really? You thought that was attractive?" Jolie scoffed. "For your information, she's a lot hotter in person." She elbowed Nova in the ribs. "And you'll get the chance to confirm that in…" She looked at the time on her bracelet. "Fifteen minutes."

"What? She's coming over here? She leaves her house?" Nova snorted as Jolie punched her in the arm.

"You're the worst. She works here as some kind of professor, but I've definitely never seen her around." I would have noticed, Jolie thought. "Anyway, she offered to help me move since she's already here today. And judging by the amount of progress we've made so far, we need it."

"That's nice of her. So, tell me how the roommate interview went. You've got fourteen minutes." Nova lay on her side and used an elbow to prop herself up.

Jolie leaned back and smiled, remembering. A warm rush cascaded through her body. "Well, things didn't quite go as planned. Remember that huge storm on Sunday?" She looked at Nova, who nodded. "Yeah, so I got caught in that. I was soaked when I got there, so she made me tea and let me wear some of her clothes while mine were in the dryer. Oh, and she made me dinner while we waited for the rain to stop." She smirked at Nova, whose eyebrows seemed to be stuck in a raised position.

"Mmm hmm. And then you made sweet, sweet love?"

"Oh my God, you are such a pervert." Jolie grabbed a pillow and hit her over the head with it.

Nova was incredulous, even as she deflected the blows. "You are such a prude. Please tell me that doesn't sound like a date to you."

"Um, I went to look at her house, and now I'm going to be her roommate. It was most definitely not a date," Jolie said, though she couldn't deny the lingering feeling that there had been some kind of attraction between them.

"So you don't have a thing for her? You did say she was hot."

"Well, yeah," she sputtered. "Objectively, she's attractive. But there's no thing. Why are you so obsessed with my love life, anyway?"

Nova ignored her. "So, if I asked her out, you would be fine with that."

"Nova. Do not. Do you realize how awkward that would be? Plus, if her bed is anything like my new bed, there's no room for that." Jolie hesitated and Nova waited. "And how do you even know she likes women?"

"I guess we'll see." Nova got up and straightened her clothes. She was about to close a half-filled box when a tentative knock came from the door. Jolie scrambled to get off the bed to the door, but Nova beat her.

"Don't worry. I got this." Nova winked and opened the door.

Jolie put her hand over her eyes, unable to watch whatever show Nova was putting on.

"Hey, there. You must be Ana. I'm Nova, Jolie's accomplice. Please come in," she said in the sweetest voice Jolie had ever heard come out of her mouth.

Jolie shot her a warning look and mouthed, "you're the worst."

"Thanks, hi," Ana said, uncertainly. She stepped into the room in a perfectly fitted suit, her dark hair pulled back in a neat bun. She carefully placed a locked briefcase against the wall, and caught Jolie's eye as she turned back to the center of the room. "Nice to see you again." A shy smile crept across Ana's face.

Jolie couldn't help but smile back. "You too. Thanks for coming by." Jolie's voice came out strained. This put together version of Ana was nothing like the one she'd seen days earlier. This Ana seemed much more mature, with an air of quiet confidence that had Jolie imagining she was somewhat more accomplished than she'd initially let on. She regarded Ana curiously, trying to piece together the little information she knew about her.

Nova cleared her throat to break the silence. "All right, ladies. How about we get this shit done? I love you, but I have stuff to do later," she said to Jolie.

"Right." Jolie gestured to the boxes. "So, Ana, we're just kind of putting things in boxes. Have at it." Jolie continued to throw items in a box, and felt Ana surveying the progress over her shoulder. She caught a familiar scent as Ana leaned in. Rosemary? She inhaled deeply, very aware of Ana's closeness, and suddenly felt lightheaded. She retreated to the wall, steadying herself against the door frame, where she had a somewhat better view of Ana in her work clothes. There was something undeniably appealing about the thought of her standing in front of a class and lecturing. Perhaps she just became interested in whatever kind of science Ana taught.

As she tried to melt further into the wall, Nova gave her a funny look. "Jo?"

Jolie shook her head almost imperceptibly, unwilling to let Nova pull her out of her daze.

Ana broke the silence. "Um, don't take this the wrong way, but you're both terrible at packing. I bet I could fit everything in this room in the six boxes you already put together."

Jolie and Nova looked at each other, amused. "Well, we're not going to win any awards for our packing skills, that's for sure," Jolie said.

Nova smirked mischievously. "I'll bet you dinner that you can't fit everything. You win, Jolie will take you to dinner. You lose, you take me. Deal?"

Jolie immediately jumped in. "Wait, you can't just—"

"Deal," Ana said. She shrugged. "Either way, I win." She took off her suit jacket, placed it on the bed and rolled up her white shirtsleeves. While her back was turned, Jolie turned to Nova and mouthed, "what the fuck?"

When she was done giving Nova the silent third degree, Jolie returned her gaze to Ana. Her undershirt was visible through the white fabric of her button-up, and Jolie could see the hint of well defined muscles in her shoulders and arms. She was a shoulder person, she'd realized recently. She had a Serena Stone action movie to thank for the epiphany. Serena's shoulders were nice, well built and able to carry insane numbers of weapons, but Ana's looked like they could lift all that and do other things she'd never imagined Serena's doing. Like letting Jolie run her hands over them as she kissed Ana's clavicle. Like holding her body tightly to Ana's. Even though this kind of thinking seemed dangerous, she was thoroughly enjoying this iteration of her new roommate, commanding and self assured.

"Actually, I'll make you another deal," Ana said, pulling Jolie out of her thoughts. "If I can do this under forty-five minutes, you both have to come watch the Orionids with me."

"The whats?" Nova and Jolie asked at the same time.

"A meteor shower in October. If the weather is good, obviously. It's my favorite meteor shower of the year, and I usually have to watch it alone."

Jolie snickered. "You have a favorite meteor shower of the year? Never mind. Fine," she said. "I'll owe you anyway if you're going to be doing all my packing, so count me in either way." Ana set a timer on her bracelet, then solemnly shook hands with Jolie and Nova.

This woman is crazy, Nova messaged.

I know! In a good way though, right?

So good. She has a crush on you.

Jolie quickly wrote, *Hey!!! Don't write things like that while she's in the room!*

You're just worried I'm right.

Trust me, I am not in the mood for a relationship.

Who said relationship?

Jolie shut her messaging app and watched Ana carefully arrange her belongings into the boxes. The last to go in was the quilt.

"Sorry, ladies, show's over. Off the bed." Jolie and Nova scooted off and handed the last piece over.

"Thirty-seven minutes and twenty-four seconds," Nova said as Ana stacked the last box and wiped her forehead with her sleeve.

"Wow," Jolie said.

"Yeah, wow," Nova echoed.

Noticing the way that Ana's skin shimmered lightly with sweat, Jolie knew that Nova wasn't only impressed by the packing. Watching Ana work, with no wasted movement, was mesmerizing. She couldn't give Nova too much of an opening, so she quickly claimed her victory. "So, unfortunately for Nova, I will be taking you to dinner, and we will both be joining you on your excursion."

"And everybody wins." Ana smiled.

"Some of us more than others," Jolie muttered to Nova, who shot her an annoyed look. "Let's take these down to the taxi." Jolie got up and picked up a box.

"Actually, I have my truck here. I think it will be easier to load up, and that way, you don't have to pay for a taxi," Ana said as she scooped two boxes into her arms and walked out. Nova and Jolie held back.

"Holy shit," Nova whispered when they were alone. "You did not tell me she was so intense."

"Trust me, I had no idea. On Sunday, she was dressed in regular clothes and she seemed pretty awkward." Endearingly so, Jolie thought.

"Girl, you have got a problem. How in the hell are you going to be just roommates with her? I'd be screwing her by tomorrow."

"You're so crude," Jolie said. "Sure, she's super nice and she could lift all my boxes at once and look good doing it, but that doesn't mean we should date."

Nova grabbed her wrists. "Are you serious? She totally has a thing for you."

"Nova, don't start." Jolie tried to suppress a grin. She wasn't oblivious, but she wasn't going to give in that easily. "She's lived alone for years. Don't you think that's weird? She'll probably realize that she actually prefers living alone and then kick me out. Oh, and also I'm her roommate. Why are we even talking about this? It's a non-issue. I'm not interested."

"You are so interested. I've never seen anyone more interested than you are right now," Nova said, and was about to say something else when they heard footsteps coming down the hall.

Ana leaned into the door frame, biting her bottom lip to hide her amusement.

"Oh, God. Sorry, we didn't mean to make you do all of the work yourself," Jolie sputtered as she tripped over Nova to get to the boxes. Nova met her eyes and suppressed a smug grin. Jolie glared back, piling an extra box onto her stack in defiance, and headed for the hallway.

The three of them quickly packed Ana's 2060s pickup truck, a little worse for wear, and Jolie left to return her key card to the resident advisor. When she got back to her room, Nova was leaning in to laugh at something Ana had said. Jolie shot Nova an angry look, realized that she was being unreasonably jealous, and turned it into a pout.

"I'm going to miss living so close to you," she said.

"I love you with all my heart and I'll miss you so much. We'll just have to make plans now whenever we want to see each other." As Jolie hugged her good-bye, Nova quietly spoke in her ear, "I think you've got an interesting year coming up."

"I'm going to fucking kill you," Jolie whispered. "Next time I see you. Which better be soon."

They all walked outside and Nova kissed Jolie's cheek before leaving, turning back once to wave good-bye and blow another kiss. Jolie looked impassively at her red brick dorm one more time, then turned toward the truck. Ana stood with her hands in her pants pockets, her suit jacket back on, surveying the campus.

"Ready?"

"As much as I'll ever be." Jolie climbed into the cab as Ana held the door for her.

The ride to her new house was much more pleasant when she wasn't alone in a taxi, riding through a storm. They bumped along the torn up road in Ana's rusty blue truck, watching the light playing off yellow foliage that covered the trees. The boxes rattled in the truck bed.

"Nova seems nice." Ana's voice trailed off as she gazed out her window.

"Yeah. She's great. She's my best friend. I mean, she was," Jolie said, unable to properly sum up her sadness at leaving Nova and her ambivalence toward staying. "I don't know. She still is, I guess, but things sort of shifted when she joined the sorority last year. You know, she's around those girls all the time, and I always have to find time between all her activities to see her."

Ana nodded. "How long have you been friends?"

"Since orientation. We hit it off right away and were pretty much inseparable for a while." Jolie cleared her throat. That was almost the truth.

Ana turned to her. "Can I ask you something weird?"

Jolie saw the uncertainty in Ana's eyes and smiled to herself. She was finally turning back into the adorable, awkward person she'd met last weekend. "Of course. Ask away."

"Okay, so I'm not really an expert in this, but it kind of seemed like she was hitting on me. Do you think she was?"

Jolie sighed, making a mental note to ask Nova what exactly had happened when she'd left them alone. "Probably. She thinks you're cute."

"Oh." Ana turned bright red and pretended to be very interested in something outside.

"Does that bother you?"

"Hmm?" She coughed. "Oh, no, I'm just not interested."

What was happening? "Not interested because?" Jolie asked.

Ana gave her a funny look and shrugged. "I'm just not."

"Good to know?" Jolie was puzzled by the whole conversation.

Ana sighed. "I just wanted you to know so you didn't think I wanted to date your best friend. Sorry. I didn't mean to make things weird."

Jolie did her best not to laugh at the ridiculousness of the conversation. Apparently Ana was a mess when it came to dating. "Ana, you're fine. I don't care who you date." She found Ana's expression unreadable.

Pulling off the ambling country road and onto Ana's long, gravel driveway, Jolie was able to see the property clearly for the first time. One side of the driveway was lined with trees, and the other was a grassy hill sloping gently up to the house. Ana's garden was at the top of the hill, looking as lush as it must have been in the height of summer. She saw what looked like five hundred square feet packed with rosettes of dark greens and the broad, spiny leaves of winter squashes. Her mind quickly ran through how many pounds of vegetables it must produce each year. It was certainly more variety than her family had ever squeezed into the land at home. She pictured the farm in Nebraska, no doubt continuing to produce less and less each year, relegated to growing cheap, drought-tolerant crops because of the water restrictions.

"Reminds me of home," Jolie murmured.

"In a good way?"

"Sort of bittersweet, I guess. Maybe I'm homesick. Haven't been back in years."

Ana raised her eyebrows.

Jolie shrugged and said, "I know, it's horrible. I feel guilty all the time, but I can't get it out of my head that if I went home, I would never leave again. It's one of those places."

"I know what you mean," Ana said. "A one-way ticket."

"Yeah. Anyway, let's get out and I can unload."

The truck slowed and Ana jumped out first, swiftly undoing the ropes fastening the boxes in the truck. She took two in her arms and turned to walk to the house.

"Wait. You really don't have to unload all of my boxes for me. I feel terrible that you've done basically all of the work. I can finish this myself." Jolie tried to take the boxes from Ana's arms, but she swung them away.

"Not a chance. You have no idea how helpful it's going to be to have you here. I really don't mind."

Jolie shrugged. She couldn't argue with a gorgeous woman showing off her sexy arm muscles. Particularly one who absolutely did not want to date her best friend. "Fine. You're very persuasive. But after that, I'll cook us dinner, deal?" She shouldered a box and they walked toward the door.

Ana smiled. "Since today is the day of deals, I think that's fair. I could use some time to relax before tomorrow." Ana's face softened as she touched the entry pad.

"You must be tired. You were in the zone when you were packing my room," Jolie said with a smile. She elbowed Ana in jest, and thought she saw her cheeks color briefly as they set the boxes down and went to retrieve more.

When the truck had been cleared, Ana headed for the shower, and Jolie perused the refrigerator for ingredients. The shelves were chock full of late season vegetables, and the wall next to it contained an electric root cellar with months' worth of potatoes, apples, and onions. She found even more in the kitchen island. She did a little dance. She'd never been in such a well stocked kitchen, and rarely had the chance to make something at her dorm that wasn't from a box.

With butternut squash soup simmering on the stove, fragrant tendrils of steam rising into the air, Jolie figured it was time to summon her dinner companion. "Ana? Dinner's on. Ten minutes until it's done," she shouted.

Now was as good a time as any to give herself a quick tour of her new home. The main section of the house was perfectly round, and the walls looked like they were lined with cozy, honey-colored wood. Jolie touched it and the material gave ever so slightly. This was some kind of smart material that she'd never seen before, not wood at all. She slowly walked around the room's perimeter, stopping every few feet to admire the high definition photographs of planets and nebulae. Ana certainly had strange taste in artwork. Even though Jolie would never have decorated like this, she had to admit that it suited the odd, space-age feel of the house. When she reached the small corridor that led to the bedrooms, she hesitated. "Ana? Are you in your room? Dinner's ready."

The hallway was dark except for the sliver of yellow light that shined from behind Ana's cracked door. She knocked on it lightly, and the door fell far enough open for her to poke her head in. The room was tidy, except for a small pile of clothes in the corner. If it weren't for that, Jolie would have a hard time picturing anybody living there at all. There was no clutter, nothing hung on the walls, and the bed was expertly made. She pulled back and closed the door almost all the way. As she turned around, her jaw collided with a muscular shoulder.

"Jesus." Jolie steadied herself against a shocked Ana. As she pulled back, she saw why. Their collision had resulted in Ana dropping the towel she'd been wrapped in, leaving her naked before her, with the towel in a heap on the floor. Jolie reached down to pick it up, and handed it to Ana, who was massaging her shoulder from the blow. "I'm so sorry," Jolie said. "I was going to tell you that dinner's ready."

"Thanks, but is your face okay? You hit my shoulder pretty hard."

In the dim light, Jolie could make out the solid curves of Ana's body as she uncrumpled the towel and covered herself. Her head swam, but she didn't think it was from the impact. She tried not to think of how close she was to acting out her earlier fantasy. Those gorgeous shoulders were exposed right in front of her. "Oh, yeah, it's completely fine." She felt her jaw, which throbbed on one side. "Totally okay," she repeated.

Ana's cheeks colored. "I guess I should learn to get dressed in the bathroom from now on."

Jolie's pulse pounded in her throat. "No, I mean, this was my fault. I ran into you. Besides, a bunch of girls in my dorm would walk around pretty much naked all the time, so really, it's no big deal. Nothing I haven't seen. Well, I'll go make sure dinner's really ready, and I'll let you get dressed." Jolie quickly bowed out without waiting for a response and practically ran to the kitchen. She steadied herself on the counter as the last of the adrenaline dissipated. What was going on with her? She'd seen plenty of attractive women naked before, and she'd never felt so off-kilter. She worked herself into irritation as she stood there pondering her behavior, considering its implications. How could she be so stupid as to let herself feel any real attraction to Ana? That was so clearly never going to happen.

When Ana finally walked in, Jolie sprung into action, making up for time lost in her thoughts. "Hey, have a seat. Water okay to drink?" she asked, opening a few cabinets. "Where are the cups, anyway?" She looked everywhere except at Ana, knowing that all she'd see was the image of her bare skin burned into her mind.

Ana pulled some glasses, plates, and bowls from a cupboard. "Feel free to go through the cupboards and drawers out here," she said. "Also, Cassiopeia has a map of the house that shows you where everything is. I'll program her to recognize you and respond to your commands."

Jolie nodded and stole a quick glance at Ana. It looked like they were both avoiding each other.

Ana cleared her throat and sat on the couch, changing the ambiance of the room to match early evening's slanted sun. Jolie brought two bowls over and they began to eat in silence.

"Thanks for dinner," Ana mumbled as she ate a spoonful of soup. "This is good."

"No problem. Glad you like it." This was getting awkward. She had to say something before their brief friendship was drowned in embarrassment. "Everything okay?"

Ana put down her spoon and wiped her mouth with the back of her hand. "Of course. Why wouldn't it be?" she said without looking up.

"I'm sorry about the hallway."

Ana frowned and looked at her. "It just caught me off guard, that's all. I'm sorry you had to see," she gestured down her body, "this, without clothes on. Not a great welcome from me."

Jolie laughed heartily, not at all sorry that she saw what she saw. Ana did not join her. "Oh, you're serious. If I were you, I wouldn't worry about someone accidentally seeing me naked." She held Ana's gaze for a moment, hoping she understood everything Jolie meant. She didn't want to have to explain that she'd happily look at Ana's naked body again someday.

Ana didn't answer, and swiped her hand over the coffee table. The wall across from them turned into a menu of media options. "Want to watch a movie?"

Relieved, Jolie nodded. "Pick something good."

"Cassiopeia, please pick a movie for us," Ana said.

"Choosing a mutually agreeable movie," the system replied.

Jolie took a spoonful of soup and turned to Ana. "Why did you name it that? Do you have a deceased pet named Cassiopeia or something?"

Ana laughed. "I have no deceased pets. It's my favorite constellation, actually. I always found it first in the sky when I was younger. And look." She pulled her sleeve up. "I have freckles on my arm that are in the exact formation as those five stars."

Jolie looked at her dubiously. "Not to burst your bubble, but I bet I could find some freckles on my arm that form the same shape." Jolie pushed her sleeve back, revealing a pale, freckle covered arm.

"Bubble officially burst. Thanks a lot." Ana rolled her sleeve back down, a faint smile playing at the edges of her mouth.

"Playing *Steel For Guns*, starring Serena Stone and Cody Warner," Cassiopeia said.

Jolie chuckled to herself and leaned back against the warm leather of the couch. "Perfect."

CHAPTER SIX

Ana checked her messages on a foldable screen before stowing it in a drawer. She didn't like to carry screens with her unless there was a real need. Besides, her bracelet performed almost the same functions. Technology was embedded so seamlessly around her property, she felt off the grid most of the time, even though she could call up the Internet almost anywhere.

She felt antsy for the first time in a while. She had no shortage of work to catch up on, but at the moment, it seemed unimportant. This week alone, she'd had six meetings with the local stakeholders, who were increasingly eager to realize their investments as the departure date drew near. She had given so many presentations about her research, preparation, and the other members of the crew, that the words she spoke were starting to lose meaning. Spending so much time presenting and answering rapid-fire questions was wearing on her. Although she was ultimately glad that Dr. Mitchell had extended her vacation in Paris, she wished she didn't have to step into her mother's role as interim public relations person.

She sighed and leaned against the back of the couch. Aside from the laboratory work piling up, she should be weightlifting and running today, but she couldn't muster the energy to change into her workout clothes. She'd rarely let her fitness regimen slide before, conscientious of the shape she'd need to be in during the trip. Even with the onboard workout machines, the reality was that she'd lose most of her muscle mass in transit. The exoskeletons would help, but she didn't like having to rely solely on technology to perform basic functions like walking ten feet. Today, Ana simply couldn't find the will to care. What was one day off over the course of years, anyway? She'd start again tomorrow, doubling up on her efforts. Pushing the guilt from her mind, she considered how to spend her impromptu day off, but nothing in particular seemed worth doing. Her mind kept leading her back to one thought: Jolie.

Even as she questioned her fixation, she touched her wrist and brought up the messaging platform. *What are you up to?* She waited a few minutes for Jolie to reply, but nothing came. She didn't want to seem too pushy, especially since they'd only been living together a few weeks. Besides, she told herself, she really didn't need Jolie around to have a nice day. Adamant about enjoying her independence, she pulled on a pair of hiking boots and set out to walk the property. It was a rectangle, about thirty acres in all, that extended from her driveway back to some fallow fields that hadn't been farmed in decades. The land contained meadows and forest, including a swath of maples and oaks lining a river that cut diagonally through the parcel. The river wasn't wide or very deep in most parts, but there was one bend in which the water had carved a deep trench over hundreds of years. Hanging from an old white oak branch near the far bank was a length of rope, and she'd spent many hot summer days swinging into the river, or sitting on the bank with a book. Beyond that was an apple orchard, long untended, yet still yielding more than enough fruit. She walked there now, relishing in the sunlight and warm air of autumn.

To get to the orchard, she had to find a section of the river with exposed rocks, which involved walking several hundred yards along the bank. It had rained heavily this year, so the water level was higher than normal and obscured all but the tops of the stones she usually used to bridge the river. Across the water, she could see the edge of the orchard, waxy apples shining through like Christmas ornaments. She had once tried to control the bittersweet that cloaked the trees, but its relentless growth was impossible to contain. Still, the old orchard produced well into November, and she could pick enough to store for an entire year while giving the rest away.

Ana walked farther down the river bank until she found an oak tree that must have been uprooted in a recent storm. The trunk was sturdy enough that she walked across easily, jumping onto the other bank with a satisfying thump. She followed an overgrown dirt path that ran through the orchard, eventually leading to the ruins of a house that had stood abandoned since the late twentieth century. The breeze carried a hint of sweetness from the ripe apples, and Ana inhaled deeply, her mouth watering.

She found a tree on the edge that was somewhat exposed to the sunlight and picked a perfectly ripe Cortland. Wiping off the natural waxy coating on her pants, she bit into the tart flesh. This, she would miss. Her own little plot of land, her apple orchard, the smell of the dirt-road dust as the wind kicked it into the air. She'd have to bring Jolie here to show her where she'd be able to harvest apples, and to see the look on her face when she discovered that she had access to an entire orchard in addition to the existing garden. Though she'd mentioned growing up on a farm, Ana would have thought that she'd never seen a vegetable in her life. She took too much joy in the piles of fresh produce in the fridge and root cellar.

Ana picked a few more apples to take back, and made her way toward the river. She hoped Jolie would be home when she got back, but she was probably busy, at school or hanging out with her actual friends, like Nova. She still winced when she recalled their conversation in the truck. Did she have to be so obvious about where her interest lay? Ana sighed and slowed her pace to a meander. As she approached the house, she watched for movement inside.

"Anybody home?" she asked tentatively from the doorway. Her heart sank when she received no response, and she felt an unfamiliar loneliness. She'd been happy living alone until she wasn't. Something had changed. She wanted company, and she increasingly wanted it to be Jolie. Ana put the apples into a bowl on the coffee table and took out a container. She walked to the back, past the bedrooms and the bathroom, past the lab where she should be working, and into the terrarium. The spherical structure reminded her of a snow globe, and indeed, if it were shaken hard enough, she could imagine the pollen floating from the flowers like snowflakes.

Through years of careful experimentation, Ana determined that these were the optimal growing conditions to produce the amount of food needed to sustain three people indefinitely. In deployment, there would be several domes producing much more food, but this was sufficient for now. She produced so much between the garden, her orchard, and the terrarium that it was impossible to go through it all in one year. She usually left produce for the local food bank to pick up, or gave it to her grateful students, who barely had time to eat, let alone grow their own food.

Ana used a bowl to harvest potatoes that grew in hanging baskets along the sides of the terrarium. The potatoes filled the flexible mesh so that she could tell exactly where each tuber was by the bulge it produced. She carefully lifted each plant and clipped off the larger potatoes, setting the rest back inside so that they would continue to grow. With a gene modification, she had created a variety of potato that would produce generously for years before the top eventually died off and she had to replant. The more longevity she could get out of her flora, the more successful the mission would be in the long run. On her way out, she picked some soybeans off lush green plants, and gathered handfuls of blueberries.

She carried her basket through the air locked door and back into the kitchen. The silence remained disconcerting. Still no sign of Jolie. Oh well, she thought. "Cass, would you put on some music? Something jazzy."

Taylor Moroney's voice filled the room and Ana instantly felt better. One of her favorite things to do when she was growing was help her mother cook dinner while they both sang along to the latest Moroney hits. She couldn't recall the last time she'd listened to this album, or done something fun with her mother, but she hadn't forgotten any of the words. She hummed as she scrubbed the dirt off the potatoes.

Most days, she cooked simply, throwing whatever she had into a pot without much thought, and eating it for lunch and dinner. It wasn't her job to cook for the crew, and she didn't have the creativity to imagine dozens of ways to serve a small number of ingredients.

She'd come up with something good that first night when she'd just met Jolie, but since then, her imagination had run dry.

"Hey, Cass. Some recipes with the ingredients I have here?"

"Three choices on your countertop," she replied.

Ana settled on roasted potatoes and soybeans with a honey mustard glaze. For dessert, fresh blueberries with whipped yogurt from some milk she'd picked up earlier in the week. Perfect, she thought. If Jolie happened to come back in time, Ana would have the chance to impress her with a good, home cooked meal. They hadn't had much time to eat together since that first night, with school in full swing and Ana pulled into unexpected meetings.

She followed the recipe the way a scientist would, with unnecessary detail and precision. She was in the process of whipping the yogurt for exactly five minutes, zero seconds, and singing loudly to "You've Got Me Feelin' Real Good" when the front door burst open.

"You have an amazing voice," Jolie said as she entered, wiping sweat from her forehead. "Seriously. You sound just like her."

"Jesus," Ana cried, putting a hand to her chest. "You scared me. I didn't realize I was that loud."

"Window's open," Jolie said nonchalantly as she pointed to a window by the door. She smiled genuinely. "It was good."

How long had she been listening? Ana's cheeks burned. She set down the whisk and watched a droplet of sweat make its way from Jolie's forehead to the base of her neck. Her face glowed and she could see the outline of a sports bra underneath the thin white fabric.

She remembered what she was doing before Jolie came in. "Are you hungry? I'm making lunch."

"I already had lunch at school, but I think it's safe to say I burned that off. I could eat," Jolie said. She leaned heavily on the kitchen island as she stretched her legs, giving Ana an excellent view of her cleavage.

"So, what have you been up to today?" Ana concentrated every ounce of willpower into not gazing at her chest.

"I was in the studio all morning, which was amazing," Jolie said. "I never had a Sunday morning all to myself until I moved here, you know? Then I had lunch with Nova. She wants to know how much of a pain in the ass I am to live with."

"A huge one." Ana snickered.

"Speak for yourself, Miss Up-At-All-Hours-Of-The-Night Scientist Lady." Ana's face must have fallen because Jolie added, "I'm kidding, I'm kidding. You don't wake me up or anything. I'm going to jump in the shower, so just call me when the food's ready. But don't come and get me. We know how that worked out last time."

The wicked look on Jolie's face challenged Ana's ability to stand. As she watched Jolie practically skip out of the room in her very short running shorts, her hair bouncing in its ponytail, she hardly noticed that she was holding her breath.

CHAPTER SEVEN

"That was excellent," Jolie said as she patted her stomach. "You should become a chef. Seriously, you could open up your own little restaurant and feed the masses with everything you've got out here. I'll be the hostess."

Ana's cheeks flushed at the thought of Jolie being a hostess. "Sounds like a plan to me. You'd have to be the hostess, the waitress, and the marketing department. I'll be too busy trying to figure out how to cook." The album was on its third run through, and Ana's head swam with the seductive music.

Jolie laughed. "Seems like you figured it out. It's nice to have someone cook for me who isn't paid to do it." She tucked her damp hair behind her ears and adjusted the collar of her polo shirt.

Ana studied her unabashedly for a moment before she spoke. "It's nice to have someone to cook for." Jolie looked away and a funny feeling settled in Ana's stomach.

Jolie cleared her throat. "Between the two of us, if we eat like this every night, we'll be living in the lap of luxury. All we need is a mud mask and a hot stone massage." She closed her eyes and leaned back against the couch.

Ana thought for a moment. "Wait here. I'll be right back."

"Oh, Ana, you don't—"

"Just wait." Ana darted out of the room down the hall. She opened a section of the wall near the bathroom that served as her overflow bathroom storage, and found a jar of clay she'd had for years and never used. Whether she'd bought it or it had been given to her, she didn't know, but she was glad to have it now. On her way back to the couch, she took a late season cucumber from the fridge.

"You don't do anything half-assed, do you?" Jolie sat on the couch, watching with amusement as Ana moved quickly around the kitchen.

"Why do it half-assed when you can have a full-on face mask just like I've seen in the movies? Seriously, I've never done this." She returned to the couch with nervous energy and placed a small bowl of cucumber slices next to the clay mixture. "You first."

Jolie smiled and dipped her hand into the clay. "Just make sure I don't miss any spots."

Ana watched her as she expertly smoothed it across her forehead and cheekbones, then her nose. "You've clearly done this before." She scooped out some clay and started haphazardly painting her own face with it.

Jolie laughed and shook her head. "Come here." She added some clay to Ana's face around her temples and nose. Ana's heart raced at Jolie's touch, and she was thankful to have the mask as a barrier to her flushed cheeks.

"There. Now lay back and close your eyes," Jolie said.

Ana slumped into the couch. She felt Jolie place the cucumber on her eyelids and instantly relaxed. She moaned. "You were absolutely correct. This is the way to live."

"I know a few things. I'm going to do your nails. Hold on, let me get my nail polish."

"What? I thought you were supposed to be relaxing." Ana already felt her skin tightening uncomfortably as the clay dried.

"Oh, come on. Your nails are full of dirt. I promise I'll make them look good."

She heard Jolie pad down the hall and into her room and return a moment later. Zippers were unzipped and dishes were arranged on the coffee table. Ana's hands were placed in a bowl of warm water. "Why?" she asked.

"Let it soak for a minute. I have to do your cuticles."

"You do?"

Jolie laughed and said, "Trust me, I used to do this with my friends all the time. What do you want on your nails?"

"Nail polish, I guess?"

"Okay, you are officially banned from making creative decisions. Obviously nail polish. What color, genius?"

Ana heard metal clanking against the table. "I don't know. You're the artist. Are you sure you're not going to torture me with whatever that is? It sounds sharp."

"Oh, you wish."

Ana laughed uncomfortably and shifted in her seat. "How am I supposed to wash this off my face if you're working on my cuticles?"

"Here, take your hand out and go wash it off now. I have to get some design inspiration anyway."

Ana picked the cucumbers off her eyes and blinked at the brightness of the room. Jolie's face was covered in light and dark splotches of clay. She concentrated hard on a projection from her bracelet in front of her. "You look ridiculous," she said as she scooted down the hall into the bathroom.

When she returned, Jolie was waiting eagerly for her. "Are you ready?" she asked. "This is going to be epic. Also, this is a great album and everything, but can we please listen to something else?"

"Anything you want. Call on Cassiopeia and tell her." Ana sat on the couch and returned her hands to the cooling water.

"Okay, Cassiopeia, play some good old bluegrass music," she said to the room, then turned to Ana and shrugged. "It's a family thing. My mom used to put it on when we couldn't sleep. My grandma used to do the same for her and my aunts. I can't imagine how it worked, but it relaxes me for some reason."

"Never listened to much bluegrass." The first twangs of a banjo filled the room, and Ana found herself bobbing her head along to the music.

"It's good, right? Give me your hand." Jolie proceeded to massage Ana's right hand with lavender oil. Ana felt the pressure all over her body as warm hands slid over her skin. It was all she could do not to moan.

She needed a distraction. "Tell me something I don't know about you," she said suddenly.

"That leaves a lot." Jolie moved onto the other hand. "Nova wasn't always my best friend. We dated for a month when I first got to college."

Ana watched Jolie's fingers dig into her palms, activating muscles she didn't realize she had, and sending waves of pleasure through her. Her body buzzed at this unexpected information. Confirmation that Jolie was interested in women. The air between them shifted dangerously. "What happened?" she asked.

"Some people are better as friends." She placed Ana's hand on top of a towel that rested on her knee and began to work on her cuticles. "Your turn."

Ana thought for a moment. "I'm a biochemist."

"The lab that you have in your house gave that away, genius. Also, I'm pretty sure you told me you taught biochem in one of our first conversations."

"Well, did you know that I conduct research in alternative drug delivery and tweaking the body to cure itself?"

"Okay, that's definitely cooler than what I imagined." Jolie glanced up at Ana. "Is it weird, though? You must be the same age as some of your students."

"They don't seem to mind. I'm clearly the smartest one in the room, anyway." She smirked and Jolie laughed.

"Brains, beauty, you've got it all."

Ana's pulse raced and she struggled to discern whether there was anything behind that comment. All the comments, really. Was Jolie flirting with her? She couldn't take this uncertain in-between she felt with Jolie anymore. She needed to know the facts, analyze them, and figure out where they stood. "Remember when I asked you if Nova was hitting on me?"

"Yeah, of course." Jolie laughed. "Oh, and she confirmed that she was. You're not as clueless as you think you are."

"Okay, well, good to know. So, what about you?"

"What about me what?"

"Are you hitting on me? Just, you know, my brains and scientific reasoning skills kicking in," Ana said, smirking.

Jolie's eyebrows shot up and she put the cuticle pusher down. "What if I am?"

"Then I'd say that you have an awful lot of confidence for somebody whose face is covered in mud."

Jolie burst out laughing. "Point taken. Next time, I'll be sure to wash my face beforehand." She picked up the tool again and continued working on Ana's nails.

Ana almost fainted at Jolie's nonchalance. She hadn't even flinched. "You know, I think I have some work in the lab to do, actually. Maybe nails another time?"

"Aww, was it something I said?" Jolie pouted as she put down the tool.

"Yes." Ana wasn't sure why she was so unsettled by Jolie's admission, but she couldn't shake it.

"Way to be direct."

Ana stood, wiping her hands on the towel. "Could say the same about you."

A look of sadness crossed Jolie's face as she replied, "One hit after another."

Ana shook her head. "Look, I'm flattered, but you're not my type." Lies.

"What is your type?"

"Someone who's not my roommate." More lies. "And aren't you a little young for me? It would be like dating a student." Ana ruffled Jolie's damp hair as she walked away. "Completes the look," she shouted back. She almost avoided seeing the shock on Jolie's face.

Once she reached her lab and shut the door, Ana slumped into the desk chair and threw her head back, running her lavender scented fingers through her hair. She should go back there and apologize, but she couldn't. She was afraid of what she might do to the woman who had just shamelessly flirted with her. Shit, she thought. This was supposed to be a one-sided fantasy, not an actual possibility. Her wrist buzzed and she touched it to open a feed. A waist up hologram of Martine appeared in front of her.

"Thank God, Martine. Great timing. I'm in deep trouble and I need your help," she whispered.

CHAPTER EIGHT

K yoko, you want to loosen the bolt and remove the silver canister." Ana stood facing the wall in her lab. "That's it. One more turn. Okay." Through her glasses, she watched the maneuver as if she were in the control deck, guiding Carlos and Kyoko through cameras mounted on their space suits.

"Canister removed," Kyoko said. She slowly pulled the weightless piece of machinery from the open engine compartment.

Even though Kyoko was safely on the ground in Japan, Ana knew she really was moving slowly in the simulator suit she was wearing right now. She touched the side of her glasses and her input changed to Carlos's view. He was tethered to the spacecraft, watching Kyoko and waiting for orders to replace the canister.

When the time was right, Ana said, "Carlos, insert the canister and turn it a half turn to the right."

"Okay, canister inserted and turned." He floated away to let Kyoko back in. Ana's stomach lurched for a moment. They'd been at this for several hours already, and she had been feeling motion sick for the last two.

"Kyoko, retighten the bolt with the pistol grip, and, Carlos, you can shut the panel when she's done."

"Maneuver completed," Carlos said.

From her virtual position next to Ana in the control deck, Martine said, "Good work, team. No mistakes."

"Thank you, Captain," Kyoko said.

Ana looked at her watch and logged the time it had taken them to replace the part. Not bad. "Okay, we have one more, and this will be a long one. Is everybody okay to continue?"

"I'm a go," Kyoko said with an audible sigh.

Carlos echoed her exhaustion and they began the final simulation of the day. If everything went well, they'd be done in the early morning hours. Ana was about to give the command to move to the solar assembly at the top of the craft when she heard the front door shut. She listened for a moment as footsteps thudded down the hallway into Jolie's room. She heard something metal clatter on the floor and held her breath. A moment later, the bedroom door shut. She looked at her watch: 10:12 p.m. She hadn't seen Jolie all day, so this was the first chance she had to apologize.

A private video feed showed up in her VR glasses. Martine was giving her a strange look. "What's going on? It sounded like we lost you there for a second. Is your connection okay?"

"Sorry, got lost in my thoughts for a minute."

"Is this what we discussed last night?" Martine looked concerned, but also mildly amused. Ana knew Martine thought she was a prude who needed to have some casual sex every now and then. She'd said as much last night. Why she focused on her and not, say, Kyoko, who also didn't seem to have any romantic attachments, was beyond her.

"I'll get it under control, I promise."

"Ana, just remember what I told you. Sex is great, but don't get attached. You can make it work, but remember that the mission comes first." It was easy for her to say. She was looking at a lifetime with her true love, Liv. Even though Martine was in France and Liv was in Antarctica, they saw each other a few times a year, and Ana was pretty sure they had virtual sex a few times a week.

"Noted." Ana sighed, shutting off Martine's feed. She didn't need to be reminded that she shouldn't fall in love with anyone, particularly her roommate. If anything happened, it had to be casual. No feelings. She refocused on Kyoko and Carlos, who had already started moving toward the front of the ship. She watched them clip and unclip on a series of rings, floating in what seemed like slow motion, and yawned. This was going to be a long night.

The repairs to the solar panels were done around 2 a.m. Ana scribbled that into her log and shut off her headset. She was exhausted, but too nauseated to go right to bed. She'd never gotten used to virtual reality, and was not hopeful that she'd adapt to zero gravity without losing her lunch a few times first.

She went to the couch where she picked up the paperback that Jolie had been reading. Judging from the dog-eared pages, she'd made it almost all the way through in just a few weeks. Ana had owned it for a couple of years and had never managed to read more than a few paragraphs at a time.

She opened the book where Jolie left off, a few pages from the end, and began to read. Soon, her eyelids began to droop and she pulled a blanket over her. She reread the same paragraph four times before putting the book down. She'd never finish it. Just as she drifted off, her wrist buzzed three times, her setting for urgent messages. Startled, she threw the blanket off and sat up, rubbing her eyes.

"Fuck. What is it now?" She projected the sender data onto the table and saw it was from her mother. She was instantly annoyed. Her mother must know what time it was, and she surely knew that they'd been in simulations all evening. At least it was a message, and not a direct call.

She rolled her eyes. "Play message," she said into her wrist.

"Ana, it's your mother. I'm at the airport in Paris and I'm going to be on the next flight out of the city. I hope your meetings with the stakeholders didn't end disastrously. You don't have the people skills that I do, but I haven't heard from anybody wanting to back out yet." Ana groaned. Clearly, an extended vacation wasn't enough to turn her into a nice person. Her mother's voice continued, "I'll be at the complex in seven hours to get an update from you in person, so be awake by then." She stopped speaking and Ana turned the app off. Her blood was boiling, and she was sure she wouldn't be able to sleep now. In a few short hours, she'd have to fill Dr. Mitchell in on every detail from the past few weeks, including explaining Jolie's presence. That was not a conversation she was looking forward to. She set her alarm and picked up the book again, rereading the paragraph for a fifth time.

Ana's wrist buzzed and she jolted awake, confused. It was dark in the room. She looked more closely and saw that the windows had been darkened to keep the light out. She could see thin beams of pale daylight slipping in around the edge of the door, and was relieved. She had slept for a couple of hours at least. Even worse than debriefing her mother would have been doing it while half asleep.

"Daylight," she croaked, and each window became clear. She smoothed back her hair and looked around. On the table in front of her was a mug with a note attached. She inhaled the aroma of the lukewarm coffee, took a sip, and read the note.

Hope you got some sleep. See you later. -J

Ana smiled and folded the note into the book. It was some kind of peace offering, a sign that Jolie maybe didn't hate her after all for her ill chosen words. The warmth that Jolie brought to the house was quickly replaced with a chill as Ana imagined her mother here, barking her orders and expecting Ana to obey. She relaxed a bit knowing that Jolie wasn't going to be around to meet her mother. That would have been the worst-case scenario. Now, technically Ana didn't even have to tell her about her new roommate at all, unless she was actively monitoring the data from Cassiopeia and figured it out on her own.

She had fifteen minutes until Dr. Mitchell's scheduled arrival. Fifteen minutes to shower, get dressed, get her notes together, and figure out if or how she was going to mention Jolie. Ana went through the motions of getting ready, but her head was elsewhere. What would she say about Jolie? What could her mother do about it? And, most importantly, why was that all she could think about?

At precisely 8 a.m., a car arrived in the driveway. Punctual as usual. Ana answered the door, still towel drying her hair, and Dr. Mitchell pushed right past her.

"Hi, Mom. Please, come in," she said, sarcastically.

"Ana, sit down and get out your notes. I don't have all day. I've got meetings with the stakeholders in an hour and I have to update them on some things we discovered while I was gone. I have six screens for you. You should read them, then throw them away."

"I know the drill." She sat next to her mother, who wore a black business suit and smelled like expensive perfume. Ana crinkled her nose.

"Here. These are the two most important documents. One is a change to the training schedule. I met with Martine and she agreed that accelerating the schedule would be prudent in light of the other document. I'll let you read it on your own. You'll probably need time to absorb the information. The high-level summary is that we have information about another mission, and it's connected to the failed colony. Martine will tell you more than you'll find on these screens. Coffee. Do you have coffee for me?"

Ana put down the screen she was holding and sighed. It didn't matter what she did or didn't do, what she told or didn't tell her mother. It wasn't going to change Dr. Mitchell's constant disappointment in her. She'd heard snippets of the story throughout her life, and had gathered that her mother had been one of the original candidates for MarsOne. She had been pretty far into the process when she became pregnant with Ana. If she couldn't make history herself, then her daughter, who had ruined all her plans in the first place, would have to do it, or so Ana had always believed. Dr. Mitchell worked tirelessly to ensure that the mission came to fruition. She might not be on board, but she would be controlling the entire operation from the ground.

Ana made a mug of coffee, heated the one Jolie had made for her earlier, and returned to the couch.

"Thank you," Dr. Mitchell said curtly. "I've had a headache for hours. Now, update me on the meetings."

Ana gave her a recap as far as she could remember. She had anticipated needing to rehash all the details, but she had been a little distracted.

"And the simulations?" Her mother recorded information with her bracelet as quickly as Ana shared it.

"All done in under the allotted amount of time."

"Good. I think that's all I need. I'm going to head over to the university now. Will you be in Dr. Brighton's lab later?"

Ana put her hands on her knees and squeezed them until her knuckles turned white. It was all she could do to keep from hitting the table in frustration. "I wasn't planning on it."

"What on Earth are you going to be doing instead? Playing in your orchard? That's not going to further the mission. You know that."

Ana steeled herself. "For your information, I wasn't going to go to the orchard today. Even if I were, at least I'd be having fun. You're always talking about positive mental health. Is there anything you do that you actually enjoy?"

"Of course. You know everything I do is to put you down in history as one of the first successful colonists."

"You didn't answer my question," Ana said.

"Ana, you know as well as anybody that you can't have a normal life. No use trying to pretend you're a regular person. You're better than them. You're smarter. You have a future that they only dream of. Everything's a sacrifice, and we all gave up things for this mission."

Ana wanted to cry, but she took a deep breath instead and stood up. "Maybe there are some things I don't have to give up." Like her orchard. Like a chance with Jolie. She thought about her childhood, which was full of quality mother-daughter time until her mother signed on as mission director. She remembered the nights Dr. Mitchell would come home after midnight, fall asleep on the couch, then leave the house before sunrise. Ana had always understood that this was a necessary part of the mission, and it hadn't bothered her before now. She watched her mother's creased face frown at the table as she sent a message. She hadn't even paid attention to her own daughter's last words as they flew into the open, then settled back in Ana's mind like a fog.

"I have work to do," Ana said. "I hope everything goes well in your meeting." Ana turned, walked out of the room and into the lab, shutting the door behind her. She heard her mother get up and leave without another word. Ana put her head in her hands and burst into tears. She couldn't end up like that.

CHAPTER NINE

Jolie typed her response to the last question on her Art History exam and pressed the submit button. She leaned back in her chair and crossed her feet, stretching her legs to the back of the chair in front of her. Her classmates continued to work on their tests, some of them with extreme concentration. She should probably care a little more, but she'd much rather be creating art than studying it. Her mind wandered to the series of sketches she'd been working on. Usually, she drew landscapes, desolate, dry places like where she grew up. But ever since she ran into Ana in the hallway, she'd been branching out and drawing people. One person in particular, really.

Her stomach growled. She hadn't eaten all day and it was mid-afternoon. Truthfully, she didn't have much of an appetite. Five days of waking up at dawn and returning to the house late at night were catching up with her. She was still a little stung by Ana's rejection, though it had faded into a light awkwardness when she imagined running into her. She'd have to work harder to contain her attraction, since her flirting was making Ana uncomfortable.

A message popped up on her screen. For an instant, she panicked, thinking it was Ana wondering why she had been avoiding her, if she even noticed in the first place. To her relief, it was Nova inviting her to dinner at the sorority house, as she had done the past few days. Jolie contemplated going again, but she was too exhausted to keep up the ruse. She was tired of making small talk with people she didn't really care about, except Nova, of course. Karlee wasn't so bad either, once you got to know her. Still, she couldn't avoid Ana forever. She would have to find some way to rise above her feelings so she wouldn't have to move back to the dorms again. Surely she could pretend not to want to kiss Ana every time she did something awkward or adorable, which was all the time. She politely declined Nova's invitation and grabbed her bag, tiptoeing past the distracted TA and out of the classroom.

The day was the coldest of the season so far, and Jolie shivered in the light jacket she had brought with her. As she waited for her taxi to arrive, she thought back to a year ago, when she bounced from class to work, then to the library, the studio, and back to her room for a few hours of sleep. She barely had any time to herself between doing everything she could to hold on to her scholarship and working in the art studio. A calmness washed over her as she stood on the curb with her tennis shoes hanging over the edge. So much had changed in that time, but mostly, she just felt older, maybe a little wiser, definitely not more in control of her life.

The taxi pulled up in front of her and sounded its telltale melodic horn. She unlocked the door with her handprint and stepped inside. As the car pulled away from the curb and began driving down the main road, she felt the anxiety well up in her chest, and did her usual counting exercises. It was so much better now than the years following the accident, and that was something to be grateful for. Still, she had occasional flashbacks of that car crossing the center line, the overwhelming helplessness of her own two hands and the car's computerized steering. The sickening crunch, the leaking chemicals, and then the sterile white of the hospital.

It had been hailing all night, and there was a tornado watch wailing through her radio. She should have waited it out at the dance studio, but she was tired and looking forward to a shower and a big plate of whatever her mother had made for dinner. She noticed the car coming toward her in the opposite lane, but didn't think much of it until it suddenly swerved into her lane. She didn't remember much else, except that her car swerved as well, avoiding the head-on collision and instead sliding through the coating of hail into a tree. It could have been much worse, said the car company, who should have been legally at fault. They had an out, since the other driver was operating his vehicle manually.

What happened after was a blur. Surgeries, physical therapy, and the promise of a fully integrated experimental leg. She could walk again, and the company who created it paid for her recovery. It had been a no-brainer in her household, even though part of her body was technically still their property.

When Jolie emerged from her thoughts, the car was turning onto Ana's driveway. She placed her hands on the smooth dashboard to cool them, and wiped a band of sweat from her forehead. She did her best to look composed, though she felt drained remembering the accident. She hoped Ana wasn't home so that she'd have a minute to relax. Seeing her straight away would keep her heart racing, though not for the same reasons. She peeked through the window next to the door and saw nobody inside. Relieved, she opened the door, set her bag down on the coffee table and sprawled on the couch.

"Cassiopeia, put on a vacation show." She closed her eyes as a panorama of pristine azure water and white sand beaches filled three wall panels. The narrator described what he called "ultimate luxury," and soothing steel drum music played in the background. Jolie pictured herself there, her toes sinking into the hot sand, walking hand in hand next to the undulating water with a faceless person she knew deep down was Ana.

Some time later, she awoke to the smell of chili simmering on the stove. She opened her eyes and lifted her head slightly, then slowly sat up. Stifling a yawn, she shrugged off the blanket that had been placed over her as she slept, presumably by Ana, who stood in the kitchen over the stove. She watched her stir the pot, taste its contents, and then add more spices. Ana was taking care of her. This, the simplest of facts, seen through a mind empty from sleep, brought a new level of clarity to her feelings. Jolie was falling for her, no matter how much she wanted to convince herself otherwise.

She stood unsteadily and walked over to the kitchen island, leaning on it. Ana turned at the noise and smiled brilliantly.

"You had a nice long nap." Ana appraised her with amusement. "I hope you're hungry. I'm always hungry after I wake up."

Jolie nodded and rubbed her eyes. "Mmm hmm. Smells wonderful." She walked to where Ana stood stirring the pot, and looked inside. Instinctively, she steadied herself by placing her hand on the small of Ana's back. She heard her draw a quick breath, and saw her hesitate ever so slightly. Jolie remembered her intention to stop flirting with Ana, but it was so hard to do. Her heart swelled and she wanted nothing more than to move her arm all the way around, gathering Ana in a warm embrace.

Ana stared straight ahead. "I don't know if you have plans this evening, but—"

"Sure." Jolie said sleepily, then realized she had cut Ana off. "Sorry. What do you want to do?"

"Do you want to go on a walk? I have something to show you."

"Yeah." She nodded. "Sounds good." Not thinking clearly, she drew her arm around Ana's waist and squeezed. Ana gripped the spoon tightly and steadied herself on the edge of the stove.

"I'm going to go sit down now."

"Okay," Ana said, breathlessly.

Jolie yawned and retreated to the couch, where she watched Ana out of the corner of her eye. She seemed self-conscious, aware that Jolie was watching, but unwilling to acknowledge it. Jolie picked up the paperback and tried to read a few lines, but she couldn't concentrate. The longer she watched Ana, the more she realized how deep she really was. To admit it to herself was sobering. She wanted more than anything to go back to the stove and hug Ana again, to memorize the way their bodies fit together. Maybe if Ana knew how she really felt, she'd rethink what she said the other night, but maybe not. If she went too far, Ana might ask her to leave, and she'd begun to love this place.

There was the small issue of no possible future together, even if they did hook up. Jolie got the impression that she was there to learn how to take care of the property as Ana slowly disappeared for longer and longer periods of time, until she was gone for good. Jolie realized she hadn't asked for any specific information about what Ana was doing, or when, and she made a mental note to find out. In a strange way, the impermanence of their situation gave her license to be bolder in acknowledging her feelings. Ana didn't want to date her roommate? Technically, they wouldn't be roommates for much longer.

Ana walked over and set a bowl of chili in front of her, breaking her train of thought. She felt a warm nervousness as the simple gesture reminded her why Ana had been so present in her thoughts lately.

"Thanks," Jolie said. "This looks delicious. You are definitely outdoing yourself in the cooking department." The steam rose from the surface, creating undulating wisps that danced upward and then disappeared. "I'd give it a ten for presentation."

"Presentation?" Ana eyed her. "It's a bowl of chili."

"Yeah, you did a good job putting it in the bowl. Whatever. I'm just trying to talk you up."

"Okay. Well, thanks. I appreciate it," Ana said.

Jolie took a bite. "This is restaurant quality. I'd give it at least a ten and a half overall."

"Good. I spent an entire half hour slaving away in the kitchen and following an actual recipe."

Jolie chuckled and shook her head. They continued to eat in silence.

"You must have been tired. You didn't even move when I put a blanket over you," Ana said, after a while.

Jolie turned to her. "It was sweet of you to do that." She turned back to her bowl, and felt Ana's gaze linger for a moment longer.

When they finished eating, Ana insisted on cleaning up. Jolie watched her put the dishes into the dishwasher. All she wanted to do was to study her from a distance, watch the way she shifted from one foot to the other as she moved from the stove to the sink, but she knew it was creepy to stare. She settled for glancing occasionally in the general direction of the kitchen, reveling in the knowledge that her infatuation wasn't just one-sided. Not if the way Ana kept glancing back at her was any indication.

"Ready to head out? Better get a coat," Ana said as she shrugged a jacket on.

"Yeah." Jolie yawned. "Let's go."

The wind had picked up and easily cut through the fleece that Jolie wore. She hugged herself tightly as they walked side by side down to the river in silence. Ana was staring straight ahead. "You're quiet. What's wrong?" Jolie asked.

Ana gave her a sidelong glance. "I'm sorry about what I said the other night."

"Hey, it's totally okay. I shouldn't have been so forward." Jolie wanted to get it all out in the open. Maybe making her intentions a verbal proclamation would get her to follow them, since just thinking she shouldn't flirt clearly didn't do the trick. "I'm completely prepared to never flirt with you again if it makes you uncomfortable. I didn't even mean to do it in the first place. It just kind of happened and then I got carried away. And I should've thought of what you would think of me, being so much younger, and you leaving, and it's ridiculous anyway because you're so cool and I'd rather just be your roommate, you know?"

Ana stopped walking, and Jolie had to backtrack a couple of steps. "Are you done?"

Jolie shoved her hands in her jacket pockets and shrugged. "Do you forgive me yet?"

Ana looked at her in a way that made Jolie's mouth go dry and her head spin.

"Ana," she whispered.

As Ana stepped toward her with eyes full of desire and fear, Jolie gulped. When Ana pressed her lips to hers, Jolie didn't care anymore about what she thought was going to happen, and what was somehow taking place. All she cared about was Ana's warm body pulling her in, her soft mouth moving over hers in a delicious motion that left her body aching for more. She cupped her hands around Ana's neck and pulled her closer, until she felt the swell of Ana's breasts and the heat of her stomach. Ana drew in a breath and kissed her harder. Her heart pounded in her ribcage, and her ears were on fire. She couldn't believe it, Ana's body pressed against hers, her tongue against her lips, then suddenly against her neck as Ana pressed her lips there. Her hands moved to Ana's shoulders, and she drew her fingertips down the well defined muscles of her biceps. They were every bit as wonderful as she'd imagined. She fit nicely in between Ana's arms, her head in the crook of Ana's neck. It was over too soon as Ana pulled away, resting her forehead against Jolie's. She could feel Ana's pulse, and she looked up, smiling.

"That was unexpected."

"I couldn't help it," Ana said between labored breaths. "You're kind of irresistible." Jolie's cheeks flushed as she watched Ana's chest rise and fall rapidly.

Jolie reached out and tucked a strand of Ana's hair behind her ears. In the evening light, Ana was radiant, glowing with a blush that colored her cheeks and lips. Suddenly, she didn't care if they made it to wherever Ana was taking them, or anywhere at all. She wrapped her hands around Ana's waist and pulled her in again for another searing kiss. Ana moaned and she opened her mouth wider to meet her tongue. With what seemed like a lot of effort, Ana put her hand on Jolie's chest to stop her.

"It's going to get dark soon," Ana said breathlessly.

"You still want to go?" Jolie was perplexed. She wanted nothing more to do with the outdoors unless it involved what they'd just been doing.

"I do, is that okay? I think you'll really like what I'm going to show you." She smiled and squeezed Jolie's hands. "We can do more of that later, if you want to."

She groaned. "If I have to wait to do that again, it better be for something really goddamned good."

"I promise it is." Ana led them down the hill to the river, past a tree where Jolie had spent some time sketching in her notebook. She blushed as she thought about the drawing she'd been working on, and slipped her hand into Ana's.

"Where are we going, anyway? I thought the river was the end of the property," she said.

"It's about halfway. There's a lot more that you have to see."

"Wow. That's half? That's almost as big as my family's farm. How did you end up here? Didn't you say you lived here for years? Wouldn't you have been a teenager?"

Ana laughed. "You're so talkative tonight."

Jolie stopped her and kissed her cheek. "I wouldn't be so talkative if I were doing something else with my mouth," she said.

Ana shivered, suppressing a smile, and continued on. "I got the land when I was twelve, and we built the house after that. I've lived here since I was about thirteen. Yes, by myself." Jolie must have had a horrified expression on her face because Ana turned defensive. "It's not as weird as it seems, I promise. I had help, especially when I was younger, but I did build almost everything on the property at one time or another." They continued walking along the river.

"That's amazing," Jolie said. "I can't imagine being alone at thirteen. Aren't you supposed to be running off with your friends and getting detention for skipping school?"

"I didn't have what you would call a normal childhood."

Jolie looked at her expectantly for a moment, waiting for more information. When she didn't receive any, she said, "I had a weird childhood too. Worked all the time. But I didn't get to live by myself in the middle of nowhere. I had to deal with the small town people I grew up with. Everything seems a lot more magnified when there are so few people around, and so little going on. I can't believe you got to skip that part."

"There are a lot of things you probably wouldn't believe if I told you." Ana looked away. They walked for a little while longer until they reached a tree that had fallen across the water.

Jolie gulped. "Oh my God. No."

"Oh, come on. I walked across it the other day. You're not scared, are you? You look a little pale." The corners of Ana's mouth curled slightly into a teasing grin.

"I'm not doing that. You're going to have to convince me," Jolie said, facing Ana and putting her arms around her waist.

Ana kissed her lightly on the lips. "Convinced?"

"You're going to have to do better than that. Lead me across. And then give me something even better on the other side." She grasped Ana's hand a little too tightly.

"I can't imagine what I can give you over there that I can't give you over here," Ana said, squeezing Jolie's hand.

"I'm sure you can think of something." Jolie drew Ana close and kissed her neck, then groaned. "All right, let's do this."

Ana laughed. "It's not deep, I promise. If you fall, which you won't, you probably won't die."

Jolie stood rooted in place and eyed Ana warily as she jumped up on the log and started across without so much as a wobble. She climbed on and advanced cautiously, led by Ana, until they were in the middle of the river. Water rushed beneath them, and Jolie had a moment of panic.

"I don't think I like this," she said, her eyes darting around for an escape.

"Hey, come on," Ana coaxed. "Look at me. Think about what you get when we cross to the other side."

Ana's eyes sparkled and her smile soothed Jolie's nerves like a balm.

"This better be good," she muttered, following Ana to the other side.

Ana hopped down to help Jolie off. "See? Easy."

"Whatever." Jolie scoffed. "Where's my prize?"

Ana smiled devilishly and closed the distance between them, her hand cradling Jolie's neck. Jolie saw the desire in her eyes, and her breath hitched just as Ana met her lips. Jolie backed into the end of the log, pulling Ana in, her hands sliding up Ana's back under her shirt. Ana moaned and pulled away.

"That's it?" Jolie struggled to control her emotions and tried to pretend she wasn't wet as hell.

"Um, yeah, Miss Greedy. Have some patience." Ana's squeezed Jolie's butt and smiled.

"You're pretty hot. It's hard to have patience," Jolie said, matching Ana's grin with her own. "Huh. Do I actually get to say that stuff now?"

"After that impassioned speech you gave up there, I wasn't sure you ever would again. But yeah, I'm glad you get to say that stuff now." Ana pushed a stray hair behind Jolie's ear. "So let's make this a relatively quick visit and then get out of here so you can tell me more things. Take a look around."

Jolie scanned the landscape behind them. It looked as though someone had planted a continuous series of hedges and pruned them so that they had regular peaks and falls. Then, she caught a glimpse of red at the edge. As she walked toward it, she saw more, peeking through the waves of vine.

"Oh my God, Ana. This whole thing—you have a giant apple orchard, too?" Jolie couldn't believe her eyes. Most of it was choked out by the bittersweet, but it was there, underneath, waiting for someone to rescue the old trees. She wanted to cry, overwhelmed by more compounding emotions than she was used to handling at one time. She'd seen the apples in the kitchen, but hadn't thought about where they came from.

"We both have a giant orchard. I'm not the only one living here now." Ana walked toward a nearby tree and ran her fingers along an exposed branch. "This is good for all year, plus some. Pies, applesauce, fresh out of cold storage. I usually give the extras away, and there's so much more left on the trees, even after all that."

Jolie could barely contain her excitement. She took a deep breath to clear the lump from her throat. If only her family's farmland was more like this, her father would be happy again. He got choked up when they harvested enough to break even. "Let's walk to the end." Jolie practically dragged Ana to the dirt path that ran down the center, cutting the orchard neatly in two.

"I tried to clear away the vines, once upon a time, but it's an impossible task for one person." The sun hung low in the sky before them, brilliantly orange and casting a warm glaze over the land as they walked to the end.

Jolie squeezed Ana's hand. It was all she could do to process their newness. Every time she thought about the fact that their skin was touching, her heart swelled with joy. Ana intertwined their fingers and ran her thumb up and down the back of Jolie's hand. If anybody had ever touched her like that before, she didn't remember. Her heart pounded in her throat, no longer from uncertainty, but from anticipation of everything that was now possible. She looked out into the orchard. She could see some patches where the bittersweet had been cleared away, and the trees were producing magnificently.

A deep contentedness swept through her and a hint of pride rose in her chest. She felt regal walking with Ana, surveying their kingdom side by side.

Too quickly, they reached the end of the orchard, abutted by a thick oak and maple forest and the ruin of a house. The sun was halfway below the horizon, close to setting completely. The sunset brought a deep chill, the wind blowing Jolie's loose hair against her cheek and eliciting a shiver.

"We should head back. I don't want you to have to cross the river in the dark," Ana said.

"So thoughtful." Jolie shouldered Ana. They laughed and Jolie sighed contentedly.

They continued to the river in silence, picking a few apples along the way. Ana offered to help her across again, but she refused.

"Teach a woman to fish," Jolie said. The light was almost gone as they headed up the hill. Ambling toward the house, Jolie told Ana about her productive day in the art studio.

"What do you do there all day?" Ana asked. "I don't think I've ever made a piece of art."

"I'm making some pieces for the student show in January. Hoping to have three sculptures and a bunch of sketches done by then. I actually have you to thank," she said carefully. For more reasons than one, she thought, remembering the nudes she'd been working on earlier in the week.

"Oh?"

"You may have given me some inspiration," Jolie said.

Ana smiled. "Happy to help, I think. What are the sculptures?"

"Well, right now I'm working on a sculpture that's about the size of your sink. On one side, there are tiny rusted metal scraps with nails poking out. The other side is just waves."

Ana thought for a moment. "That sounds neat. I'd like to see it sometime. What does it represent?"

Jolie shrugged. "It's sort of an evolving explanation." It had been a piece about her unrequited feelings for Ana, but now, everything had changed, hadn't it? She wasn't sure which side of the sculpture she'd eventually land on. "I'll let you know when I figure it out."

Just then, Ana's bracelet buzzed three times. Jolie watched as Ana's expression steeled.

"I'm sorry, I have to take this," she said. "Hopefully, it won't take long. I'll find you when I'm done, okay?"

Jolie's heart sunk. She knew how long Ana's calls usually lasted, and if this was anything like them, she wouldn't be seeing Ana for the rest of the evening.

Trying not to sound too dejected, Jolie said, "No problem. I'll get ready for bed and probably be in my room." She gave Ana a soft, lingering kiss on the lips, one that would surely make her wish she was with Jolie instead. As she stepped inside, she caught a glimpse of Ana staring after her with a look of utter desire.

CHAPTER TEN

Ana woke around noon. She had been up at various points during the night talking to the rest of the crew about the intel that had been uncovered by an anonymous informant. The developing story chilled her to the bone. The whole world knew the story of the MarsOne disaster a few decades before. A crew not that different from her own tried to establish a colony on the red planet and, several months in, all indications pointed to cautious celebration. One of the female crew members was pregnant, the habitat had been built, and everyone was as happy as could be expected in a barren wasteland. Then, suddenly, they were all on the floor, dead. The initial investigation determined that one of the crew members had looped the video feed before everyone perished in a carbon monoxide leak. The video tampering pointed to murder or a group suicide. The data were inconclusive, but most of the world preferred the murder explanation. Suicide pointed to sinister forces in the universe that could preclude humans from colonizing another planet, and an inability to take refuge from a dying Earth was too depressing to consider.

Now Ana knew there was more to the story. Much more. And it scared the shit out of her. The Hammer team was still investigating, but it looked as though someone had hacked the encrypted systems from Earth. Signs pointed to the director of a newly discovered rival mission to Mars as the hacker. With a competing mission and only one ready built habitat, the HammerOne mission could not afford to be the second to leave.

Until suspicions were confirmed, there was nothing for the crew to do but push forward with normal mission preparations. Ana yawned, her body aching with exhaustion, and wiped her eyes. She'd never quite gotten used to interrupted sleep, but it was the reality of her work. And last night, knowing what she could have been doing instead left her feeling enormously turned on and eager to see Jolie. She mentioned the turn of events to Martine during the night, who said it was her "sexual awakening," and strongly suggested that she get it out of her system on this planet. That way, she'd have a lot less to figure out during a time when they'd all be under a lot more stress.

Now, replaying the evening in her tired mind, she felt a deep pleasure at her core, and wished she could have silenced her bracelet last night. If only they'd gone inside together, what would she have done? Followed Jolie to her room, maybe, and lifted her onto the desk. Ana moved her hand under the elastic band of her shorts as she imagined kissing Jolie, pressing her hands against her perfectly sized breasts. She wanted Jolie's legs wrapped around her hips, pulling her in as she slipped her hands under Jolie's shirt. Ana's fingers moved over the wet folds of her skin and she shuddered as they touched her clit. In her mind, Jolie was kissing her deeply and grasping her hips tightly, like she'd done the night before against the tree trunk. Jolie had looked so radiant in that moment, Ana had almost led them back to the house right then.

Ana breathed rapidly as her fingers moved faster. She imagined they were Jolie's fingers, moving roughly, then slowly, teasing her and testing her response. She wanted Jolie on top of her more than anything right now, her hair cascading against Ana's cheeks, her pale breasts grazing Ana's own. Ana let out a sharp cry as she came hard. She lay with her hand still down her pants for a while. It felt amazing imagining Jolie's hand in place of her own, but it seemed somehow wrong to fantasize when the real thing was within reach.

She wiped her hand on the sheet and touched her bracelet to send Jolie a message. *Miss you. Will you be home today?* She checked the calendar. It was Monday. What did Jolie do on Mondays? She couldn't remember, but she guessed it involved classes and the studio, like most other days. When five minutes had passed and she received no response, she sighed and got up.

Ana made herself breakfast and ate it absentmindedly. Every thought she had was hijacked by Jolie. It was exhilarating, but also time consuming, and Ana had work to do. She took a shower, relishing in the hot water pouring over her skin that was still sensitive from her earlier activity. The slight breeze from an open window raised goose bumps on her bare shoulders. She'd never felt so feral before, so intimate with her emotions and distant from logic. A small part of her was raising an enormous red flag, afraid that if she let herself fall for Jolie completely, she'd let down her guard, hurting both of them and the mission. She could see herself giving up all of the confidential information she was supposed to keep near if Jolie asked her at the right time, in the right way. But she also didn't have to end up like her mother. She could have both her life's work and the affection that she desired.

Clean and dressed, Ana was restless. She unfolded a screen to try and find a distraction, then shut it when none seemed worth pursuing. Any kind of focus seemed elusive. She peeked into Jolie's room, but that didn't help. What would she do in there, anyway? Go through her desk? She laughed out loud at herself. What in the world was she doing? Resigned, she returned to the kitchen and stood with her hands on her hips. The sun shone brightly through the windows. That was one advantage of her occasional late waking schedule. The morning fog had lifted, revealing the prime of the day. She sighed heavily. She didn't have enough time left on Earth to spend this morning wishing she was doing something with Jolie. Her days as she knew them were numbered.

She put on a jacket and went outside. As she walked through the garden and past the shed, a pang of nostalgia hit. She would miss this place, its warmth, the feeling of wind moving across her bare skin, and the way the sun cast shadows on all of the life around her. She'd never go outside again in just a shirt and pants. She breathed deeply to record the exact way that dying leaves smelled on a warm fall day. She wanted to remember the aroma of Earth when she was on a monotonous, lifeless world.

Ana stopped walking, stunned. She had begun to think of the mission as a chore rather than the greatest accomplishment of her life. She'd spent the last thirteen years focusing on it as the holy grail, the culmination of countless hours of training. She quickly shook the doubt from her mind and replaced it with a hollow shell of the excitement she was used to feeling, but still it lurked, like a virus, waiting for the right time to awaken. She knew she'd have to tell Martine if this continued. A mission specialist who wished she were somewhere else was as good as a sack of bricks, as far as the team was concerned.

She continued her slow stroll until she reached the top of the hill that sloped down toward the river. She looked over the trees lining the water to the orchard. It looked nothing like a formerly cultivated orchard from here. You had to examine it up close to find the hidden treasure. She scanned the horizon and came to rest on a small figure sitting under an old oak tree at the edge of the river. Her heart leapt and she broke into a sweat. Jolie sat by the river with a pad of paper on her lap, drawing with more focus than Ana had applied to anything in days. Had she been here the whole morning? Ana's first instinct was to walk away and not disturb her, but her eyes remained fixed on the spot.

She watched as Jolie leaned against the sturdy tree trunk and stretched her legs, then her arms. She wore blue jeans and a flannel shirt. On her head was a worn cowboy hat that Ana hadn't seen before. She probably lived in those clothes growing up, working on her farm. Ana's mind wandered to what she imagined Jolie looked like doing farm labor. No matter what she pictured, she found the images impossibly appealing.

Jolie looked like she belonged under that tree, enveloped in the land. Ana stared until the image was safely stored away in her mind. She wanted to walk down here every day for the rest of her life and find Jolie under that tree. She'd have to settle for the few months they had left. She began to walk back toward the house, unwilling to abandon her usual levelheadedness so easily. Soon though, she found herself descending the hill toward Jolie.

"Hi," she called out when she got close.

Jolie looked up with a start and put a hand to her chest. She adjusted her hat and squinted up the hill. "Holy shit, you cannot sneak up on someone like that."

"Hardly. I've been crunching grass the whole way down. What are you doing, anyway?" Ana craned her neck toward the pad of paper.

Jolie quickly concealed the sketch she was working on before Ana had a chance to look. "Just drawing. Not much, really."

Ana saw her cheeks color and smiled. "Can I see?"

"No way," Jolie said. She looked embarrassed, as if Ana had walked in on her doing what she'd just done to herself. The relief she'd felt earlier dissipated and she ached to kiss Jolie again. A part of her couldn't believe that someone so gorgeous, smart, and sexy liked her as much as she liked them.

"Nice hat." Ana knelt and tapped the front of Jolie's hat over her eyes. "Looks like something you'd find in the great state of Texas."

"That's hilarious. If you did your research, you would know that's insulting to someone from Nebraska." She grinned.

Ana sat down and laughed. "I'm not as uninformed as you might think."

"Oh, so you're just a huge jerk, then." Jolie pushed Ana onto her side. "Come here."

Ana got up and moved close to Jolie, leaning in for a lingering kiss.

"Mmm, that was good," Jolie said. She rested her head on Ana's shoulder and they relaxed into each other. "It's so peaceful here."

"Yeah. What was it like where you grew up?"

Jolie shrugged. "I don't know. Dry. Poor. Lots of dust storms, some tornadoes."

"What about your family?" Ana couldn't believe she still knew next to nothing about Jolie before she moved out east for school. "Were you close?"

Jolie nodded. "We were close. I'm the asshole who left and didn't look back. There just wasn't anything there for me."

Ana sighed. A vision of Jolie growing up returned to her mind, this time colored with reality. "I'm surprised people can still live there. At some point, you just have to give up and let the weather win."

Jolie lifted her head off Ana's shoulder and scrunched her face in annoyance. "They have, for the most part. They grow millet now. I built this huge greenhouse with my dad a few years ago, so they'd have more luck growing some vegetables for themselves." Jolie rolled a small pebble in her fingers. "My mom used to talk about when the drought was just starting. I think she heard stories from my grandparents, actually, since it was probably before she was born. Anyway, they'd go plant water-intensives, as if doing that would make it rain. Obviously, we all know how that turned out. After a while, you just accept that you live somewhere difficult, and you go on living." She looked at Ana with hurt in her eyes. "My family isn't stupid for wanting to stay. That house has been on my mom's side for generations."

Ana felt Jolie's pain as deeply as if it were her own and felt awful for causing it. "No, of course not. I didn't mean to imply that. I know how hard it is to leave the place you love."

"They're so ingrained in the Nebraskan landscape, they wouldn't know what to do with themselves if they moved anywhere different. They haven't even been out to visit me."

Ana put her arm around Jolie's shoulders and pulled her in. "That's too bad. At least you get out there sometimes for a visit, right?"

"No," Jolie said. "Not since I've been here. Like I said, I'm the asshole who hopes everybody's okay, but doesn't have the balls to find out. I feel horrible about it, but now it's been so long, it would be weird to go back. I'm afraid to see how much more desperate they are now. As for them, even if they could afford it, I don't think they would come. It's too far out of their comfort zone. They're country people. I don't think they've ever been on a plane, if you can imagine that."

"You kind of ran away," Ana said after a moment.

"I guess. I think they're happy knowing that I'm in a good place, making good decisions about my future. And you're one to talk."

"What?" Ana looked at Jolie.

"Running away. Isn't that what you're doing?" Jolie spoke carefully. Ana was sure she was going out on a limb. Jolie didn't know anything about what she was planning.

"No. Yes, but it's not the same. It's more like running to somewhere."

"Well, depends how you look at it. You can't run to somewhere without running away from somewhere else," Jolie said. Ana avoided Jolie's gaze and played with a blade of grass. Jolie took Ana's hand. "I'm running toward something too, I'm just not sure what it is yet. Running is running. You end up somewhere else or back at the beginning." She paused and looked into Ana's eyes. "Wherever you're running, is it better than what you already have?"

Ana shrugged and shook her head sadly. Jolie was right. Over the last few days, it had become more and more apparent that if there was one place that was better than another, it was right here, present company included.

Out of the corner of her eye, she saw Jolie regard her with concern. Would it really be so bad if she found out? Discussing the mission with someone outside of the small team would be an enormous relief. It was also guaranteed to bring the wrath of her mother, the Hammer Corporation, and everyone else involved. Her mouth opened, lulled by the security she found with Jolie. She could almost feel the weight of her future dropping from her shoulders.

"I owe you dinner," Jolie said suddenly. "You up for lunch instead?" She stood and held out a hand, breaking Ana's spell.

Ana blinked up at the gorgeous woman standing above her, her breath catching as a halo of sunlight illuminated the flyaway strands of strawberry blond hair. She wanted so badly to share all of her secrets with Jolie, but she wouldn't. Instead, she pushed a dark wave of hair from her face and, shivering from the brief collapse of her willpower, took Jolie's hand. "How could I say no?"

Chapter Eleven

The waiter brought a bottle of sparkling water to the table and skillfully poured it into their glasses.

Ana looked around the dimly lit room, a stark contrast to the bright sunlight streaming through the windows. "Well, this is a surprise. I had no idea there were any restaurants left with old-fashioned service."

Jolie smiled under Ana's admiration. "I have a few surprises up my sleeve. So, how did last night's call go?" She lifted her water glass to her lips and took a slow sip, not taking her eyes from Ana's.

"Oh, you know, the usual chatter." She wanted to think about anything other than last night. While the truck was parking, Ana had received a chilling one word message from Martine. *Confirmed.* She knew what that meant. The rival mission director had indeed hacked the MarsOne systems and caused a slow carbon monoxide leak that led to the colonists' deaths. Of course, no law enforcement would be notified because it would bring attention to the Hammer Corporation's own secretive plans. Ana and the team had to be even more careful than usual.

"You okay?" Jolie asked, running her fingers across Ana's arm. She shivered, completely taken aback by the way a simple touch could make her dark thoughts vanish.

"I am, thanks. I was hoping you'd be home today. I'm sorry for running off on you last night." Ana looked into Jolie's eyes and saw her imagining the course the night could have taken.

"It's okay. I know you have your stuff to do. And I have mine," she added defiantly. "Anyway, I'm glad you found me today. It's nice to get dressed up and go somewhere fancy. And you look really sexy. Does this date mean we're officially dating, then?"

Ana blushed and fidgeted with her button-up. "I guess it must. This is the first date I've ever been on. Is that sad?"

Jolie kicked at her foot under the table. "It's even better because I get to take you on it."

Ana gave her an appreciative look. "You look pretty hot, too, you know."

Jolie gulped a sip of water and looked down at her lacy black dress. "I do, don't I? You know, I want to date you, but you're going to have to be a little more open with me about your life."

Ana felt the blood drain from her face. If only Jolie knew how important it was that she not say anything, and how close she had come to telling her everything, she wouldn't make such a difficult request.

Jolie continued. "You're going to have to give me some kind of timeline, at least. That's all I'm asking for."

Ana sighed. "Okay. That, I can do." It wasn't technically allowed, but at least it wasn't a full run down of their plans, as she had feared.

Jolie smiled. "Good."

She reached across the table and intertwined her fingers with Ana's. A rush of heat shot through her and she wondered how much longer they were going to be here.

"Have you decided what you'd like to eat, ladies?" The waiter materialized at the side of the table.

Ana looked across the table. Jolie nodded and said, "Go ahead, I'll figure it out."

"I'll have the millet-encrusted cod, please," Ana told the waiter.

"I'll have the same," Jolie said in a rush.

"Very good, we'll have those out to you shortly."

The waiter took the menus, and Jolie sipped her water again as he walked away. "I just ordered millet, didn't I?"

"Yep," Ana said. "You could just have him come back, you know."

"Nah, might as well eat the fruits of my family's labor. Besides, I kind of want to get this over with. Not because I don't want to spend time with you, but because I'm realizing the things we could be doing instead."

Ana's breath caught in her chest. "Yeah, I was thinking the same thing."

Jolie's eyes darkened as they looked up and down Ana's chest. "You want to get it to go?"

"Definitely," Ana said. She got up and walked over to the host, a pimple-faced college student who immediately assumed that something was wrong. She assured him that everything was, in fact, better than okay, and asked for the food to go. As she swiped her bracelet to pay for the meal, she looked back toward the table. Jolie was giving her a challenging look.

"Hey. I thought I was taking you to lunch," Jolie said as Ana returned to the table.

"Oh, yeah. Sorry. I just want to get out of here. It's not a big deal for me to get it."

Jolie's brow was creased. "Okay, but I don't want you to have to pay for everything. Even though I talk a lot about not having money, it's not a hint that you need to pay for everything. You know?"

Ana grasped her hands across the table. "Of course, it won't happen again. I honestly was only thinking about when I get to kiss you again." Jolie's smile told her she was forgiven.

"I'm going to run to the bathroom before we go," Jolie said. A few minutes later, Jolie emerged from the bathroom, limping. Ana stood and rushed toward her.

"Are you okay? Why are you limping?" She grasped Jolie around the waist and helped her the rest of the way to the table.

"I'm fine. My leg's just acting up for some reason." Jolie sat carefully.

"Did you twist it or something?" Ana knelt beside Jolie's chair, her fingers resting against her leg. The skin felt cooler than normal, which struck her as odd. If she'd pulled something, it should've been warmer. Ana frowned.

"I'm fine, really. I'll just go to the lab tomorrow. They fix my model for free there."

Ana's eyes widened as it dawned on her. "You have a bioleg? Wow." She examined it further. "This is one of the best I've seen. Can't see the seam at all."

"Yeah, it was an experimental model. I don't think it ever made it to market, but it's better than the ones out there. Usually."

"Amazing." Ana ran her fingers along the back of her calf, and Jolie let out a quick breath, prompting Ana to look up. Her eyes were closed and her cheeks were bright red. Well, it looked like there was at least some sensation in her leg despite the malfunction. Ana drew her fingers upward, beyond the hem of her dress, and brushed Jolie's smooth inner thigh.

"Jesus." Jolie gasped.

Ana grinned and withdrew her hand. "I'll take a look at it when we get home. I can probably fix it."

Jolie sucked in another breath. "I don't give a shit about the leg. When the hell's the food coming?"

Ana looked behind her. "Right about now. Good timing." She stood and took the bag of food containers from the waiter. The aroma made her stomach grumble, but she was sure that could wait.

Jolie pushed herself out of the chair, and Ana was quickly by her side, her arm firmly around Jolie's waist. She felt Jolie lean into her, and she picked the pace up a little. The short walk to the truck felt like forever. The second they were both inside, Jolie pulled Ana on top of her.

Their mouths met roughly. Jolie ran her tongue over Ana's bottom lip, moaning against her mouth. Jolie slid her hands underneath Ana's shirt, cupping her breasts through her thin bra. Ana smiled to herself. This was already so much better than this morning. Waves of pleasure ran through Ana's body as Jolie's fingers grazed her hard nipples.

Ana broke away, panting. "Wait." She reached over Jolie and brought up the control panel to tint the windows, then turned up the overhead light. "Okay." She collapsed into Jolie, kissing down her freckled neck to the top of her achingly sexy cleavage. Jolie moaned as Ana pulled her dress lower and kissed in between her breasts. Ana wanted to stay there forever, her mouth on Jolie's fair skin.

"Oh my God, you're making me dizzy."

Ana slowed her study of Jolie's chest. "Are you okay?"

Jolie nodded and took some deep breaths. "I'm fine. I'm not saying it's a bad thing." Ana felt her shoulders being pulled up until she was kissing Jolie's swollen lips again. Jolie pushed her backward and climbed on top. "Can anybody see in here?"

"I don't think so. I honestly don't care right now," Ana said.

Jolie reached behind herself and unzipped her dress halfway, pushing it toward her waist. "You're right, neither do I. Except that we might get arrested." They both giggled. Ana's reputation had always come first, but she knew she would ruin it for five more minutes with Jolie.

"Again, do not care," Ana said, staring at Jolie's chest. "Just want to touch."

"Thank God. If you didn't, I might have to touch them myself. You got me pretty worked up in there."

"Either way sounds hot." A smile crept across Ana's face, and she didn't move her hands from Jolie's thighs. She could wait.

"Fine, that's how it's going to be?" Jolie reached across her chest and twisted her nipple. Her hips began to move rhythmically against Ana's pelvis.

Heat flooded Ana's entire body. She'd never seen anything so devastatingly sexy in her life. Her breath sped up as she slid her hands underneath the dress, feeling the place where Jolie's skin met her underwear. She moved her fingers across the fabric, along the slippery wetness that soaked through. Ana's entire body radiated like a pulsar. Her instincts took over as she watched Jolie throw her head back in ecstasy. Her only goal was to make Jolie feel like this for as long as she could.

She slid her fingers beneath the hem of Jolie's underwear and into her warm folds. Jolie looked like she wanted to scream, but she kept it at a medium groan. Ana stroked her inside and out as she watched her face twist from restrained pleasure to something more wild. She was transfixed, watching Jolie squeeze her breasts and play with her nipples roughly as she rode Ana's hand. How could she possibly need anything more in life than moments like this?

Finally, Ana felt her tense against her fingers, and Jolie leaned down to kiss her so hard that she thought her lip might bleed. Jolie shuddered against her as she came, moaning into Ana's mouth as their tongues clashed frantically. Ana caught her breath as Jolie came to rest on her chest. She smoothed her hair and stroked Jolie's sweaty back.

"You're really hot," Ana said.

"You're really hot, too. I've never done that before with anyone." Jolie lifted her chin so that she was looking at Ana.

"What? Sex?" That didn't seem right. She was way too confident with her body to have kept it all to herself. Ana wasn't quite sure how hers would respond to another person touching it like she touched herself, but she knew she would never feel as unselfconscious as Jolie.

Jolie laughed, her breath tickling Ana's neck. "No, dummy, sex in the cab of a truck in broad daylight with the whole town right outside."

Ana lifted her head to peer outside the window. She could see the shadows of people as they passed, but their features were obscured by the window filters.

"You know, that was pretty amazing, but maybe we should take this party home."

Jolie sighed contentedly. "I've got nothing to do for the rest of the day."

"And there is the small problem of your leg. I might as well try to fix it to save you a trip." As much as she wanted to continue this activity, part of her was suddenly nervous about baring everything. She needed Jolie's mouth all over her, but the intimacy would threaten the only barrier she had left to protect her other life, and she was dangerously close to toppling it.

Jolie kissed her sweetly and put her dress back on. Ana watched her cover up with a pang of regret, then started the truck and untinted the windows, squinting at the bright afternoon sun. They rode back hand in hand, Jolie resting her head on Ana's shoulder.

CHAPTER TWELVE

To Jolie's chagrin, Ana didn't seem to want to continue what they'd started in the truck, so she showered and put on a clean dress, one that was a little too sexy for hanging around the house. Ana was waiting for her in the lab, so she took her sweet time brushing her hair, and even put on a little makeup. She needed Ana to feel the small rejection she was experiencing at her sudden disinterest.

Eventually, she made her way across the hall and into the small room crammed with machinery. The look on Ana's face was worth it, annoyance at having to wait mixed with deep appreciation of her presence.

"You look...really good." Ana's eyes darkened with desire.

Jolie ignored the compliment. "So where should I sit?"

"Um, over here. Just sit on this table." Ana gestured to a clean work bench in front of her, then lowered her chair so that she was almost eye level with Jolie's knee.

It was an interesting position for her to be in, and she was still feeling slightly cruel, so Jolie parted her legs a bit more than she needed to. She could see down Ana's shirt, and watched her chest rise and fall rapidly.

Ana cleared her throat and gingerly touched the seamless area where the two parts of Jolie's body, original and prosthetic, met. "I'm going to see if I can get a clean nerve map."

She reached out and took a scanner off of the shelf, then touched her bracelet to bring up a hologram of the leg. As the scanner passed up and down the limb, the image became more complex, a web of veins, bones, and nerves that Jolie had seen many times before. Ana worked silently, her focus mostly on the image, every so often catching Jolie's eye. Her plan was working, but she also wanted her leg fixed, so she temporarily suspended her slow seduction.

"Cassiopeia, analyze for abnormalities. And throw this on the wall in front of me." Jolie saw the reflection from the screen behind her dance on the wall across the room. She turned her head to see what Ana was looking at.

"That's cool," she said as she watched the blood move through her veins with each heartbeat. The nerves didn't look so good, though. The one that ran down the back of her leg appeared to have atrophied.

"That's definitely not normal," Ana said, looking around the room. She took another instrument from the shelf and held it near Jolie's calf. "Okay, so they probably used Neuropten to regulate the nerve growth. It probably just needs to be replaced, since your body doesn't produce it and the self-regulating mechanism seems to have failed." Finally, she looked at Jolie. "Do you know if this Neuropten is supposed to be replaced every five years or so? That's the standard these days."

"I don't remember. I just go to the lab when I need something."

Ana chuckled and shook her head. "Okay. No problem. I just need you to get some saliva on this." She held out a small plastic stick, which Jolie licked. "Give me a minute." Jolie sat patiently as Ana put the stick in some kind of receptacle, which projected its reading back onto the screen behind her.

"Low on Neuropten. Good thing we did this today. Once the regulators fail, it only takes a day or two to completely leave the system. You wouldn't have been able to walk at all."

Jolie shuddered at the thought. That had been her reality for over a year as she'd dealt with all of the problems of an experimental limb, and she'd spent most of it on crutches or in a wheelchair, yearning to walk again.

"How do I get the Neuropten?"

Ana came over and kissed her gently. "Lucky for you, I work with it pretty frequently. I'll have to modify it for your DNA, but shouldn't take more than a few hours." Jolie watched her gather everything she'd need for her science project, moving furiously around the lab to find the right equipment and chemicals. She loved the way Ana worked, so fluidly, like she belonged in the lab. "I even have regulators that will probably last ten years. Maybe more," Ana said excitedly. "All experimental, of course, but the science is sound. They'll work."

Jolie caught Ana's enthusiasm and laughed. "I bet you make a great teacher. You even have me excited about this."

Ana shot her the cutest grin from across the room.

"What do you have to do to modify it?" Jolie asked.

Ana gestured to the saliva sample. "I just have to put it in this machine, get some of your DNA, and let it do its thing. You get a highly customized serum that we'll inject later."

"Not looking forward to that," she mumbled as Ana connected the plastic stick to a small machine.

"Okay. We're done here for now." Ana stood before her with her hands on her hips, her face flushed from running around.

Jolie's cheeks burned. "I don't know if we are done here," she said suggestively.

"What do you mean? We have to wait for—oh," she said as Jolie hooked her fingers into the belt loops of her pants and pulled her close.

"What's with the one and done attitude? You give me what was probably the best orgasm of my life, and then you're not interested anymore?"

Ana looked away. "It's not that." She took a deep breath and squeezed Jolie's shoulders. "I'm nervous, I guess."

Jolie pulled her in for a kiss. "You, my gorgeous scientist, don't need to be nervous. In fact, you don't need to do anything at all." A bold idea was coming to her, and she wasn't sure Ana would be on board, but she had to try. "Do you trust me?"

Ana gulped. "I think so?"

"I need something like a tie, or a long ribbon. Do you have that?"

"Probably. Why?"

"Help me into my bed, find one, and meet me there. And take off your clothes, okay?"

Ana helped her hobble to her room, and then left to find the ribbon. Jolie reclined in her bed and took off her dress again. Today, it seemed that clothing served no practical purpose.

When Ana returned, she was holding some kind of fabric, and had taken everything off but her underwear. She glanced nervously between the floor and the bed.

"Underwear. Off. Now." Ana reluctantly complied and Jolie took in the sight of her muscular body, feeling her own flood with desire. She pulled Ana into the sleeping pod, which was barely high enough to sit up in, and crawled onto her lap to kiss her. Ana's thighs were warm and smooth, and Jolie ran her fingers to her hips and up her back. Ana smiled against her mouth and let out a sigh. She took that as her cue and gently pushed Ana back onto the pillow.

"Hands above your head," she instructed, looping the fabric around a plastic component connecting the bed to the wall. Ana tentatively complied, watching Jolie as she tied snug knots around her wrists.

Ana chuckled. "Is this how you seduce all your women?"

Jolie tugged at her bound hands. "Only the ones I want to feel extra good," she said.

If Ana was jealous, she quickly forgot as Jolie positioned herself on Ana's torso and kissed her passionately. She felt her wetness against Ana's stomach as she slid down to lick her nipples. Ana moaned loudly and pressed herself harder against Jolie's tongue. She took her time with Ana's breasts and stomach, drawing out her pleasure as if they had days to spend in bed like this.

"Oh my God, I don't know how much more of this I can take." Ana groaned.

Jolie stopped her exploration of Ana's lower stomach and met her lips. "What would you make me do if you weren't tied up?"

"You're cruel, you know that?"

"What would you make me do? Say it and I'll do it."

"Put your fingers inside me," Ana said desperately.

Jolie did as instructed and Ana's face twisted. "What else?"

"Move them in and out?"

"I'm going to take pity on you and not make you tell me anything else, but only because I don't think you'll ask for what I'm about to do." Ana opened her eyes wide and stared as Jolie lowered herself between her legs. She heard Ana gasp as she touched her tongue to Ana's clit. The taste drove her wild and she lost herself in Ana's rhythm against her tongue. Jolie wrapped her arms around Ana's muscular thighs and pressed her tongue harder against Ana, who gasped then came with a string of moans and expletives that made Jolie throb. Afterward, she untied Ana's hands, falling against her lips in a sensuous kiss.

"I love how you taste," Jolie said. She felt Ana smile as she buried her face in Ana's neck.

A while later, while Jolie was drawing circles on Ana's abs, she heard Ana clear her throat. "Do you think we should talk?" Ana asked.

Jolie propped herself up on her elbow. "About this?"

"About this."

Jolie took a deep breath. "I don't know what to say except that I'm glad it happened. I had been thinking about it for a while."

Ana nodded. "Me too. I just want to make sure we're on the same page."

Jolie didn't really want to know what page that was, so she just nodded her head and kissed Ana's cheek.

They didn't talk for a while, only held each other as the sun cast a long glare into the sleeping pod. Finally, an alarm sounded and it was time to get up. Jolie took a deep breath and let it out in a groan.

"Your leg will be fine, don't worry," Ana said, kissing her forehead.

"I know. It just brings back a lot of memories. It's not just that, though. I don't want to get up. You feel too good." She returned her head to Ana's neck and inhaled deeply. She could get used to this, except for the lingering notion that she couldn't let herself.

Back in the lab, Ana was more deliberate and much calmer. Nova always said you could never underestimate the power of a good orgasm, and right now, Jolie couldn't agree more. She wanted to send her best friend a message and tell her everything that had happened, but she'd have to wait until Ana wasn't in the room. No way was she going to discuss this anywhere within earshot.

"You're going to have to take this pill, then I'm going to give you the shot, okay?" Ana had thrown on a tank top and some underwear, and Jolie was eyeing the way neither of them did much to cover her up. Ana put her hands on Jolie's thighs and leaned in for a kiss. Jolie sucked Ana's bottom lip, still swollen from before. "Did you hear me?" she whispered.

"Uh huh," Jolie murmured. "Do whatever you want. I'm just enjoying the view."

"Naughty." Ana laughed. "Here."

The pill went down easily, and the shot didn't hurt as much as she expected. "How long?"

"A day or two until you're back to your old self, but you should start to feel improvement right away," she said, her hands grazing Jolie's pale shoulders.

Jolie shivered as a chill radiated down her spine. "I feel better already, actually. Want to take these annoying clothes off again?"

"I thought you'd never ask."

CHAPTER THIRTEEN

S he kissed me," Nova said as she repositioned herself on her bed. Jolie leaned on her elbow in rapt attention. "Karlee fucking kissed me. And then fucking fucked me."

"You sound sort of mad about that," Jolie said.

"Yes, I'm mad, because you know what she said when we were messing around in her bed?"

"I really can't wait to hear."

"I think you can." Nova huffed. "She was drunk, so I'll take about five percent of the responsibility away from her, but it's still no excuse. She said your name."

Jolie popped straight up. "What? That's a thing that actually happens? I always thought that was an urban legend to discourage extramarital affairs or something." She shook her head.

"I wouldn't have believed it either. But it happened. Apparently, she has the hots for you so bad that she has to sleep with me and pretend it's you."

"That's messed up," Jolie said solemnly.

"No kidding. I don't even look remotely like you. How she managed to fool herself into thinking that is beyond me."

"Wow." Jolie smiled. "I'm almost sorry you told me that." She quickly cascaded into full-blown laughter. A moment later, Nova joined her.

"Oh, man, I needed that," Jolie said.

"After the week I've had, me too. So. Tell me about your love life." Nova's face lit up with anticipation.

"Hold onto your britches." She paused for effect. "So, I told you that we had that super romantic night in the apple orchard, right?"

"Yes, you did. Did you finally get to home plate?"

Jolie covered her face in her hands. "Maybe. Maybe a lot of times."

"Oh my God, I'm so happy for you. It's been way too long since you've been properly laid."

"You sound like a frat boy." Jolie rolled her eyes.

"Frat boy, sorority girl…"

Jolie rolled onto her back. "I just don't know what to do."

"What do you mean?" Nova asked. "It sounds like you know who to do, at least."

"I just moved into her house like a month ago, and I'm acting like an idiot. You don't go and sleep with your roommate. That's like Roommates 101."

"Okay, but it's Lesbians 101 that you do." Nova chuckled.

"Also, the reason she wanted a roommate in the first place is because she is going on some lifelong work trip and she wants me to stay at her house for who knows how long. Who wants to be in a relationship that will last a few months at most?"

"You're looking at her." Nova pointed to herself. "Also, Karlee. She would be happy to be in a relationship for a few minutes, especially if it's with you."

"I don't think she wants a relationship. It's called sex addiction."

Nova laughed. "So true. And I am, apparently, more than happy to be her sex toy."

"Clearly not that happy. If she were less annoying, I'd be happy to be her sex toy. I mean, before Ana happened."

"Christ. How did we end up back on Karlee again? We were talking about your roommate-slash-love interest. Anyway, I'm happy for you. It was pretty obvious from the beginning that you two had the hots for each other. How was it, by the way?" Nova wiggled her eyebrows and poked Jolie in the stomach.

"Wonderful, obviously."

"Obviously."

They lay side by side in silence for a moment. "So, have you figured out what her job is yet? I think she's some kind of spy." Nova giggled.

"You're ridiculous. She's a biochemist."

"That's what a spy would say. Plus, biochemists don't just disappear off the face of the Earth all of a sudden."

Jolie shrugged. "I don't know. She fixed my leg. And she's always up in the middle of the night doing science things in her lab and talking to her friends from all over the world. Especially a hot one from Paris. Anyway, apparently I'll find out her real deal after she's gone for good." Jolie gazed out the window into the night. "Which is unfortunate because I am fucked. I know that we just got together, but I really, really like her. And I'm pretty sure the feeling is mutual."

"Oh, honey." Nova put an arm around her. "Not that I want you to be sad, but I do want to point out that at some point, it will end, whether or not she leaves. Eventually, one of you would die, even if you made it through everything else. You might as well live it up while you have the chance."

"Great, lovely thought, Nova." Jolie rolled her eyes. "It's not the same, though. It's different when you know that it's going to end soon."

"Isn't it better this way? You know exactly what's going to happen, so you can plan for it. It sounds kind of perfect to me."

Jolie sighed. "How so? I'd rather be in the dark and have hope that it could last forever. Otherwise, what's the point? You don't make yourself vulnerable for someone if you don't think it will last. How could we even really be together if we're both holding back?" She rubbed her face with her hands. "Let's talk about something else. This is depressing me."

"Okay. How's the prep for your art show coming?"

"Fine," Jolie said quickly.

"Fine?"

"Yep."

Nova looked at her with feigned annoyance. "Want to go get a drink at the Station?"

Jolie wasn't usually one to use alcohol to forget her problems, but that seemed like the perfect solution right now. Just then, she felt the familiar buzz of a message against her wrist. She held it up to her ear and listened.

Nova's eyes went wide. "Who is it? Is that Ana? Does she want to come to the bar with us?" Nova practically inserted herself between the bracelet and her ear.

"She wanted to know if I'd be home soon."

"Booty call." A wide grin swept across Nova's face.

"Booty call, or making sure I won't be around for some top secret spy stuff."

"I told you," Nova said, smugly.

Jolie ignored her. "I'll ask her if she wants to come." She pressed the phone icon on her wrist and it immediately connected with Cassiopeia, who would notify Ana of the call. She heard a click.

"Hi," Ana said, shyly.

"Hi." A slow smile formed on Jolie's lips. She saw Nova roll her eyes and realized she was taking too long. "Nova's here with me and we're going to Station Bar. Want to join?"

"A bar? Not normally my thing, but I'm not getting anything done here, so sure."

Nova gave her the thumbs up. "Okay, it's pretty swanky, just so you know," Jolie said.

"Got it. See you in a bit."

Jolie ended the call and turned to face a suspicious Nova. "It's not that swanky," Nova said.

"Oh, that was just for me. It's not my fault she looks hot all dressed up."

Nova laughed. "I love the way you think."

They both turned at a knock on the door. Karlee stuck her head in and Jolie cringed before catching herself. The last thing she wanted to do was fend off Karlee's advances all night.

"Did I hear something about Station?"

"Yeah, want to come?" Nova asked. "Otherwise, I'll be the odd lady out."

"I'll be ready in five." Karlee disappeared as quickly as she had come.

Jolie turned to Nova. "Did you have to?"

"Oh, she's harmless. And she's a good friend, if you give her a chance."

"If you say so," Jolie said, stretching and cracking her neck. "Let's go do our faces and make sure we look sexy."

"Double dating. I never thought I'd see the day."

Jolie smiled and tugged Nova toward her by the waist. "We've come a long way, babe."

CHAPTER FOURTEEN

Ana twisted her hair into a bun for the fifth time. It looked okay, but not exactly perfect. She took it down again and hastily brushed the thick strands with her fingers. She didn't understand why she was getting so worked up. It was a downtown bar, not a meeting with the CEO of Hammer Corporation. She'd feel much better wearing a suit, but that wasn't really appropriate for a night out. Three black dresses were thrown in a heap on her desk, none of them worn. Her mother had bought them for her years ago, and she wasn't even sure if they still fit. They were the only garments in her closet that screamed swanky.

She turned her bedroom walls into a 360 degree mirror and appraised herself. The long-sleeved, shimmery dress she had chosen was fairly conservative, but she imagined the lack of skin would have Jolie wishing she could see what was underneath. Satisfied, she grabbed a coat and headed out the door. She was in such a hurry to get into the truck that she barely registered her wrist buzzing. It was Martine, who had projected a small hologram of herself that floated ghost-like against the backdrop of night.

"Calling an emergency meeting of the HammerOne crew," she said in her Parisian lilt.

Ana sighed and went back to the house. She hoped this one was short. She didn't want Jolie waiting for her all night. After sending a quick message apologizing to Jolie for her impending lateness, she projected her own hologram to the group. Soon, she was surrounded by the faces of her fellow crew members, several of whom had been awakened and were in various states of yawning and stretching. Luke was actively falling back asleep, and she sent him a private ping to wake him up. He smiled at her and ran his hand through his mop of blond hair.

The entire crew was family at this point, but she had favorites, and carefree Luke was one of them. They rarely talked outside of meetings, but they had the most similar personalities in the group. When they lived together full-time in a few months, she was sure they'd become closer.

Martine had an indecipherable look on her face, and Ana braced for the news. "Thank you for meeting on such short notice. I'll make this quick. I've received word from Hammer's intelligence division that our competition, let's call them Mission 2, is on a time frame to leave one week earlier than we plan to. With what we know about the MarsOne incident, and its connection to Mission 2, we should all watch our backs. I ask that you keep your eyes and ears open, and don't share information with anyone outside of our group. Never has this been more important than now, since we are only months away from departure. Please be advised that we will have to make changes in our mission schedule based on this."

Nobody spoke, but Kyoko, Udeme and Carlos nodded. Liv and Luke both look like they'd already fallen back asleep. Ana wondered if Martine had heard of a threat against one of them. A competing mission could mean, at best, a jump in funding and preparation for their own, or at worst, direct sabotage and cancellation over lack of resources if the other one left before theirs did. There was only enough ready built shelter for one small team, and the privatization of the missions meant that neither would be working together.

"What do we do?" Kyoko asked.

"At this point, we wait," Martine said. "I've been discussing mission details with Dr. Mitchell, and she'll make the final recommendation after she talks to the rest of the stakeholders. I'll keep you all apprised. That's it for now, have a good night, or morning."

Martine shrunk back into her wrist, and one by one, the rest of the crew followed. A sick feeling replaced the excitement she'd had at going out. Nothing had changed about the mission, not exactly, not yet. But she knew it would, and all she could think about was how Jolie would react to a change in the timeline for their already abridged relationship. She didn't feel like going out anymore, but she hadn't seen Jolie since this morning, and she missed her. Reluctantly, she gathered herself and made her way to the truck.

The town center was busy for a Thursday night, and Ana had to park several blocks away. She navigated around couples and through a group of loud college students, bristling at their recklessness. When she finally got to the entrance, an unassuming, poorly lit wooden door, she was anxious and annoyed, not to mention exhausted from the day.

The hostess pointed her to a table at the back of the long cylindrical room. It resembled the belly of a steam engine, dark walls lined with small tables, almost all of them occupied. She spotted Nova, who was laughing at something said by a petite blonde seated next to her. The blonde leaned across the table and touched Jolie's arm, too intimately as far as Ana was concerned. She fumed inside and turned back toward the door. Maybe she should just go home. It was a mistake to come here in her current mood. She started toward the door when she felt a hand on her arm.

"Hey, didn't you see us?" Jolie stood before her, puzzled at her attempted departure.

"Yeah, sorry, I wasn't feeling well all of a sudden, so I thought I'd go home."

"Aww, don't leave. Come hang out with us." Jolie looked at her with such disappointment and hope that she cracked inside.

"Okay," she said unhappily. "I'll stay for a little while."

She felt slightly more herself as Jolie took her hand and led her to the table. They passed table after table of nice jeans, T-shirts and sweaters, but nobody was dressed half as nicely as she was. "Hey, I thought you said this place was swanky."

Jolie stopped walking and turned toward her, snaking her arms around her waist. "Maybe I just wanted you to dress up for me. Is that a crime?"

Jolie leaned in for a kiss that tasted like whiskey. Under other circumstances, she would have enjoyed dressing up for her, and may have even liked the taste of her lips, but today was not that day. Ana fell further into a funk as they approached the table. Nova greeted her first, giving her a tight squeeze.

"It's so good to see you again. You look fabulous in this dress," Nova said.

"Thanks," she said, annoyed that her appearance was affording her more attention than normal.

"This is my sorority sister, Karlee." She saw Karlee size her up as she stood and stuck her hand out.

"Hi, you must be Ana," Karlee said, too sweetly. "We've all heard so much about you."

Ana shook her hand briefly, not at all impressed with this Karlee character, and took the seat next to Jolie.

The service robot didn't miss a beat, maneuvering toward their table between the standing, chatting patrons. She ordered a seltzer with lime, reminding herself of the importance of being sober and not sharing secrets she knew might slip out innocently in a moment of weakness. As they made small talk, she noticed that Karlee avoided looking at her, instead focusing on Jolie and touching Nova's arm.

"So, Jo, you coming to our talent show next week?" Karlee asked.

"I don't know. Maybe." Jolie shrugged. "What's your talent going to be?"

"You don't want to know." Nova rolled her eyes. "Worse than her usual performance."

"Hey, no fair. At least I'm participating, you wimp. I'm doing a burlesque type dance to our song."

Ana almost choked on her drink. "You have a song?"

Jolie blushed and shook her head. "Not like that. Nova, Karlee and I used to drive around last year listening to 'Touch Me, Touch You' by The Grinders."

"Oh. Sounds fun," Ana said, unconvinced. Of course, Jolie could do what she wanted, but if she had to think about Karlee doing a striptease for Jolie to a song about touching each other, she thought she might throw up. Especially if it took away precious time from Ana that she and Jolie could be spending together.

"Hey, I'm going to run to the bathroom," Ana said to Jolie in a low voice. Her head was spinning and she wondered if she'd been given the wrong drink.

There was a six person deep line for two single bathrooms. Ana sighed and queued up, avoiding an appreciative gaze from the man in front of her. She wasn't in the mood, and his cologne was making her nauseous. She felt a hand on the small of her back and turned around to admonish the person who'd accidentally touched her.

"Whoa. Easy there, tiger," Jolie said.

"I'm sorry. I thought it was a stranger."

"The way you were acting back there, I might as well be," Jolie said.

"I'm sorry. I got some bad news right as I was leaving the house and I shouldn't have come. It's like, you guys have your own thing. I thought being around people was a good idea, but I feel worse than if I had just stayed home alone." Ana took a deep breath and sighed loudly.

"Hey, I'm glad you came." Jolie put her arms around Ana's waist and pulled her close. "Karlee was being a little too flirty with me and I was kind of thinking she'd stop if you were here. Ever since I told her we were together, she's been acting weird."

"Thank you for saying that. I thought it was just me in my terrible mood."

"Aww, were you jealous?" Jolie pushed a stray hair behind Ana's ear.

"No," Ana said, scrunching her face up. "Why would I be jealous of a hot woman closer to your age who won't be running off soon?"

Jolie just smiled and looked into her eyes. "Let's go home and see if we can't make each other forget about all that." She squeezed Ana's butt, bringing an immediacy to her need to get out of here.

Just like that, Ana's doubt and jealousy melted away, and even the weight of the mission news didn't seem all that bad. Of all the things she would miss, how was she going to leave this behind?

"Come on." Jolie dragged her from the bathroom line, out into the bar, and back to the table. "Hey, guys, we're going to head out. I just realized how tired I am."

Nova raised her eyebrows. "Really. Okay, you two, have fun sleeping." She snickered to Karlee as Jolie shot her a withering look.

"Bye," Karlee said to Jolie, not bothering to acknowledge Ana.

Jolie shrugged as they walked to the door. "Okay, then," she said.

"I'm sorry I cut your night short. I feel a little bad." Ana squeezed Jolie's hand.

"Don't be. You're allowed to have a crappy day. You're only human, after all."

But I'm supposed to be better than that, Ana thought. She thought of the newspaper scrap she'd saved, hidden in a picture frame in the living room. The short article came out after the investigation into the MarsOne mission. It wasn't accurate anymore, of course, not since the discovery of hacking in the outpost. It didn't matter, though. The danger that she and the rest of the crew would face on their journey could not be overestimated. She had to be much more than human to overcome the threats of life on Mars.

Chapter Fifteen

Jolie lifted her welding mask and examined the sculpture. She kept trying to attach the small red figurine to the base, but it just wasn't perfect yet. She yawned and took off her leather gloves. Long days and passionate nights with Ana were starting to wear on her mind, if not her body.

She'd been staring at the sculpture for so long, it had become a collection of its components, its meaning lost to her. This piece was a long time coming. After the accident, she'd been so depressed that her parents insisted she see a therapist. After a few weeks of saying nothing during her appointments, her therapist suggested she draw during their sessions. It turned out she had a natural talent for art. It spoke for her when she could not speak for herself, and landed her a scholarship at Singer.

Resigned to finishing the work another day, she sat on a metal stool near the window. The day was fading with a burst of orange that illuminated the campus, casting long shadows behind the buildings. Sunsets here were beautiful, but nothing compared to home, if she could even call it that anymore. Nebraska had the best in the world, she was sure, and she'd spent many evenings on her back porch overlooking the fields watching the sky fade into brilliant hues of orange and red.

She barely registered footsteps across the linoleum floor until they were right behind her.

"Beautiful, isn't it?" Professor Anderson leaned her sinewy arms on the window sill and gazed out.

"I was just thinking that. I used to watch the sunset every night back home."

Her professor turned back into the room. "This your latest?" She nodded at the sculpture Jolie had been working on.

"Yeah. It's not going well, though."

She smiled. "Mind telling me a little about it?"

"It's meant to show the aftermath of an accident I was in a few years ago," Jolie said.

"I love it. The way you twisted the metal into a sort of tornado is lovely." She walked around to the other side of it and stooped to take a closer look. "Actually, I was hoping to find you in here. I've noticed how dedicated you've been lately, and I'd like you to be the featured artist in the Winter Art Show."

"Really?" Adrenaline pumped through Jolie's body, a mixture of excitement and fear. "You think my work is good enough?" The Winter Art Show was not big or very prestigious, but the featured artist always garnered quite a bit of extra attention.

Professor Anderson rolled up the sleeves of her black cotton shirt. "It's very good. I have some people I think you should meet. One of them owns a sculpture gallery in Boston, and I think he'd be a big fan of your work."

"Wow, thank you." Jolie was shocked at the suggestion a big city gallery owner might be interested. "That would be great."

"You earned it." Professor Anderson smiled. "I'll need you to fill the space, though. Do you think you'll have enough ready?"

"Definitely. I'll make it happen. I have a bunch of sketches I'm working on, too. It's a whole series of nudes and I think it would fit in with this well. A kind of before and after situation." Jolie beamed with pride as they worked out the details of her part of the gallery. When her professor finally left, Jolie jumped up and down and did a little dance.

"You look like you just won the lottery," Ana said as she slipped into the room.

"Hey. Guess you found the elusive art studio. You won't guess what just happened to me."

Ana made her way over to Jolie and slipped her hands around her waist. "You better just tell me then." Ana leaned in for a slow kiss that left Jolie smoldering.

"I'm going to be featured in the Winter Art Show." Jolie looked into Ana's eyes and saw the pride she was looking for.

"That's great. I'm so happy for you. What does it mean?"

"It means that I anchor the show. Most of the pieces will be mine. It could be a foot in the door for me. Lots of people come to the show, and there will even be a dealer there."

Ana's hands caressed the growing gap between Jolie's shirt and skirt waistband. "I'm actually done early at the biochem lab. Do you want to go celebrate?"

"I don't know if I want to go anywhere." Jolie brought her lips to Ana's.

"Okay," Ana said, confused. Jolie clarified her meaning by kissing Ana's neck.

"What if somebody sees us?" Ana's voice was breathy, like she only half cared that another student or faculty member might walk through the door at any moment.

Jolie dragged her into a dimly lit utility closet that held packages of clay, tubes of paint, and boxes of plaster. The chemical smell was overwhelming, but so familiar to Jolie that she didn't mind. She pushed Ana against an old wooden ladder that leaned against the poorly organized shelves, and kissed her without restraint. Ana moaned as Jolie reached her arms around and unclasped her bra. She took her time looking at Ana's soft, heaving chest, framed by her gorgeous shoulders and her waves of dark hair. "You're so beautiful," she said.

Ana blushed under her appraisal, and Jolie watched goose bumps cover her skin. Jolie discarded her own shirt on top of a bucket. She needed to feel every inch of Ana against her.

Jolie took a break from Ana's lips. "I still can't believe I get to do this to you."

Ana moaned and pulled her in again, gently biting her lower lip. A swell of emotion crashed through Jolie, and she felt something deeper than the amazing sex they'd been having. She needed all of Ana, right here, right now. She raked her fingernails across Ana's firm stomach and followed the red marks with her tongue, kneeling on the linoleum floor. Ana looked down at her, acutely aware of what she was about to do, and the fact she was going to do it in a university utility closet. The fear of possible discovery flashed across her face, but only for a moment as Jolie pulled her jeans down, and her underwear with them. Jolie brought her tongue to Ana's folds, kneading her thighs with her hands. She licked Ana a long time before she made her come, reveling in the control she felt at the moment Ana went over the edge.

Mostly naked, Ana leaned back against the ladder, her skin glistening with sweat. Jolie loved looking at her in the calm after an orgasm. She was vulnerable and beautiful, and it was in these moments that Jolie realized she was falling hard.

"I thought this was supposed to be your celebration, not mine," said Ana.

"Being able to do that to you is almost as satisfying as having you do it to me," she said as she hugged Ana. "Will you come to my show?"

"If I can possibly make it, I'll be there." She tucked Jolie's hair behind her ears and held her face between her hands. "You're pretty incredible, you know that?"

In the unromantic LED light that shone from the ceiling, Jolie looked deep into Ana's eyes, seeing her own joy reflected back. She didn't think about what came out of her mouth next. "I love you." She hadn't planned on saying it, and was almost as surprised as Ana was to hear it. The silence afterward quickly became unbearable. She could see Ana struggle to find the right words. Jolie placed a hand on her chest and kissed her. "It's okay, you don't have to say anything."

Painfully, she moved away and put her shirt back on. As she watched Ana do the same, her stomach lurched and she thought she might throw up. The smell of the paint wasn't helping, and she suddenly rushed out the door. In the empty studio, she felt slightly better. She leaned against the window sill and looked out over the campus. She watched a couple walk hand in hand down the sidewalk, furious at their apparent happiness with each other. Why couldn't it be that easy for her?

She was in the middle of thinking how unfair it all was when Ana joined her. A tear ran down Jolie's face, and then another. Her throat burned as she tried hard to hide her raw desperation, but it was no use. Ana scooped her into her arms and held her tightly.

After a while, she was able to speak again, and it took even more time for her to find the right words. "I don't want to lose you," she said before she dissolved into another round of tears.

"I know," Ana said. "I know."

CHAPTER SIXTEEN

Ana crawled out of bed quietly, tucking the blanket around Jolie as she slept. She picked up a T-shirt from the floor and pulled it over her head. Safely in her lab, she turned on the light and locked the door in case Jolie happened to wake up. Pulling a screen from the drawer, she connected to the secure portal. She hadn't showered since the utility closet workout Jolie had given her, and she hadn't been able to sleep either. She wasn't sure exactly what had come over her when Jolie declared her feelings. Everything had happened so fast, and even though she felt the same way, if she said it aloud, it meant she had gone against Martine's strict orders not to fall in love. The timing was disastrous, just as the mission was ramping up. She had explained the unclassified parts to Jolie after they returned home, and the gesture was enough to make temporary peace between them.

"Commander Mitchell?" Udeme's image appeared on the screen. Ana didn't have the energy to use her bracelet and the usual holographic meeting space, so she opted for the less intrusive version. "Nice to see you, Ana. How are you?"

"I'm exhausted," she said. "How are you?" She relaxed in her chair, tilting the screen toward her so she wouldn't have to hold it.

"I'm up," Udeme said. "Just another morning. Waiting on Captain Legrand to arrive."

Carlos yawned. "I was sleeping."

Liv smiled, surrounded by brightness. "Me too, but you can see it's practically daytime here anyway. Who cares when I sleep?"

Ana chuckled. "I forgot that you're on 24 hour daylight right now."

"Trust me, I haven't. The sleeping pills only do so much, and I'm groggy the next day."

There was a murmur of sympathy from the crew, and Martine's image popped up on the screen.

"Captain Legrand, welcome. So, business we need to attend to? I'm tired." Carlos seemed impatient to move the meeting along. Ana didn't blame him. She'd give anything to be beside Jolie's warm body instead of in the laboratory, pretending to the rest of the crew that she was still gung ho about the mission.

As second in command, Ana ran the check-in meetings. "First order," she said, looking at her notes on the wall screen. "Kyoko's cancer drug."

"Indeed, I have developed a new therapy for cancer treatment. This one can detect and target anything more than 100 cells within the body..."

Ana was aware that Kyoko continued to speak, but her mind drifted. Tomorrow was Wednesday, and Jolie would be gone almost all day at Singer. Ana was looking forward to the separation, especially after the rocky and emotional night they'd had. Maybe she'd go talk to her colleagues in the Biochem Department to take her mind off of things. After all, she'd missed the last two departmental meetings because she was otherwise occupied with Jolie.

"Ana? Earth to Ana?" Martine snickered at her joke. "I would tell you to stop daydreaming, but it's probably closer to actual dreaming. I have an update for the structures. I've designed them to have five percent more surface area for windows, which will increase the passive heating by three degrees per day. That will save a very small amount of energy in the short term, and a whole lot over the course of five years."

Ana straightened up. "That's great news. Any other business?"

"Someone's in a hurry to get back to sleep," Luke said with a casual smile. "I'll just sign off with a note that everything's ready for the training month. Looking forward to seeing you lot in a few months' time."

"Thanks, everyone. Have a good night, or day." Ana signed off, put the screen away, and quickly snuck back into the room. Jolie had rolled over so that she took up most of the sleeping space, which was not difficult to do, since it was designed for one person. She gently nudged her over and slipped in beside her.

Ana woke with a start to a bright room, banging her head on the lip of the bed pod.

"Damn it." She breathed heavily, slowing her racing heart. Jolie was no longer next to her, and she wondered how long she'd been alone. She lay back down, hoping that Jolie would reappear, but there wasn't a sound in the house.

The dream that she'd been having only moments ago left her with a clenched stomach, and as she closed her eyes, pieces of it began to reappear in her mind. She'd been alone, isolated in a tiny house she sensed was in the middle of a vacant and deserted place. She was lying in her bed, but was afraid to fall asleep because she knew that if she did, everything would change by the time she woke up. She tossed and turned to elude the exhaustion, yet felt herself slipping away. There was nothing she could do. She'd jerked awake just as she had surrendered to sleep in the dream. Her forehead was drenched in sweat. She breathed deeply to calm her racing heart. She needed Jolie to calm her down, kiss her forehead, and make her some coffee.

But she was as alone as she'd felt when she was asleep, and it struck her that soon, this would be her normal. No Jolie to wake up to, go to bed with, or kiss anytime she wanted. Her heart sank as she remembered why she'd frozen at Jolie's words. I love you. It was because she couldn't give that much of herself up, even though in her heart, she knew she already had. Ana rose from the bed and a note fell to the floor. Jolie must have slipped it next to her on the bed before she left.

A,

I had to get to class and I didn't want to wake you—I know you were in the lab last night working. I made you some breakfast. I guess I'll see you tonight when I get home. It's going to be a long day!

XO, J

Ana clutched the note to her chest and smiled. She was hopeless. Today would be a good day to bury herself in the lab at Singer, the ultimate distraction of pipettes and microscopes. She got up and ate breakfast, and was about to walk out the door when Martine called.

"Ana. How's everything going with Jolie? You seemed far away last night."

Ana sighed and spoke to Martine's projected image. "Can you blame me? It was the middle of the night."

"You're usually sharper, even in the middle of the night." Martine raised an eyebrow. Ana could tell she wasn't really upset, just making sure Ana stayed on track.

"To tell you the truth, things are going really well. I haven't exactly been getting a lot of sleep." Ana felt her cheeks redden.

"Okay, that's good to hear. Just make sure you can leave it behind when we go to training." She heard something behind those words. Martine knew how far in she was. She had to. They'd known each other for years. Ana wanted this conversation to be over as soon as possible.

"Not a problem, Captain."

"Call me if you need any advice, okay? I just want what's best for all of us."

Ana nodded, praying it would be easy to untangle intentions and consequences when the time came. "I've got to run over to the University. I'll talk to you later, okay?"

"Bye."

Ana threw her head back against the door frame. "Fuck."

CHAPTER SEVENTEEN

"Hey, you almost ready?" The loud voice came from the kitchen, where Ana was busy making midnight snacks for the meteor shower.

Jolie put her drawing pencils down and checked the time. "Sorry, I didn't realize it got so late." She tucked the half-finished sketch of Ana in the desk drawer.

"Grab a coat. It's cold out," Ana yelled.

Jolie leaned toward the hallway and said, "Okay. I'll be out soon."

"Hey, cutie." Ana appeared in the doorway. "Don't like yelling at you."

Jolie pulled a sweatshirt over her head. "That's very sweet of you."

Ana raised her eyebrows. "Nice sweatshirt. Where'd you get it?"

Jolie looked down at the ISS Trainee sweatshirt she'd slowly taken from Ana's wardrobe. "I'm sorry, it's just so comfortable. I'll give it back, I swear." She stood on her toes and kissed Ana on the lips.

"I don't believe you, but that did help make your case."

Jolie ran her fingers over the blue button-up that Ana had put on this morning for some meeting. "Is this what you're wearing?"

"No, I think I'll need something warmer."

"I'll keep you warm. Plus, if you wear this, I can guarantee you'll get lucky." She kissed Ana's scrunched nose.

"I already am lucky." Ana blushed deeply and wrapped her arms around Jolie's waist. "Anyway, I don't think Nova will appreciate me getting lucky anytime soon. She should be here in—"

They both froze as they heard the front door shut and a tentative, "Hello?" come from the main room.

Jolie pressed her hand to Ana's chest. "Good timing. Get changed and I'll show Nova around."

Ana pecked her on the cheek and disappeared into her room.

"Anybody here?" The voice was moving closer, at the end of the hallway.

"Coming," Jolie shouted. She peered into the hallway and broke into a fit of laughter. Nova had on the puffiest coat she'd ever seen, a hat, gloves, and a rolled sleeping bag tucked under her arm.

Nova narrowed her eyes and huffed. "What? I'm just prepared, that's all."

"For the winter apocalypse?"

Nova raised an eyebrow and put her hand on her hip.

"Okay, okay, let's get you out of that for the moment and show you around. Wouldn't want you to knock anything over with that thing," she murmured. Nova play punched her shoulder.

She gave Nova the two minute tour of the house, showing her the hidden drawers and closets, the coziness of her bed pod.

"What's in here?" Nova asked, dipping her head into Ana's lab.

"That's where the magic happens," she answered, remembering the slow seduction she'd executed after the restaurant, and how it led to many, many seductions thereafter. She felt her face flush as she heard Ana moving around in her room, in some state of undress.

"I don't think I want to know. What's down there at the end?" Nova pointed toward the terrarium door.

"You can go look. It's the terrarium. Ana told me there are solar panels that light up the room, even though it looks like daylight. I don't know. It's cool in there."

Nova pushed the door open halfway and stuck her head in. "Oh my God, what is that fucking divine smell?"

Jolie inhaled the air as it seeped into the hallway. It smelled like Ana. "It's rosemary. Ana even gave me some infused in oil to wear. Isn't it just sexy and so delicious?"

Nova closed her eyes and took a deep breath.

"Ladies, how's it going over here?" Jolie felt Ana's arm circle her waist as she pulled her in.

"Good. We were just admiring your creations," she said seductively.

Nova rolled her eyes. "You sure you want me here tonight?"

Jolie stepped away from Ana. "Sorry, we'll behave. Want to get out there?"

"I'll get the food and drinks and you two can set up outside," Ana said, moving toward the kitchen. "Whoa, is someone planning to camp out all night?"

"Not you, too." Nova groaned.

Jolie doubled over in laughter. "Let's take this show outside."

She and Nova spread blankets on the cool ground and settled down. Ana emerged a few minutes later with piping hot chocolate and containers of snacks. They ate and drank and Jolie couldn't remember being happier, laughing her head off alongside her two favorite people.

"Hey, did you see that?" Jolie pointed at the sky where a streaking meteorite had just crossed.

"First shooting star gets a kiss. That's the rule." Ana leaned over and kissed Jolie's cheek.

Nova folded her arms. "Aww, man. How about the second?"

"Stop trying to steal my girlfriend." Jolie pushed Nova onto her side and Ana cracked up.

"Please, I don't think I could. You two are ridiculously cute together. Jo, I've never seen you this happy."

"Aww, thanks for saying." She rested her head in Ana's lap and watched the sky. "How big is that out there?"

"Hmm?" Ana asked, absently running her fingers through Jolie's hair.

"You know, the universe."

"Really, really big. Whenever I think about it, I feel like an ant. Smaller than an ant. Like a bacterium stuck to a cell, which is part of a leaf, which is on a tree, which is only a tiny part of the forest."

"Wow. That's a neat way to think of it," Nova said with wonder.

"It's huge, and we're only starting to explore the galaxies closest to us, which are so far away that you can't see most of them without a telescope."

"I'd hate to be out there, on the moon or wherever. It's so far away. It just seems so lonely." Jolie felt Ana inhale sharply and remove the hand that was massaging her scalp. She sat up and squeezed Ana's thigh. "Everything okay?"

"Oh, yeah. I just had a cramp. A hand cramp."

Jolie shot Nova a questioning look. She shrugged.

She didn't bring up any more universe sized questions for the rest of the night, and they all settled into a companionable silence as the shooting stars flew.

CHAPTER EIGHTEEN

W e should think about getting a bigger mattress to put on the floor," Jolie said sleepily as she ran her fingernails up and down Ana's bare torso. They had shared each other's cramped sleeping pods for the past couple of months, and Jolie's muscles ached as much from the sex as from sleeping in such a small space.

"We could get one today. We'll be going into town anyway for Nova's party. That's tonight, isn't it?"

"Shit. I almost forgot. See what you turn me into?" Jolie groaned, imagining Nova's anger if she ever found out about her slip of mind. "We have to get a present. Well, you don't, I do." She scrambled out of bed, almost knocking her head on the way out. She felt Ana's hand brush the small of her back.

"We've still got hours until we have to leave. There's no rush."

Jolie stopped at Ana's logical words, calling her like a siren back to bed. Her insides melted as they had every time she thought about their bodies against each other. She leaned over to place a slow, languid kiss on Ana's lips. I love you, she thought, but she hadn't said it since the first time. "Okay. You're right. But I should get up and do some things I have to get done before tonight. I think I actually have something I can give Nova, but I'll have to buy some supplies for that."

Ana nodded, then sighed loudly. "I might need a few more hours of sleep, actually. Can you wake me up at one?"

"I will." Jolie closed the door and went to shower. Being away from Ana, even for a few moments, brought back the pit in her stomach that grew larger each time she thought too much about how quickly they'd become entrenched in each others' lives. So far, she'd been able to keep the fear of what lie ahead at bay, shielding Ana from the knowledge that she couldn't, in fact, handle being in a relationship she knew was ending. Beautiful, sexy, brilliant Ana had become far too precious to her for there to be any kind of clean break at the end. You have to get used to this, she repeated each time they separated. And each time, it seemed more difficult to believe that she could. She let a couple of tears escape her eyes before damming the flow, knowing that they'd find some way to escape later.

After her shower, Jolie went through her sketches to find the best ones for Nova. She'd spent hours at the riverbank sketching Ana's naked body from memory, but had luckily also drawn the landscape a few times. She stared at the sketches for a while, finally choosing three to make into a triptych. All she needed were three frames and some matting. She glanced inside Ana's lab and found her 3D printer. It could produce whatever custom frames she wanted without having to leave the house. After making sure Ana was still sleeping, she quietly entered the room.

She hadn't been inside since Ana fixed her leg after their first date, and she guessed that she shouldn't be. A small fume hood sat in the corner next to a larger humidity chamber. She peered in at rows of petri dishes inside, some with small colonies of multicolored bacteria, and some lying empty, waiting to be used. A collection of glassware sat on a cart in the corner. The whole room looked messier than she'd seen it. She spotted the printer on a shelf in front of her, and could tell right away that it was a higher quality model than she'd used before. If she was quick about it, Ana wouldn't even have to know. After connecting a screen, she quickly modified three different frame designs. There, she thought. Nova would have no idea that she was so distracted she almost forgot about the party. She set them to print and left the room.

She spent the next hour lounging on the couch, reading an old paperback, when she heard Ana stir. She emerged from the bedroom in a tank top and a pair of boxers, her hair sticking out at wild angles. They hadn't discussed it, but Jolie knew that the erratic days and nights of their sexual escapades were catching up to both of them. She'd fallen asleep twice in her classes that week. Still, even fatigue could not quell desire, and Jolie found herself aroused again at the outline of Ana's breasts through the thin fabric.

"You can't wear things like that if I'm trying to focus on something other than your naked body."

"Oh, I'm sorry." Ana didn't sound sorry at all. "I guess you'll have to use sheer willpower. You still have that, don't you?"

"You're an ass." Jolie chuckled. She remembered the frames still printing in the other room, and decided it was better to be up front about going in there. "I used your printer. I hope that's okay." She grimaced in embarrassment. "The door was open."

Ana looked stricken for a moment, then relaxed slightly. "I haven't been keeping on top of things lately. Not just keeping that room closed, but everything, really. All of my experiments are ruined, and the data is a mess."

Jolie paled. "I'm sorry, I didn't mean—"

"You didn't do anything. I should be paying more attention to my work."

"And less attention to me," Jolie said, sadly.

Ana walked over and knelt beside the couch. "There is nothing in my life I've ever wanted more than you." She kissed her sweetly, and Jolie believed it. "Don't forget that, no matter what happens."

"Is there anything I can do to get you to stay?" Jolie meant it half jokingly, but she felt the energy drain from the room.

Ana's face fell and she shook her head. "Even if there were, I wouldn't tell you. I don't want you to spend the next month trying to change my mind."

Jolie was silent. Was that what she would do? She couldn't be sure. "I'm not trying to change your mind."

"I wouldn't blame you. If we switched places, I can't say that I wouldn't try to get you to stay." She sat down on the couch.

"Can you at least tell me if there's a chance I might see you again?" Jolie's stomach turned as she asked the question. She already knew the answer.

Ana shook her head and almost whispered, "It's unlikely." A flicker of pain obscured Ana's features before it vanished just as suddenly.

"Do you think you'll fall in love with someone else?" Jolie asked. Ana had never acknowledged she was in love with her, but there was no way she didn't feel this too.

Ana started to say something, but it fell away and she looked at the floor.

Jolie felt like she'd been punched hard in the gut. "I see."

Ana cleared her throat. "I'll probably have other relationships, eventually. You shouldn't wait around for me."

Jolie gulped. She shouldn't have started this round of questioning, its answers making her increasingly unhappy. "It doesn't matter what you want me to do. I don't plan on keeping in contact with you after you leave." Her tone was bitter, and she could tell from Ana's twisted expression that her words had stung as intended.

"You knew this would happen." Ana looked her in the eye. "What did you expect?" She shook her head. "I knew this was a bad idea." She stood. This time, she began to walk toward her room, emerging with some sweats a moment later. Without a word, she walked out the door. Jolie did not try to stop her.

Almost a full hour passed before Ana returned. Jolie was at the small desk in her room assembling Nova's present when she heard the front door open. Most of her anger had dissipated, but she didn't acknowledge Ana's return. She heard footsteps approaching her bedroom door, which was cracked open a few inches. Jolie's breath caught as she felt Ana hesitate, then knock lightly.

"Come in," she muttered.

Ana peered into the room, then pushed the door open and walked in. Her cheeks were rosy, and Jolie thought her eyes looked a little puffy. She leaned against the wall, then slid down into a squat. Jolie swiveled to face her. Despite her frustration with their future, her heart broke to see Ana like this, as close to an emotional wreck as she'd seen her. Jolie got the feeling that before she came along, Ana wasn't prone to emotional swings.

"I've never felt like this before," Ana said, as if in answer to her thoughts. Jolie couldn't tell if she meant her feelings about her, or the pain she was in. "I didn't mean to hurt you by telling you the truth. I'm trying to be as straightforward with you as I can."

"I know," Jolie said, her head lowered. "I'm sorry that I made you say things I knew I didn't want to hear."

Ana nodded. A moment passed with Jolie looking at Ana, who was looking at the floor. "I walked down to the river and sat under that tree where you like to draw. The entire time, I couldn't stop thinking about my reaction when you asked if I would fall in love with someone else." Jolie waited as Ana drew in a long breath. Ana looked up at her, her eyes sparkling. "I can't imagine ever feeling like this with anyone else. You tear me apart, Jo. I've never felt so vulnerable and so strong at the same time. I don't think I'll ever find that again."

Jolie slid off her chair and moved next to Ana, cradling her to her chest.

"Look at me," Ana said. "I'm a mess. I'm neglecting my work, which has never been more important than it is right now. A month from now is training camp. I'm not staying in shape, at least the kind I need to be in." She cracked a smile at her insinuation, and Jolie held her tighter. "I don't know what to do. I keep thinking of how this will end," Ana said, forlornly.

Close to tears, Jolie struggled to keep her composure. "Me too. But that's still a few weeks away. You'll go to training camp, then we'll still have time after that. But I can move out before you come back. We can stop seeing each other before then, if you want."

Ana shook her head. "I don't want that."

"I don't either. Maybe we can just make more time for you to do what you need to do."

"That sounds reasonable," she said quietly.

"Okay. I love you, Ana. It kills me that I won't get the chance to see if we could have made this work." Jolie ran her fingers through Ana's soft hair, memorizing its earthy scent.

"I'm really sorry that we won't."

Jolie sighed, trying not to think about how difficult it would be to part ways in a few short months. "Let's try to enjoy this while we can."

Ana nodded. "Do you still want me to come to the party with you?"

"Of course," Jolie said.

Ana relaxed into her arms with a deep breath.

"Why don't you jump in the shower, then we can go into town and walk around until the party."

"Okay." Ana kissed her on the cheek. Jolie helped her up, then returned to her desk. Sliding into her chair, she wondered at the mysterious future that was somehow bigger than their love for each other. She knew Ana felt the deep, raw emotions too, she just couldn't bring herself to say the words, for whatever reason. Jolie sighed, powerless against fate.

By mid afternoon they were parked along Main Street near the common, which was full of college students, young families, and a group of underdressed women engaged in downward dog. The sun was high in the sky, warming the cool November air, and Jolie beamed as they walked across the busy street to the strip of locally owned shops that sold tchotchkes to the upper class locals and tourists. As much as she loved being at home with Ana, she also wanted to show her off.

"Let's go in this one." Jolie pulled Ana by the hand into a store called Coyote Dreams.

"Really?"

"Oh, come on, it'll be fun." She grinned. "Don't you ever window shop?"

Ana looked at her. "Why would I do that?"

"For fun, genius."

"If you say so," Ana muttered as they walked inside. She'd been moping ever since their talk, and all Jolie wanted to do was make her smile.

The store was a maze of tall shelves filled with kitschy local crafts, geodes, and overpriced jewelry. Jolie squeezed Ana's hand as they perused the shelves, giggling at the sappy sayings etched into glass and embroidered into pillows.

As they rounded a corner into the next room, Jolie felt Ana stiffen beside her, letting go of her hand as if it had shocked her. A distinguished looking woman with dark hair pulled back into a perfect bun, stood staring back with narrowed eyes, her hand outstretched toward a glass figurine. Jolie flitted her eyes between the two of them as the elder woman slowly lowered her arm, smoothed her fitted jacket, and walked calmly over. Ana stood rooted in her spot, and Jolie watched her fly through a series of emotions, her face twitching with embarrassment, annoyance, and finally resignation.

The woman stood directly in front of them. She was a few inches shorter than Ana, but Jolie sensed the familial tie in their cool regard for one another.

"I'm Dr. Mitchell, Ana's mother," the woman said as she held out a hand to Jolie.

Dumbfounded by her politeness, even as her gaze was suspicious, Jolie shook her hand silently, looking to Ana for help.

"This is my new roommate, Jolie." Ana flinched when her mother looked back at her.

"Is that so? Roommate seems like a rather anachronistic term for it. Seems we have a bit of catching up to do on personal matters, wouldn't you agree? And we need to talk about other things, as well."

Ana didn't respond. With each passing second, Jolie felt the tension growing between them, until she couldn't take it anymore.

"Hey, Ana? I'm going to go sit on the Common. Why don't you get me when you're ready." She began to turn around. "Oh, and it was really nice to meet you, Dr. Mitchell." She could tell that the woman was appraising her as she walked out of the store.

What the hell was that all about? Jolie shook her head. Ana hadn't mentioned that she had any kind of relationship with her mother, though that would certainly explain the frostiness. In fact, she hadn't even mentioned that she lived around here.

She sat down heavily on the lawn. She hadn't expected to be waiting, so she had none of her usual distractions with her besides her bracelet, and it was too nice a day to be glued to a game or the news. She watched the group of women doing yoga. A large oak tree shaded them, its leaves occasionally fluttering down to land on one of the mats. The women moved through a series of poses and finally settled into child's pose. She stopped watching when she realized she was staring at indecently thin fabric over their backsides.

The family next to her sat on a picnic blanket, while their cherub faced toddler ran in circles around them. She thought of her sister Danielle, who had just given birth for the third time. She had married her high school sweetheart and never left the small town in Nebraska where they had grown up. They'd settled down the street from her childhood home, and her husband worked at the local hardware store. Her sister's days were spent catering to the whims of three young children, and managing playdates with the kids of friends she'd grown up with. That kind of future made Jolie uncomfortable. She couldn't imagine not wanting more than their town had to offer, which wasn't much. It was a dying place, populated by those who stayed and reproduced, and while almost nobody left, nobody moved there either.

Still, Jolie felt a pang of nostalgia. Her childhood had been simple, mostly free of the relentless technological progress that put screens in every pocket, bracelets on every wrist, and giant wall screens in most every room. She hoped there were still places like that left, but couldn't be sure that her hometown was one anymore. She hadn't been back since three summers ago, and she knew her parents had long since given up on trying to get her to buy a plane ticket. She'd make it there soon, she thought. Maybe after Ana was gone, she could take a few weeks and attend classes remotely. Holing up in her childhood room, probably untouched with its lilac walls and flower border, became more appealing the longer she considered it. There were certain kinds of pain that only a long visit home could remedy.

She was lost in her thoughts as she felt Ana sit down next to her, her arm encircling Jolie's back.

"So?" She turned to face a brooding Ana, who looked so deeply unhappy that Jolie couldn't believe this was the person she'd awakened to that morning. "Oh, no. What happened?"

"That was my mother."

"I know. She said so."

Ana sighed. "Well, she isn't pleased that I'm in a relationship, or that I have a roommate and didn't tell her."

"I thought she might be shocked that you're with a woman. I know there are people who still have strange opinions about that," Jolie said, shaking her head.

"No. It doesn't matter who you are. It's a bit of a liability. I convinced her that it was a good idea to have someone stay at the house while I'm in training, though. That wasn't easy." Ana played with a blade of grass.

"I don't get it. You've lived alone for years. You only have yourself to answer to. Even if you didn't, you're definitely old enough to make your own decisions about dating and living with someone. Why does she care?"

"She has a good reason to care, even though I see your point." Ana looked at Jolie and lowered her voice. "Without going into too much detail, I will tell you that she's in charge of the operations for my upcoming departure. There are a lot of resources that went into this, and it's irresponsible of me to jeopardize them. But, Jo, there's more." She took a deep breath.

Jolie felt an ache in her gut as she prepared to hear the next statement.

"She confirmed some changes in the original schedule that I was kind of expecting. The training has been moved up. And the final departure date is sooner than I expected." Ana stared ahead stoically.

Jolie thought she might throw up. She wanted to stand and walk away, avoid finding out the details, but her head was dizzy and her legs were paralyzed. "When?"

"I'm sorry. I didn't know this was going to happen."

"When?"

Ana stared down at her hands. "Tomorrow. I leave tomorrow morning for training camp. When I get back, I have less than two weeks."

Jolie didn't speak as the burn of tears reached her eyes, then rolled down her cheeks. This didn't make sense. Ana seemed happy being with her, so why wasn't she more upset at this turn of events? It was almost as if, in a small way, she was relieved that things had turned out like this. She hadn't realized how much anger had bubbled up inside her until it burst forward, catching them both off guard.

"So that's it?" she spat, glaring at Ana.

Ana looked at her strangely, almost annoyed. "You knew this was coming. Do you think it's easy for me?"

"Honestly? These last couple of months have been a whirlwind and now, you don't seem to care that it's being pulled from us by your mother, who you say has a right to control your life, even though you seem pretty in control of things yourself. Why aren't you angry? Do I mean that little to you?" Jolie had forgotten about everyone around them, and now that she looked, the toddler had stopped running and was staring at them. Several other heads were turned, and she looked down in embarrassment.

Ana looked around. "I don't want to have this conversation here. Can we at least go to the truck?" she whispered.

"Fine." Jolie huffed. In a new rush of tears, she got up and marched to the vehicle without looking back to see if Ana followed her.

When they were both inside, Jolie stared straight ahead, unable and unwilling to look Ana in the eye. Her pulse pounded in her ears and she shut her eyes tightly to will the forming panic away.

"I know it doesn't seem like it, but I'm upset about this too. I'm just in shock about the whole thing. As painful as it is for you, you have no idea how much this affects me." Ana's words were muffled as she held her face in her hands. "This gives me two weeks to get the house ready, and say good-bye to everything I know." Ana leaned her head back against the seat and squeezed her eyes shut. "Will you stay at the house like we talked about? I know we haven't really discussed it, but it would mean a lot to me. I don't trust anyone else with it. I'll sign the papers over to you. You'll take care of it?"

Jolie looked at her, pain etched into every feature, ready to shatter like a tower of glass ornaments. She realized that this wasn't about her at all. As much as it hurt, she was not the one who would be displaced, at least not physically. She reached out and placed her hand on Ana's arm. It was all happening so suddenly. She didn't think she could continue her new life without Ana in the place where it all happened.

"No, Ana. I'll stay in the house for the next month, but after that, I can't see myself wanting to live there without you."

She looked disappointed, but nodded. "It's a lot to ask."

They sat silently, the air between them thick with bitterness and longing. Jolie looked at her hands in her lap. She had been the catalyst behind the early departure, she was sure. "I can't help but feel like this was partly my fault. If I hadn't held your hand in the store, or if I hadn't moved in at all, I—"

"Stop." Ana took one of her hands. The touch felt warm, but heavy with regret. Nothing like the contact they had shared just hours earlier. "This has nothing to do with you. There's a threat of danger with what we're doing. If we don't move the timeline, everything that hundreds of people have been working toward for decades will be lost."

Jolie just looked numbly at their connected hands.

"Remember when I was upset at the bar?" Ana asked.

Jolie nodded.

"I got the initial confirmation that something like this might happen. That's why I was unhappy." Ana's eyes filled with tears, but she didn't let any of them fall.

Jolie wanted desperately to remove some of the burden she was carrying. "Is there anything you can do about it?"

"Nothing." Ana sniffled.

"Okay. Will you at least come to the party still?"

Ana looked completely broken. She pressed her fingers into her eyes to keep her tears at bay. "I can't. I'm so sorry. I have to pack and make sure everything is ready."

"So, this is good-bye."

Ana's silence was answer enough. Jolie nodded, wishing that she'd wake up and find that she'd dreamed this entire conversation, that Ana was lying in her arms and they'd spend the day in bed.

Mechanically, Jolie said, "Drop me off at Nova's, please."

They drove down the street in a deafening silence. As she got out of the truck and shut the door, Jolie heard the distinct sound of a sob. Fighting back tears, she strode forward without looking back.

CHAPTER NINETEEN

Ana rolled down the windows in her parked truck, inhaling the heady scent of fall. She'd arrived in her driveway in a daze, barely aware of having ridden home at all. Her eyes were puffy and irritated, and she was unable to muster the strength to get out and start packing.

As much as it hurt her to leave Jolie like that, she had to admit the mission schedule acceleration made sense. They had no choice but to react to the information that someone else would try to take their place on Mars. As it was, Hammer would be spending millions extra to put all of the pieces into place for a six week launch date. Ana knew it had to be close to impossible to pull off, and it made her nervous. She knew that haste translated into mistakes.

On top of all of the moving parts, there was Jolie. She'd watched her walk away from the truck, her steps heavy with the same brokenness that pierced Ana inside. Maybe she'd change her mind and stay beyond the next month, but would she really risk another good-bye after that? Ana doubted it. If today was the last time she'd ever see Jolie in person, Ana knew she would regret it for the rest of her life.

"There's nothing I can do. Nothing," she said aloud. She slammed her palms against the steering wheel. Steeling herself against the pit of anxiety in her stomach, she mentally ran through a list of things she'd need to do before tomorrow morning's flight to Chile. With the last of her energy, she pushed her emotions deep underneath the surface and stepped out of the truck.

Hours later, as the light was fading, Ana finally sat down on the couch to rest. She couldn't remember the last time she felt so completely drained in mind or body. She looked at the time. The party would have just started. She knew Jolie was probably sitting by herself, perhaps being consoled by Nova, unable to join in the fun because of Ana, Ana's life, Ana's timeline. She'd never felt so dependent on another person, and so depended upon. Jolie wanted, maybe even needed her for tonight, and the next few months. And now everything had changed, leaving Ana empty and Jolie lost. The sting of separation that she felt was far greater than her annoyance about having to change her travel plans.

Ana looked at her wrist to see if Jolie had messaged her and she'd missed it. There was nothing. Her hand hovered over the messaging app, but she couldn't think of what to say. Nothing she could write would persuade Jolie to love, or even like her, again. Besides, it was selfish to want that. Jolie should get on with her life, just as she would have to. Desperate for someone to talk to, she called Liv and Martine.

She waved to their images on the screen. "Hi, I'm sorry to call so late. I just wanted to touch base before tomorrow. I can't believe we have to be there in less than a day. How are you handling it?"

Liv spoke first. "I told Martine a while ago that something like this would happen. We find out last minute so nobody has time to leak the plans."

"There are so many people involved, I can't see how it's a good idea to rush this," Ana said.

Martine jumped in. "I know. We have to work extra hard to make sure no mistakes are made. Are you up for it, Ana?"

She heard the pointedness of the question, and realized she wasn't ready by a long shot, but she couldn't let them down. "Totally up for it. I'm going to go try and get a couple hours of sleep. It'll be good to see you after such a long time."

"I know. Holograms are nothing compared to skin touching skin." Martine didn't say it suggestively, but Ana knew she was talking about Liv.

"I know you two just saw each other, so don't start."

Liv chuckled.

Martine smiled, confirming her suspicions. "Okay, well, I must finish packing now. My flight is longer than either of yours, so I leave in only a few hours. I'll see you on the other side of the world." She dropped from the call.

Liv stayed on a moment longer. "You seem sad, Ana. Are you okay?"

"I'll be fine." She hesitated a moment. Apparently Martine hadn't shared Ana's relationship news with Liv. That was a small comfort. It meant fewer eyes on her degrading performance.

"Okay. I don't believe you at all, but you know where to find me if you want to talk."

"Thank you," Ana said.

She shut off the transmission. She envied Liv and Martine, who'd been in an open relationship for years. Of course they were excited about the schedule change, she thought bitterly. It meant they could start their lives together even sooner.

"Cassiopeia, program the truck to give Jolie full access while I'm gone. Start the paperwork to transfer the title to her. Restrict access to the house to Jolie only and anyone she authorizes. Pull up all of the house plans and any information you have stored about the upkeep, and advise her of them when she returns. And wake me up at 4:30 a.m." She yawned deeply. She laid her head back on the couch and, breathing deeply for many minutes, finally fell into a restless slumber.

A taxi ride to the airport was the last thing Ana wanted to experience so early in the morning. Her head still pounded and she felt sick to her stomach. The drive took her through the dark, sleeping town, past where she had dropped Jolie off the night before. She hadn't heard from her, and hadn't really expected to. She had a momentary thought of stopping the car, running in and finding Jolie, and telling her...what? That she loved her so much it almost made her want to give up her well laid plans? That if millions of dollars had not been spent on specialized training and equipment over the years, she'd give it all up in a heartbeat? No. It wasn't rational. She couldn't throw out something so monumental based on a relationship that lasted a few incredible months. She sat on her hands and resisted changing the coordinates. When she was thousands of miles away in Chile, she'd give Jolie a call and make sure she was okay.

Hours later, Ana stepped from the private jet onto a deserted runway in the middle of the Atacama Desert. She blinked at the sudden brightness that bled through her sunglasses like they were made of clear glass. A small outpost made of a mottled reddish material was the only structure in sight, and even that was hard to see. She knew their training camp would be designed with the same material, making it almost impossible to see from planes or satellite images. Three ATVs were parked next to the building, meaning Ana was the fifth to arrive. That would leave Martine and Luke as the last two. The planes were scheduled to land far enough apart so as not to alert anyone beyond a few members of the Chilean government, with whom they had a worked for years to build the base. She watched the pilotless jet take off again, and found the ATV with her name on it. Placing the suffocating helmet over her head and the gloves on her hands, she revved the engine and took off, following the GPS on the dashboard.

The camp was six miles southeast of the landing strip, and by mile four, Ana felt the desert's oppressive heat and the high altitude beginning to take its toll. She wore clothing designed to keep the moisture close to her body so she wouldn't become dehydrated, but it had the other, unwanted effect of creating a steam bath. The helmet contained vents that collected oxygen as she raced along, combating the thin air that would have otherwise rendered her dangerously lightheaded.

The vehicle raced over the reddish sand toward a speck in the distance that appeared to be a wide, flat topped rock. As she drew closer, she began to make out the connected pods, hidden so masterfully in front of a larger rock outcropping. She parked next to the vehicles that had arrived earlier, and stepped into the airlock.

The base was designed to mirror their Mars settlement exactly, and by now, they all knew it by heart.

"It's Ana," Liv shouted as she stepped into the main room. She pushed off the floor where she was sitting and ran to Ana, enveloping her in a long hug. "It's so good to see you—in person, I mean."

"I know." Ana laughed. "It's been too long." She looked into Liv's eyes, finding familiarity and taking comfort in it. She didn't need Jolie, she told herself. The people she really needed were here, and would be here for the rest of her days.

"Carlos and Udeme are making up some lunch for us." Liv broke their contact. "Kyoko is sleeping. She had a particularly rough flight, it sounds like. Plus, the time change." Liv's words rolled off her tongue like honey, in an accent that Ana could never place. Somewhere between German and British, if she had to guess. Only her platinum blond hair and bright blue eyes hinted at her Scandinavian ancestry.

Ana saw a happiness in Liv's movements that extended beyond the excitement from training and seeing her friends. She didn't have to ask why. Soon, Martine would arrive. Ana could practically hear her counting down the moments until she heard the next ATV pull up to the base. She smiled to herself. She knew what it felt like, for the first time in her life, to anticipate the arrival of the person you loved. It must have been difficult for them to live on opposites ends of the Earth for so many years and still maintain their love for each other. If only Jolie found out where she was going, got on a plane, and made the trip down here. If only the hum of the motor outside the door right now was her. Ana winced involuntarily as Luke stepped inside the airlock and removed his helmet. She smiled the biggest false smile she could, and welcomed him with a kiss on each cheek.

"All right then, I see almost everyone's here, aye?" Luke grinned, his floppy hair settling playfully over one of his eyes.

"Nice trip from the big island?" Ana asked after Liv gave him a hug.

"The best. A little sore from surfing the reef last night, but it had to be done. Not much time left for reefs."

Ana smiled genuinely. Of course, Luke wouldn't have wasted a moment of his precious time on Earth sitting around, ruminating on what he would be missing. Luke's economy of time and motion was breathtaking to experience. He rarely did anything without a purpose, even if it wasn't evident at the time. Even now, as he made small talk, he was unpacking a shirt from his bag and taking off his sweaty one. Ana barely noticed until he was half-naked.

"Where's my main man?" he asked, chuckling.

"You mean your only man?" Liv asked. "He's in the kitchen with Udeme, making something to eat. Leave them alone or we'll never get fed." She swatted at him with the back of her hand.

Ana sighed contentedly. This was just like summer camp when she'd been young enough to be allowed to play with other kids, before she was separated from the rest of the world. She'd only been twice, but the feeling of camaraderie dredged up the memories as if they had happened yesterday. What a pleasant way to think of it—a perpetual summer camp, with more work, no swimming, and on a completely different planet. Almost the same. She might have been satisfied with the idea if Jolie hadn't been on her mind, her ghost following Ana everywhere and lodging itself in her consciousness at the most inopportune times. Like now, when she was supposed to be interacting with the team and preparing for the greatest moment of their lives.

With a forced smile, she hoisted her backpack on her shoulder and made her way to her room. It looked almost identical to her minimalist quarters back home, and as she ran her hand along familiar white sheets, there was Jolie again, her naked body inviting Ana to come back to bed and spend the day there. Ana stepped back quickly, remembering their abrupt end. No, she couldn't torture herself with the memory of pleasure when she had brought about so much pain. Stop it, she said to herself, over and over. She wanted nothing more than to lie on that bed and take a quick nap, but she couldn't stay there, not until she figured out how to turn off her imagination. She heard excited voices rise in the main room, and smiled to herself. Martine.

Like the heroine of an old French movie, Martine shook off her helmet and stood almost arrogantly, a light coating of lipstick balancing her honey waves of hair, somehow undisturbed by the trip here. Though she, Luke, and Liv were glued to Martine with looks of awe and, in Luke's case, a touch of jealousy, Martine's eyes fixated on only one of them: Liv.

"My love." She stepped into Liv's embrace. If anyone ever made a movie about the mission, Ana thought, this would be the main romance. Enduring through the years, bolstered by distance and longing. What she'd had with Jolie didn't even come close, not in so little time. If they'd had more months, or even years, could it have been as epic a story?

Luke cleared his throat as Martine tipped Liv's head back and kissed her passionately. "Okay, well I'll leave you to it and go find Carlos," he said, turning, almost running directly into the wall next to the doorway. Ana followed shortly.

"I think we should save some food for Martine and Liv," Ana said to Carlos and Udeme as she hugged them. "I don't expect they'll be able to join us for a few hours."

Udeme smiled and shook her head. "Tell me, how was your trip, Ana?"

"Uneventful. How was yours?"

Udeme shrugged. "It was difficult to get out of Abuja, as it has been for the last two years. I made it, though, in one piece." Her sad eyes betrayed her upturned mouth. Ana knew she was talking about the civil war that raged in West Africa and had taken her mother and sister years ago.

"I'm sorry, Udeme." Ana placed her hand on her arm. "I can't pretend to know what you've been through. You know I'm here if you ever want to talk about it."

She nodded and smiled again with dark eyes that had surely seen more than the rest of the crew put together.

"Looks like lunch is done," Udeme said, her face relaxing into a neutral expression. She nodded toward Carlos, who was recounting some story about sharks to Luke, with the enthusiasm of a child. "Want to leave these two to catch up, and eat in the main room?"

Ana nodded, taking her bowl of reconstituted rice, beans, and algae into the other room.

"It seems like you have something weighing on you, my friend," Udeme said as they sunk into a section of floor designed to be slightly cushiony. "The other night during check-in, you were distant. Now you are distant in a different way. What happened?"

"I wouldn't even know where to start," Ana said.

"That bad?"

Ana took a bite of her food and chewed absentmindedly. "It's still too fresh. I'm sure by the time this month is over, I'll have moved on completely. I just have to work harder at doing my job in the meantime."

Udeme nodded and squeezed Ana's shoulder. "You will be okay. We are trained in resilience, after all. If anybody can move forward, it's us."

Ana smiled briefly. Udeme was right. She'd spent years working on her coping skills, and this was the perfect situation to prove them to herself and her crew. She would allow this crack to heal, then she would so thoroughly forget about Jolie that when she went back home, it wouldn't matter if she was there or not. Ana would be the second commander they were all expecting her to be.

CHAPTER TWENTY

Jolie woke late in an unfamiliar room. As the fog of sleep and alcohol began to lift, she felt the night before slowly coming back to her. Her head spun and her body ached with the heaviness of a hangover. She remembered the pulse of the music and the heat of dancing bodies all around her. She was dancing with someone—who had it been? Her dance partner had been wearing a skintight tank top and low cut jeans. She remembered hooking her fingers in the belt loops and pulling the woman closer to…kiss her? Jolie shot up, immediately regretting moving at all. Karlee. She clutched her head and looked for signs that anything else had happened with Karlee, relieved when she found none.

Nova knocked lightly on the door and opened it a crack. "Oh, good, I'm glad you're up. I got you some breakfast." She brought a small bag over to the bed and sat down. "How are you doing, sweetie?"

"My head." Jolie moaned, burying her face in the pillow.

"You had a lot to drink last night." Nova stroked her hair.

"No kidding. I'm sorry if I ruined your party."

"You didn't ruin it, hun. I had Karlee keep an eye on you so you didn't do anything stupid."

Jolie looked up at her and didn't see any hint of sarcasm. So, she didn't know what had transpired between them during the party. Good, she thought. She'd keep it that way. No use ruining relationships with her best friend and her best friend's best friend-slash-occasional sexual partner. The previous day came rushing back now, the rawness of Ana's departure burning a hole in her stomach. She hadn't said much to Nova when she'd shown up early at the house, but her mood relayed enough for her to get the general idea.

Tears began to flow down her face, and she choked back the harder sobs that threatened to escape. Nova curled around her, but she hardly noticed being held. She had been inconsolable after the crash a few years ago, realizing that she'd lost a physical part of her body, but this pain was deeper. She'd lost something she couldn't replace with a bionic limb.

She heard Nova in the distance. "Honey? You need to eat something. Please? Eat a bite of this?"

Jolie smelled the food and it turned her stomach. She shook her head, but Nova persisted. Finally, she complied, finding it easier to be told what to do than to do any thinking of her own.

"Here. Drink this too." Nova handed her a bottle of orange juice.

Jolie took a sip and unwrapped the sandwich. On any other day, she would have welcomed breakfast in bed, but this morning, nothing was the way it should be. She took a bite and felt the warmth of the egg and cheese slide past the lump in her throat. She swallowed hard, and the emptiness returned.

"I can't," she said.

"You need to tell me what happened. Maybe it will help put things into perspective."

"She doesn't want me," Jolie said, breaking down again. Even as she said it, she knew it wasn't true. Ana just didn't want her enough. "I knew it was a bad idea to be with her, but the whole time it was happening, it felt right, like nothing has ever felt for me. It just fit. Now she's gone and I'll probably never see her again."

"I'm sorry, sweetie. I know this is difficult. But it sounded like it would have happened this way anyway."

"Not if she loved me more than this thing she has planned for herself," Jolie said bitterly. "I wish I never met her," she muttered.

"Do you really? Before yesterday, I'd never seen you happier."

"I'm miserable."

"I know." Nova shifted uncomfortably. "Will you tell me everything later? Do you want to stay here? We're going hiking today and you're welcome to come with us."

"Who is we? Karlee?" She blushed as she said her name, and hoped Nova didn't notice.

"Yeah. I hope you're not mad. Karlee and I have become pretty close since you moved in with Ana."

Jolie wanted to say, "Not as close as we were last night," but quickly realized that Karlee and Nova had indeed been closer on at least one occasion. That wasn't a conversation she wanted to start, though she couldn't deny that being desired by Karlee gave her a boost in confidence when she so desperately needed it.

"Fine, I'll go." She sighed. "I just don't want to intrude."

Nova looked her in the eye. "You will never, ever be intruding, understand? You're my best friend and I love you more than anything. Let's all have a good time and try to take your mind off things."

Jolie nodded and flopped back down on the pillow.

"Twenty minutes to mope, then you're done."

She shut her eyes tightly and willed them to go by quickly.

An hour later, Jolie and Nova stood outside next to a taxi, bundled in fleece jackets. The air was cool, the sky overcast with gray clouds. Jolie silently thanked whoever or whatever was responsible for the weather. If it had been a nice day, she would have felt compelled to reflect it with her mood. Now, she matched her sulking to the sky's dullness and figured she had an excuse if anybody gave her a hard time. She wore a pair of hiking boots borrowed from one of the sorority sisters, along with some sweatpants and a shirt that she borrowed from Karlee. The faint lavender scent of the shirt reminded her of being close to Karlee last night, and although it felt terrible to betray Ana like this, she also welcomed the distraction.

Karlee shouted from her open window, "Be down in a minute, you two." She was way, way too perky for Jolie today.

"Hurry your ass up," yelled Nova.

Jolie chuckled without joy. "This is going to be an interesting trip."

The trail was less than an hour away, off a winding mountain road that appeared deserted, save the occasional mailbox next to a long dirt driveway. Jolie hadn't eaten more than a bite of the breakfast sandwich and was starting to feel like she might throw up. During the ride, she was vaguely aware that Nova and Karlee were trying to distract her with car games, but she couldn't muster the strength to participate. Instead, she'd rested her forehead on the cold window and stared at the rolling mountains as they passed in the distance.

Karlee and Nova walked ahead of her on the trail, sensing that she needed space. She thought she could hear them whispering about what had happened between her and Ana, but it took too much focus to listen in. Instead, she put all of her brainpower into putting one heavy foot in front of the other. When they reached the summit a half hour later, Karlee handed out peanut butter sandwiches and juice pouches. Jolie ate in silence, peering out into the valley below, studying its geography. A river ran horizontally across the ground, and she wondered if it was the same river that intersected Ana's property twenty-five miles away. She wondered what Ana was doing, and where she was doing it. Was she getting on with her day as if nothing had happened? Was she as empty as Jolie felt?

Jolie felt her bracelet buzz and opened up the messaging app, hoping it was from Ana and dreading it at the same time. Her heart fell as she saw a message from her mom, concerned that she hadn't called in over two weeks. Guiltily, she ignored it and resolved to call back later, though she knew she wouldn't. Ana wasn't thinking about her at all, or else she'd at least have told her she'd arrived safely.

Karlee glanced at her and did a double take. "Hey, are you okay?" She put her hand on Jolie's arm.

Jolie felt the blood pulsing through her ears as her head spun.

Karlee pulled her into her shoulder and rubbed her back. Jolie inhaled Karlee's smell, a mixture of fresh clothing and a hint of sweat. It was nice, safe, different from Ana's. She so desperately needed nice and safe right now.

"Don't pass out on us," Karlee said sweetly into Jolie's ear, her blond hair tickling Jolie's cheek. She swatted it away.

Nova patted her shoulder. "You'll be fine, sweetie. I promise." She looked at Karlee. "Maybe we should go. She doesn't look good."

Karlee nodded and they both scooped Jolie up, steadying her as they started back to the trailhead.

The ride back was quiet. Nova sat in the back seat with Jolie, who fell asleep on her shoulder. When they got back to the sorority house, Jolie wanted to hide in embarrassment. As awful as she felt, she knew she had ruined the hike. She said as much to Nova, who assured her nobody was upset. The three of them retreated to Nova's room, up two flights of stairs and down a long hallway. Jolie walked across the creaky wooden floor to a bean bag chair and plunked down into it, sinking as far into the fabric as she could.

Nova stood in the doorway. "I'm going to run out and get some much needed comfort foods. Karlee, would you mind staying?"

Jolie weakly protested, "Oh, no, that's okay, I can be by my—"

"No problem. I'll be right here." Karlee turned on the bed to face her. They were alone.

"I'm such an idiot," Jolie said.

Karlee got up, and sat on the edge of the bean bag. "You are not an idiot. You're brilliant, gorgeous, and sometimes fun to be around." She squeezed Jolie's shoulder.

"I'm sure I was fun to be around last night. What exactly happened?"

"You kissed me. You passed out pretty soon after that." Karlee looked away.

"I didn't mean to. I mean, I'm sure I did at the time, but I'm sorry if it made you uncomfortable."

"Jolie, I think you know that I like you."

"I heard you hooked up with Nova. How did that go?" Suddenly, Jolie found herself needing to make Karlee as uncomfortable as she was hurt. It was unfair, but in her state, she would take any ounce of pleasure.

Karlee looked at her, annoyed. "I know you know the whole story."

Jolie deflated. "I know. I'm sorry."

Karlee looked sympathetic. "Ana is an idiot for giving you up. I don't care what she had planned. I can go kick her ass for you."

Jolie exhaled sharply. "I'm pretty sure Nova is also interested in doing that."

"She doesn't want to see you get hurt, either."

Jolie looked at Karlee. She really was gorgeous, and probably good in bed, though she couldn't even remember the kiss, and barely remembered the time they hooked up last year. It was a shame. Karlee deserved more than that. She deserved someone who was attentive and not drunk, and who really liked her. Jolie suddenly found herself mildly interested in being that person, though she knew it was unfair, using Karlee as a rebound. She knew she was a horrible person for this, but she would do anything to be able to imagine that Ana was kissing her again. And what did Karlee care if she liked Jolie in the first place? She reached over and played with stray pieces of blond hair that fell in front of Karlee's ear. She did want to feel wanted, didn't she?

"Why are you looking at me like that?" Karlee gave her a paranoid sidelong glance.

"I don't know." Jolie looked away, but now Karlee was studying her profile. Jolie turned slowly back to face her. She looked so inviting, her lips slightly parted and her eyes determined. Karlee wanted her. She'd told her as much. Silently, she raised her lips to Karlee's and kissed her softly. She felt the thrill of kissing someone new, unadulterated by the haze of alcohol. The passion and raw need she had experienced with Ana was mostly absent, but the feeling was pleasant anyway. Karlee's chest rose and fell rapidly, and Jolie caught the heat radiating from her body. When she closed her eyes, it was easy to picture Ana there, roughly pulling her closer, needing her as though nothing had happened.

She kissed Karlee harder, moving her hand to Karlee's smooth neck and pulling her deeper against her mouth. Her mind went blank as Karlee leaned over and straddled her, her hands moving under Jolie's shirt and over her bra. Karlee's hands. Ana's hands.

They didn't hear the footsteps in the hallway, or the whine of the door opening. Jolie opened her eyes to find a confused Nova standing in the doorway, holding a cloth bag. She quickly broke contact with Karlee and pushed her away.

"Well, this is certainly unexpected," Nova said. She left the bag on the floor and walked mechanically back to the front of the house.

"Jesus, I have to go talk to her." Jolie scrambled to get up, but Karlee grabbed her arm.

"Wait."

"Karlee, I can't."

"I know. I get that you're using me, but as long as I know that, it's okay, isn't it?"

Jolie stopped pulling and let her body sag. "It's not okay. I'm sorry. I shouldn't have done that. Nova—"

"She's just weirded out, but she'll get over it. She knows how I feel about you. I made a mistake sleeping with her the first time because I have a thing for you, but it's fine. We hook up sometimes anyway. She knows everything."

Jolie shook her head. "What the fuck is wrong with everyone? I have to go find her." Jolie practically sprinted out of the room, hoping she wasn't too late.

She found Nova sitting on the porch swing, staring at the street. She didn't turn around at Jolie sat down beside her.

"That was weird," Nova said distantly.

"I'm so sorry you saw that. I didn't mean to make things awkward between you and your two best friends. Well, the whole little triangle, really. I honestly don't know what came over me." She spoke softly, her feet dusting the ground with each swing. "Can I ask you something?" Jolie turned her body so she was facing Nova. "Do you have a thing for Karlee? Because you used to try to get me to date her, remember? Are you really that upset?"

Nova laughed, then shrugged. "Nah, I like our relationship just like it is. I just didn't expect you to move on so soon, and you know I want you both to be happy, but you don't even want to be with Karlee, remember?"

Jolie sighed. "I'm an asshole. The whole time I was kissing her, I was imagining it was Ana. I don't know what my problem is."

"You've been broken up for one whole day. Don't you think you should give it some time? You won't always be devastated about Ana, you know. Look, I love you both. So don't go getting Karlee's hopes up if it's not her you're after," Nova said.

"I get it. I'm just full of fucking good ideas lately, aren't I?" Jolie groaned. "Oh, and while I'm on a roll, you should know that last night, at the party, I kissed Karlee. Apparently, she's my go-to when I'm drunk enough not to consider the consequences."

"I knew about last night. She told me."

Jolie's eyes widened. "Oh. You didn't say. Aren't you upset?"

Nova shook her head. "Not really. You were drunk."

Jolie put her arm around Nova's shoulders and held her close. "You're the coolest, most smartest, and most understanding best friend I have."

"Don't you forget it." Nova held her close, rocking along with the swing. "Your most understanding best friend reminds you that you promised to tell me what exactly happened between you and Ana."

"Right." Jolie recounted yesterday's events to Nova as well as she could remember. Everything was cloaked in a haze of sadness. "Then it just ended. I don't really want to talk about that part."

"Okay, okay. How about we go in and see what the rest of the girls are up to. I think this might be a movie afternoon."

"Yeah," Jolie said as she got up. Her mind was fried from processing so many conflicting emotions in such a short time. She couldn't think of anywhere better to be than watching a movie with her best friend by her side.

CHAPTER TWENTY-ONE

Jolie awoke late for the second day in a row, this time with a clear head and solid memories of the night before. Karlee rolled over and gave her a peck on the cheek.

"Did you sleep okay?" she asked sweetly. Everything about Karlee was sugarcoated, which would normally have pissed her off. For the time being though, she found it comforting.

"Yep, I did. Thanks for letting me sleep in your bed."

"Of course. Anytime," Karlee said.

Jolie saw in her eyes that she meant it in every way, even though Jolie only wanted a comforting body nearby.

"I should probably get going. I have things to do at home, and I haven't been there in two days." She sat up and swung her legs over the edge of the bed. She felt Karlee watching her and wondered if she should stay longer. Surely that's what Karlee wanted, but she couldn't bring herself to kiss her again, not with the knowledge that she was just trying to feel Ana.

After a moment, Karlee said, "Okay. Maybe we can get together soon, though."

Jolie nodded toward the wall, feeling like a real asshole. Despite her intentions, she'd continued to lead Karlee to think that they might get together, even though she already realized that Karlee would never fill the void.

Jolie rode to the house deep in thought, considering how she might feel when she arrived. Her mom messaged her again along the way. "Fine," she said under her breath. She pushed a button on her wrist.

"Hi, sweetie. I was getting worried about you." Her mom's shrill voice played clearly from her wrist and Jolie stopped short of rolling her eyes.

"Hi, Mom. I'm fine. You know, you really don't have to worry about me so much. Sometimes I'm busy and I just can't call back for a while."

"Oh, I know, dear. How have you been? You look tired." Jolie wondered how her mother could see the dark lines under her eyes in the tiny image, but not much got by Iris Dann.

Jolie sighed. She usually glossed over the difficult aspects of her personal life in order to save her mother the worry, but today, she was seeking comfort and safety, and perhaps her mom had some advice.

"I've had a rough couple of days. I was dating someone, and we broke up," she said.

A flash of joy passed across Iris's face, and quickly turned to concern. "Oh, honey, what happened? Why didn't you tell us you were dating someone?"

Jolie sighed. "I don't know. It was pretty new. Her name is Ana. I moved into her house so that I could get off campus. Then we started dating."

"Okay," Iris said, puzzled. "So why did you break up then?"

"She already had plans to go off on some work thing. I don't really know. She's leaving in a few weeks, and actually she's training for it right now. That's why we broke up. Because her training started early and it just seemed like a good time to end it." She realized she was crying and wiped tears off her cheeks with the back of her hand.

"I'm sorry, honey, your father is calling me." Jolie listened to the muffled conversation in the background. "Sweetie, why don't you come home for a while? We haven't seen you in too long. Your father could really use your help with the farm while I help your sister with the kids. Your nephews only know you from a screen."

"I have to be here for the next month because I said I would. Oh, remember the art show I told you about? I'm being featured, so

0

I have to get ready for that." Jolie took a deep breath and continued, "Anyway, after a month, Ana comes back for a week or two. I don't know what I'm going to do. I already told her I would leave before then, but I guess I'll see how I feel. I just don't know what I'm going to do when she's gone for good. Get another job and an apartment, I guess."

"Why don't you take a little time off school and come down here until the next semester starts up?"

"I can't really do that, Mom. I have a scholarship to keep," Jolie said.

"What about attending remotely? Surely they'll let you do that, especially if you have a good reason."

She was right. Jolie could make it happen, if she wanted to. Right now, all she wanted was for Ana to be gone for good so that she wouldn't need to make these decisions anymore. Everything would be easier then.

"I'll think about it, okay?"

Iris smiled broadly, the battle not yet won, but leaning in her favor.

"Okay, I'll let you go, Mom. I have some things to do around the house." She squinted at the sky, the day as gray as yesterday.

"Okay, honey. Please call again soon. We'll have a decent harvest this year. Your father wants to tell you about it."

"I will. Bye."

The house was silent, as she had suspected. Ana's room seemed particularly devoid of life, but then so did the rest of the house when it was clean. Upon further inspection, most of her belongings were scattered behind the walls and in the drawers, as if Ana had packed in a hurry. She took a cursory look through them to see if she could find any clues as to her whereabouts, but nothing stood out. Though she'd been alone in the house many times before, the silence was suffocating. She braced herself against one of the walls, her head throbbing. She needed to get out.

Without a plan, she grabbed her coat and ran out the door, across the meadow, and down the hill. Her legs took her automatically to the bank of the creek, and she sat against her usual tree trunk.

This was what she wanted in the first place, wasn't it? Peace and quiet? Out here, a few miles from town and hundreds of feet from the nearest neighbor, she felt utterly alone. She hoped it would get easier as the month wore on, but then what? Could she stay for the week after Ana got back? And after that? Ana had wanted to give her the property, but it would remind her too much of what they'd had. She couldn't take the gift. She'd have to get a job this month to afford another apartment, or maybe she could stay in the sorority house for a while. Both options were disappointing.

Jolie called Nova in the late afternoon. "Hey, do you think you can stay with me tonight?" she asked, her voice strained.

"Hey, love, I have a lot of work to do, but I could swing by, maybe for dinner."

"That would be nice, thanks." She thought about calling Karlee to stay the night, but she knew she'd have to sleep here alone sooner or later. Probably best to get it over with tonight.

She was about to go out again to harvest some apples when Cassiopeia sprang to life. "Jolie, Ana is calling for you. Will you accept?"

"Jesus fucking Christ," Jolie said. She considered rejecting the call, but figured that if Ana was calling her from wherever she was, it had to be important. "Fine. Yes, Cassiopeia, I can talk."

An image appeared on one of the wall screens of a landscape jerking around violently. Ana's face came into the frame. She wore a thin white jacket and sunglasses, and the sun rested low in the sky behind her. Jolie scanned the landscape, which was a sparse peppering of reddish rocks and a distant mountain range. She saw no structures, no people, except for Ana.

"I had to get away from everyone for a minute." Ana breathed heavily as though she'd just sprinted there.

"Who's everyone? It looks like you're stranded in a desert."

"Oh, just my team." She ignored Jolie's other comment.

"Are you okay? You sound like you're going to pass out. And where the hell are you?" Jolie tried her best to act put out, but secretly, she was glad that Ana had finally called.

Ana let out a laugh that dissolved into a dry cough. She panned the camera around her, revealing more of the rocky ground and a better view of the mountains. Jolie saw nothing growing and immediately disliked wherever this was. Ana lowered her voice to a husky whisper. "I'm in Chile."

"Very specific," Jolie said, annoyed. "Why did you call, Ana?"

"I, uh." She turned to look at something in the distance. "I just wanted to say that I'm sorry, for hurting you. And I owe you more of an explanation."

Jolie was mildly intrigued. "Okay." She sat against the back of the couch and crossed her arms. Whatever Ana had to say, wherever she was and whatever she was doing, Jolie was pleased that she was distracting her.

Ana adjusted her coat and sunglasses, clearing her throat before beginning. "I'm a part of a…program. I can't say what kind, and if you figure it out, you have to promise me you won't say anything to anyone. It's extremely expensive, and involves a small team of people, sort of. No, it involves hundreds of people, really, but I'm the second commander of the small team at the core. I've been training to do this half my life. I signed up years ago. Building that house, everything I did there, was preparation for where I'm going." Jolie adjusted her posture as she waited for Ana to continue her monologue. "I can't just stop being a part of this, Jolie. They've invested too much time and money into me, and I'm one of the only ones fit for the job." Ana spoke as if trying to convince herself, feeding the rising anger in Jolie's chest. "I wasn't expecting—" Ana stopped and looked down for a moment. "I wasn't expecting you."

"You don't expect love, Ana." Jolie rolled her eyes. "Can I be honest with you?"

"Of course."

"You seem to be convincing yourself that you want to be there. I don't really want to hear it. You're there, you're leaving, and we're not together anymore. Don't make me think that you still want me. I'm happy to talk about the house with you, but that's it. We're not friends. Please don't call me again unless you have something to say that I actually want to hear. And in the meantime, figure out what you want, for your own sake."

Ana's brow furrowed as she stood there, dumbfounded. "What I want? You know—never mind." She opened her mouth to say something, but quickly shut it. "Okay. I won't bother you again. I have to get back to the base anyway."

Jolie thought she saw the glint of a tear as it trailed down Ana's cheek.

"Bye." The screen cut out and Jolie flopped down on the couch, pressing the back of her head against the back. "Fuck." She took a deep breath. If the edge of their relationship had been dotted before, it was unquestionably drawn with a thick black pen now. It felt good to be in control for once, Jolie thought. A cruelness crept into her. Ana could go away and have relationships with other people, but she could also stand her ground and build walls to keep Ana out. Two could play that game.

Jolie sat for a while, looking at the smooth white ceiling, when she heard the rumble of thunder. She closed her eyes and relished in the sounds of the storm coming closer, until it was right there. Even with her eyes shut, she could see the flashes of lightning. The wind had picked up and was whistling around the house. It had almost lulled her into a light sleep when she heard the crash. She jumped up immediately from the couch, her eyes wildly searching for what had fallen.

On the wall near the kitchen, she saw a bare nail where a photograph used to hang. She walked over to the broken glass shattered on the floor, and cleared the big pieces away. She carefully picked up the photo and was about to place it on the coffee table when she saw a piece of old newspaper float to the ground. She hadn't seen a newspaper for years, and even then, it was at an antique store back in Nebraska. The delicate paper was yellowing and unfolded easily.

MarsOne Disaster, the headline read. *All twelve colonists living in the MarsOne settlement dead, Mars One Foundation reports.* Jolie put the paper down. She didn't have to read further. She hadn't been born at the time, but everybody knew about the failed program. The story stood out ominously in her mind. She pictured the archival footage she must have seen in history class, and mentally replayed the newscaster's chilly delivery of the news. The footage they looped was the colonists waving into the camera during happier times. Their faces were obscured by the headpieces of their space suits, with no indication of what was about to happen. She couldn't remember if anyone had figured out the reason for the deaths. There was an official explanation, murder maybe, but it had fallen flat, even on her civilian ears. No colonists had returned to Mars since the disaster, and Jolie hadn't heard of any plans to send any more.

She thought about Ana's words, and began to shake with the realization. Suddenly, it all made sense. Ana was going to Mars. She was on a one-way trip to a planet millions of miles away in hopes of recolonizing. Of course she couldn't tell Jolie, or anyone else. It was considered a suicide mission after what had happened to the last crew, and the media would have a field day with it. She covered her mouth as a sob escaped. The pieces fell together in her mind as she saw the entire landscape of Ana's world. The house, the terrarium, the pleasure she took in picking an apple or looking out over her property. The desert, where she was now. How could she have been so stupid to think Ana would choose her over the most important spaceflight event in thirty years? Of course Ana would choose the mission. She was destined to do things for the greater good, make sure humanity had a second chance, and here was Jolie, crying over a broken heart. Ana would make human history. She would touch generations with her courage and bravery. What they'd had together was inconsequential compared to that, and Jolie felt like a fool for allowing herself to think it was important. Who would want that when they could have so much more?

Her eyes watered and she felt a tightness clutch at her chest. She wished desperately that she had been kinder when she had spoken to Ana earlier, and cursed their distance from each other. It was possible that Ana hurt as much as she did, but had no choice other than to press onward. Jolie couldn't imagine having to switch her feelings off and be partly responsible for the success of such a mission. She was about to call out to Cassiopeia to get Ana back on the screen when she heard a vehicle approach.

"That better be Nova."

Sure enough, her friend tentatively opened the door. Jolie quickly stashed the article in a drawer.

Nova looked at her with concern and came over to give her a hug. "I'm sorry, hun. Have you been crying?" She wiped Jolie's wet cheek with the back of her hand. "You know what? You don't need her. She's a jerk and she's playing with your emotions. You need someone to treat you better than that."

Jolie just closed her eyes and shook her head, new tears flowing down her face. "It's complicated."

"There's nothing complicated about a woman who goes and breaks my best friend's heart," Nova said coldly. "Even if she is mind blowingly hot." She squeezed Jolie.

Jolie's heart broke even more for Ana as she listened to Nova berate her. "Can we talk about something else?" she asked with an edge in her voice.

"Um, okay, sure. Whatever you need." Nova looked unsure for a split second before her confidence was restored. "What do you want to do? I'm starving."

"Can you make us something to eat? I can find a movie."

"Sounds good to me." Nova got up and walked over to the kitchenette, catching sight of the mess on the floor. "What happened here?"

Jolie remembered the picture frame still on the floor and burst into tears again.

"Oh, honey, come here," Nova said soothingly as she rushed over to her. "I'll clean it up, okay? You don't have to worry about it."

Jolie shook her head, unable to think. "Can we go back to your house?"

Nova covered her face in her hands and shook her head, chuckling. "You are impossible. Okay, let's go."

CHAPTER TWENTY-TWO

Ana walked quickly back to the base. She had trekked two miles out so that she wouldn't be followed or seen, and the walk there had emptied her canteen. She coughed from the dry air in her lungs. She still stung from Jolie's superficial assessment of her actions, but how could she blame her? It didn't matter though, in the long run. She couldn't hurt Jolie more than she already had by trying to smooth things over between them. Sighing, she saw the reddish pods drawing closer. It would be a long month.

As she entered the main unit through the airlock, she tried to focus her attention on the work she had to do to get the laboratory up and running, but she couldn't shake Jolie's disappointed stare from her mind. The rest of the crew was already there, seated in a circle on the floor of the sparsely furnished sterile room.

"Where have you been?" Carlos demanded. His slight frame disguised a sinewy musculature that would be employed in building and repairing the habitat left by MarsOne.

She had known the members of the crew for years, and though Carlos was never her favorite, she had nothing but respect for him. This change in demeanor annoyed her, and on top of everything else, she snapped. "As your ranking officer, I don't need to justify my whereabouts to you. If anyone gets to question me, it's Captain Legrand." She took a seat and did not look at Carlos, but could see him scowling in her periphery.

Martine and Udeme looked at each other, then raised their eyebrows at Ana. She knew she shouldn't have barked at him, and certainly shouldn't have pulled her rank card this early in training, but she had no patience.

Ana took a deep breath. "I'm sorry for being late to this meeting."

Carlos raised his eyebrows as Martine cleared her throat to begin the meeting. Ana knew she'd have to explain herself later, but was glad to be out of the spotlight for now. "You've all received details of the training exercises for the next month. Since the timeline was accelerated, you can disregard those except the first one. I'll be drawing up new plans tonight and pushing them out early tomorrow morning. This isn't going to be easy, but I know we can be as prepared as we would have been. Does anybody have questions, or shall we start the first training simulation?"

"Please, would you clarify the policy on space skins for this month?" Kyoko asked. In her early thirties, Kyoko had been the youngest senior scientist at a pharmaceutical company in Tokyo. She was brilliant in medicine and had developed key drugs to treat Lyme disease and multiple sclerosis. Her contributions would be missed in the scientific community, though her work on Mars would be just as important.

"Of course. They are to be worn during simulations only for the first week, and then because of the turn of events, for the last three weeks, we will wear them as if we were already on Mars. If you are having trouble with your suit, Liv will fix it for you." They all knew that, of course, because Liv had been fixing suits and other components in their virtual trainings for years. By this point, if something happened to any one of them, they could mostly fill each others' roles. Still, it was important for each of them to have their own set of tasks. It would help keep team morale up, and ultimately, it would mean the difference between a successful mission and one that failed.

Kyoko nodded her thanks.

"Anybody else?" Martine asked. The room was silent, waiting for permission to start. "Ana, please set the timer."

"We are a go," Ana said with authority.

The crew stood and quickly dispersed for the first training exercise. Moments later, an alarm went off and the walls flashed blue and white. Ana took out a screen and set it to display the locations and movements of the crew. She saw body shapes converging upon the source of a simulated leak, located in the west facing wall of the anterior pod. In this scenario, debris had struck the wall material which had just cracked, allowing the inhospitable Martian atmosphere to seep in.

Udeme temporarily patched the wall while Liv printed a wall modification to attach to the inside. Ana watched the screen as Luke's outline donned a space skin and made its way outside, attaching another piece of wall there. Ana went through the motions in her mind. The material was responsive, and the patch would be absorbed into the existing wall.

The team began to filter toward the main room again, emergency averted. Luke came in last through the airlock, taking his helmet off and puffing his cheeks.

Ana checked the time. "Great work, everyone. You did it in 75% of the time it took in VR."

"Let's resume our baseline activities and meet back here at 2100 hours," said Martine. Ana saw a brief but penetrating look she gave Liv, and was struck with a surge of jealousy. She wanted that for herself.

"Ana, I'll talk to you later, okay?" Martine hooked her arm through Liv's and moved in close. Together, they were radiant. Over a decade ago, the crew was chosen based on psychological stability and genetic strength, their beauty the expression of the latter. All except for Ana, chosen for her lineage, daughter of the mission director. The fitness of the group would make it easier to perpetuate their colony when the time came. She thought of the children she'd have to bear in a few years, with either Carlos or Luke, and her mind wandered to Jolie. Ana wasn't sure she even wanted children, at least not on Earth. On Mars, it was an obligation, one that would be more palatable with a partner like Jolie.

Ana spent the next hour documenting the results of the training scenario. As second in command, she would be required to send a daily, or if needed, more frequent reports to mission control on Earth. Of course, the team on the home planet would receive an almost constant stream of data from the Martian base detailing who was where, for how long, and even what they were doing. There would be no privacy, though the remoteness of the training base at least made it seem otherwise. The data feed was necessary to avoid another MarsOne situation. The sponsors would do everything in their power to make sure this mission was successful, down to terminating one or more of its crew members if necessary. Ana cringed at the thought. She wasn't sure anybody else knew about this contingency besides her and Martine. If there was anything the scientific world learned from the previous disaster, it was that any leak in their tight preparations could spell doom.

When she finished, she went to lay down on her bed. She was close to drifting off when her bracelet pinged.

I hope you are well. I'm sorry I was angry. I understand everything now. Sadly, Jolie.

Ana drew in a breath. She hadn't expected Jolie to figure it out this quickly, just from their conversation earlier today. She was light and dizzy with relief. She had someone on the outside who knew, a huge liability, but she felt only elation. Maybe this meant they could at least be friends. Maybe Jolie wouldn't have to be completely gone from her life. They could send video messages through space to one another in a sort of very, very long-distance friendship. She wanted desperately to write back and have an actual, out in the open conversation about her future—their futures, but she quickly tempered her emotions. *Sadly, Jolie.* It would be unfair of her to pounce on this opportunity while she knew Jolie still hurt. She closed the message and took off her bracelet, stowing it in a drawer. She needed to be strong and loyal to her mission. There were six people, and scores more behind the scenes, depending on her right now, and she wouldn't let them down.

With renewed purpose, she made her way into the room across the hall. Their next exercise was to add a laboratory pod onto the back of the base, but that would take days and the efforts of the whole crew. The last time they'd all been at this base was two years ago. Some enhancements had been made, but adding a functioning laboratory wasn't one of them. She'd used part of this small room last time, but it wasn't conducive to keeping a sterilized environment. For now, while they built the new one, she'd have to set up a makeshift space in here again. The hair samples she'd asked everyone to leave sat in vials on the end of a small counter. As the rest of the crew spent the end of their first day winding down, she began the process of screening for abnormalities and establishing current baseline biomarkers. Jolie didn't creep into her thoughts until it was time to sleep, and Ana knew that was the best she could hope for.

CHAPTER TWENTY-THREE

Yes, they're tonight. You have to come over." Jolie peered anxiously out the window at the fading light.

"What's this again?" Nova asked.

"The something-ids. I don't remember, different meteors. Remember how much fun we had last time?"

"You mean that time I chaperoned your little outdoor sex party? Listen, I really want to, but I have to finish this paper. It's due tomorrow." Nova's tone became more annoyed by the second. "I can ask Karlee if she wants to come over."

Jolie slumped her shoulders, defeated. Nova wouldn't understand why she just had to look at the same night sky Ana was watching, on a night she'd surely be looking at it. Ana had been gone for two weeks and Jolie hadn't heard from her again, but it comforted her to know they'd probably be watching tonight's meteor shower together, in a way.

"Yeah, okay. See if she can come over," Jolie said half-heartedly.

Nova chuckled. "You sound thrilled by that idea. I'll go ask her, then send you a message."

"Okay. If you finish your paper, will you come later?"

"Not a chance that's going to happen, but sure. I can promise that if it does, I will."

Jolie hung up and sighed. She was tired. In addition to her schoolwork and spending long hours in the studio, she had been doing some heavy lifting around the property getting the garden ready for winter. She wanted to make Ana's last few days there carefree, though she was still torn about whether she'd be sticking around. Now that everything was out in the open, she felt a sort of reverence toward Ana. To give up everything in order to do something so extraordinary, you had to be a special sort of person, and it only complicated her feelings. How could Jolie feel anything but love toward someone so loyal to a cause, even to the death? Two weeks had given her enough space to realize that the most loving thing she could do was to support Ana while she could, then let her go.

Her bracelet buzzed with an incoming message. *Sorry babe, Karlee can't make it either. Have fun.* Jolie sighed with relief. As much as she wanted the company, she'd just be wishing that Karlee was Ana the entire night. That could lead her down paths she hadn't fully explored with Karlee, and wasn't sure she wanted to.

Jolie made her way outside with a chair and one of Ana's long, warm coats. The air carried the sharp scent of fallen leaves, and she hunkered down into the chair, drawing the coat tightly around her. It smelled vaguely of Ana's skin, and she buried her face in the collar, inhaling deeply. She couldn't help remembering the last time she was out here at night, during the Orionids. Her chest ached at the memory of Ana's strong arms around her, the heat of Ana's skin making her wish Nova had cancelled. Apparently, Nova had wished the same thing.

Jolie sat down and looked up into the sky, shivering at the thought of her Ana, floating through that vast nothingness in a tiny ship, living out her days in a few square miles of a desolate planet. Hot tears formed in her eyes, stinging in the cold breeze. Suddenly compelled to make sure Ana knew she was very much wanted right here on Earth, she took out a screen and composed a message. When it was finished, she reread it, and knew she shouldn't send it. Ana had been very clear, after all, about her plans and her determination to carry them out. Her silence the last two weeks sent an unmistakable message, but Jolie was feeling nostalgic, and the cloak of darkness suppressed her inhibitions. She swiped the message with a finger and sent it.

She folded the screen up and put it in her coat pocket, not expecting a response tonight, or even at all, so she jumped when her wrist buzzed ten minutes later. She projected the message into the darkness.

Thank you for writing. I've been thinking about you a lot as well, which is why I haven't written or called you since the first day. I don't want to complicate things. I'm so glad that you are watching tonight's meteor shower even without my encouragement! I hope Nova is with you. If you feel like it, we could talk to each other face to face. That would be almost like watching it together. Jolie's face flushed at the thought of being so close to Ana again, even if it was only a virtual connection. The darkness and small screens would add an air of intimacy that she'd missed desperately. *There have been a few hiccups, but otherwise, it's been a productive couple of weeks. I do miss home, though. This will be a difficult transition. XO, Ana.*

Jolie read the message over and over. Some small part of her was hoping that Ana would add a postscript that read, *Just kidding. I'm coming home to live with you forever.* She chastised herself for wishing that. As she was deciding whether or not she should call Ana, a feed came through on her bracelet. She found herself looking at a thinner, less put together version of the woman who had left two weeks ago.

"Hi," Ana said.

Jolie felt giddy. "Hi, yourself."

"I can't see you," Ana said as she smiled.

"It's kind of nice. I get to stare at you all I want and you have no idea what I'm doing."

Ana chuckled. "Let me guess. You're sitting outside, close to the house because I see a tiny bit of glow from the right side of the screen. Turn on night vision so I can see."

"You won't be able to see the stars if I point it at the sky with night vision on."

"That's okay. I would rather see you." Ana seemed almost shy, and Jolie felt herself break into a sweat despite the temperature. Even after everything, Ana's words still had that effect on her.

"Okay." She switched the camera setting. "Better?"

"Much. It was nice to hear from you tonight." She saw Ana set her device on some kind of shelf and lean back against her pillow.

"You seem a lot more settled. Are you doing okay?"

"I'm doing okay. It took a little while, but now it's halfway over."

"Are you looking forward to it being done? Aren't you supposed to want to stay there forever?" Jolie studied Ana's conflicted facial expressions.

"I am."

"You are what?"

"I don't know. Both?" She looked away from the camera as if gathering her thoughts, then turned back to look at Jolie. "I'm glad you figured it out. It's nice to talk to somebody uninvolved."

"I'm not really uninvolved," Jolie said.

"You know what I mean. I just need to talk to someone who's not here." She adjusted her position and leaned a little toward the camera. Her next words started out in a whisper. "I don't feel the same way as I used to about it, but I can't step down, and I can't really tell anyone. I signed that contract a long time ago. I miss home, though, and I'm looking forward to going back again. Maybe it'll help me get back into the correct mindset." Ana's voice trailed off.

Jolie didn't know what to say, so she changed the subject. "Do you want to see the sky?"

"Yeah." Ana smiled again. "You really look good, by the way. Country living agrees with you."

"Oh, please. If that's what you got from a night vision camera, then you should have your eyes checked. I'm the same as when you left."

"You looked good then, too. You've lost weight, though." Ana moved the device so it was on her lap and Jolie was looking up at her.

Jolie hadn't considered that she was thinner, but now that Ana had mentioned it, she wasn't eating as well. She had lost her appetite in the drama of two weeks ago, and it was only starting to return. "You're thinner too. I hope you're eating enough."

"I'm eating okay. Haven't had much of an appetite lately."

"Me neither." They were silent for a long moment. Jolie angled her bracelet upward. "So, here's the sky. Can you see the stars?"

"A little," Ana said. "Oh look, did you see that shooting star?"

"No, I was trying to get the camera adjusted for you. I can't believe you saw one first. You're not even here. Not fair." Jolie laughed.

"I love nights like this. It just makes you feel so insignificant, like nothing matters."

Jolie was about to disagree about what mattered when she heard the crunching gravel of a car approaching.

"Um, someone's here. I'll be right back." Jolie set the screen down on the chair so Ana could still see the sky. She walked around the house to the front door, the dim light from indoors illuminating her way. The blonde about to knock on the front door was unmistakable. "Karlee?"

"Hey, girl, sorry I just showed up. It sounded like you might need a friend tonight and I finished what I had to do." Karlee enveloped Jolie in a long hug.

"Well, I did, but—"

"No buts, I'm here now and we're going to make a night out of it. I brought some wine and a blanket. We can sit out and watch the stars. A few more hours until the big show anyway."

"Okay. I was talking to Ana and kind of watching them with her." Jolie shifted uncomfortably.

"Oh. Ohh. Oops, I should have called."

"That would have been nice," said Jolie.

"Sorry, I didn't realize you were talking again. Well, I can go." She began to back away toward the car, a pained expression forming on her face.

"Wait. You clearly put a lot of effort into this, and you're already here, so…"

Karlee returned with a sweeping grin and handed the blanket to Jolie. "Are you sure? I don't want to intrude."

Jolie shook her head and laughed. As if Karlee cared about intruding. "Let me go tell Ana and hang up with her. Give me a minute?"

"You got it, boss."

Jolie shuffled back to her chair, not looking forward to hanging up with Ana for many reasons. She couldn't help but feel like she was doing something unethical by spending the night with Karlee instead of Ana, but Karlee was here and Ana wasn't. Karlee was emotionally and physically available. Ana was ultimately neither.

She picked up the screen. "Hey."

"Everything okay?"

"Yeah. So, a friend of mine actually just came over. I didn't know she was coming, but I think we're going to watch the rest of the show together," Jolie said tentatively.

"Oh." Ana paused. "That's great. I should really be sleeping now anyway, so it's really no problem at all," she rambled.

Jolie noted the drop in Ana's confidence and was secretly glad she seemed jealous.

"Can I ask who it is, though? I'm just curious who would come all the way out there at this time of night," Ana said nonchalantly.

"It's Karlee." Jolie knew as soon as she said it that she should have lied.

Ana's face fell. "Right. Great. Well, have fun. If you want to reach me in the next two weeks, you know how. Bye, Jo."

Ana signed off immediately, and Jolie stood there trying not to cry.

"Hey, are you ready for me now?" Karlee called boisterously from around the house.

"You can come around," Jolie yelled back with little enthusiasm, her voice catching in her throat. As Karlee made her way around and bent to lay the blanket out, Jolie blurted, "I'm not sleeping with you. Just so you know. We're just watching the meteor shower."

Karlee reeled. "Well, that was a little presumptuous, don't you think?"

"Don't try to tell me that wasn't on your mind."

Karlee sat on the blanket. "Okay, I won't tell you it didn't occur to me. Although I don't see what the big deal is. We've already done it. What's one more time?"

Jolie knelt beside her. "Why do you settle for that? Why not find someone who's actually available and wants to be with you, and go sleep with them?"

"Last I checked, you were actually available. Maybe that's changed? And you came on to me in Nova's room. Anyway, I don't have time to date, and honestly, it's more fun for me this way. I get that new hookup feeling every time." She winked and ran a finger over Jolie's hand. "Seriously, though, look at all the shit you're going through with this girl. It's because you're trying to make it more than it has to be. Embrace the hookup."

"You don't understand. It is more. I mean, it was more than that. We were in love." Jolie looked away. She felt ridiculous admitting this to Karlee, whose views on love were clearly more pessimistic.

"But it seems like that's over now. You have to pick up and move on, not talk to her like you're old friends or something. You broke up, right?"

Jolie shook her head. "God, you've been spending too much time with Nova. Is she feeding you this through an earpiece?"

Karlee simply smiled and put her arm around Jolie. They sat silently for a while, watching the sky. Eventually, Jolie settled in and began to enjoy her company. Karlee nodded off around midnight, and Jolie practically carried her inside.

"Here, you can sleep on the couch." She deposited Karlee in the living room and handed her a blanket. She watched Karlee's breathing even out, and was glad to have a guest. It brought some life back to the house.

Once Jolie got to her room, she crawled into bed and read Ana's message again. It made her giddy to know that Ana was thinking of her, even though she knew she was giving in to false hope. She reached over and pulled a piece of paper out of a drawer in her desk. She hadn't looked at it in two weeks, but tonight she allowed herself. It was a drawing of Ana, naked and peacefully lying on the couch. She'd drawn it from detailed memories of Ana's curves and edges one morning by the river. She meant to give it to her as a present, a token of her love. Now Jolie regarded it in a different light. This image was an ordinary moment in an extraordinary life. It was meant to be saved and framed, and someday sent to an archive to mark this small moment in history. It was a reminder of her place in Ana's past, and not her future. She tucked it into the ceiling of her bed pod so that when she opened her eyes in the morning, she'd remember everything.

Jolie vowed right then to do her part to make Ana's next few weeks as drama free as possible. No distractions, no calls, no messages. No trace of herself when Ana returned.

CHAPTER TWENTY-FOUR

"Martine, I love it." Ana clapped her hands together as Martine brought her into the finished laboratory pod. "This is incredible. I see you improved on the design since we saw it last."

"Of course. Do you think I would sit around for two years and not make changes? This is a work in progress. I will make it better yet, up there." She flicked her eyes to the ceiling, and Ana knew she was looking far beyond their camp.

"Thank you. You're an amazing architect." Ana touched her arm and Martine smiled. "Hey, where's Liv? I figured she'd be eating breakfast with us this morning."

"She is with Luke right now. I think they are sleeping together."

"Doesn't that bother you?" Ana knew that Liv and Martine had both been involved with others, and, eventually, many of the crew members would pair up, but she couldn't wrap her head around her own jealousy toward Karlee. She didn't want to think about the guilty look Jolie had given her the other night after Karlee had interrupted them, or what may have happened afterward.

"Oh, no, she can do what she likes," Martine said. "Besides, you think he is a better lover than I am?"

"Point taken. Well, we're almost done with this place and onto the real thing. How do you think it went?" Ana asked as she sat on her newly constructed bench in a laboratory she probably wouldn't use more than a handful of times. At least it would be here for the next crew that would begin training almost immediately after they left. Ana hadn't met them, but she knew they were a group of young adults similar in makeup to their crew.

"I think you should tell me what is going on with you. This whole time, you don't seem yourself, and you brush it off when I ask you. We can't leave like this, with you pining over someone. You don't talk to anyone about it, you go crazy." Martine leaned against the wall and crossed her arms. "So?"

"It's nothing, really. It's over. I made the mistake of falling in love with someone who isn't part of this mission. Before I left, it ended. There was no other option." Saying the words out loud forced Ana to realize how untrue they were. Being over Jolie would take far longer than a few weeks.

Martine cocked an eyebrow. "You would have ended it if you weren't going to Mars?"

Ana sighed and let her head fall back against the wall. "No, but I guess we all have to make sacrifices."

Martine laughed. "Yes, well that is the hard part. I had to leave behind some lovers because of this. I have Liv now, and she is the best parts of every one of them."

"I would be lying if I didn't admit that I'm a little jealous of you two."

Martine sat down on the bench beside Ana. "You know, we worry about you. You have a job to do, that is for sure. But you also need another outlet. You cannot work all the time. You need to relax somehow. The question is, will your feelings for this girl mean you cannot love someone else?"

Ana looked into Martine's eyes. "I don't know."

"Think hard. If you will spend the rest of your life pining for her, will it be worth it to leave?"

Congratulations, you just hit on the million dollar question, Ana thought. When she couldn't answer, Martine left quietly, closing the door behind her.

Ana didn't emerge from the lab until hours later. She had immersed herself in isolating a protein that could be made into a lotion that would help their skin retain water in case their humidifier malfunctioned. This project might not yield results for months, but she needed a reason to be by herself. Over computer analysis of each genome, and between targeting sequences that would prove useful to express, she thought of Jolie. She thought of being with her, and not being with her, and the uncrossable chasm between the two. Martine was right, she would be unfit to continue if she couldn't get Jolie out of her mind. She'd just have to try harder.

At the debrief that night, Liv and Luke sat close to each other, occasionally sneaking sidelong glances, while Martine kept near Ana. The rest of the crew either hadn't formed any lasting intimate relationships, or weren't interested in making those known. Udeme started the conversation by explaining the upgrades she had made to the wireless network that ran through almost every object in the base.

"I wrote a program that will allow us to control the temperature and humidity in each pod with any wall or pocket screen by using a series of swipe motions." She took out her screen and, in three movements of her fingers, turned on the compressor in the main room. "See? Simple."

A chorus of praise echoed through the room. "Nicely done, mate. Can you send me the code for that? I'd like to take a look," Luke said. Udeme nodded. Luke continued, "I'll go next. I've been mapping out the contingency plans if we have to land farther than one and a half kilometers from base camp. I'll share them when I'm through, probably when we're home." He nodded in satisfaction and ran a hand through his floppy blond hair.

The team finished their updates quickly, and it was Ana's turn to lead a self-improvement discussion. Liv had termed them "fireside chats," to everyone's amusement. Not only was fire dangerous to their compressed oxygen systems, the room was far from cozy, its shiny, sterile white walls forming a circular barrier around them.

"Since we're almost done with our time here, I thought we should talk about regrets. Martine, do you want to start?"

"I have none. I have lived well, and will continue to live well with my best friends and my love." She focused squarely on Liv, who blushed and smiled back. "I cannot imagine a life without this in it. Ana? I will pass the baton to you."

Ana gave her a withering look, then turned to the group. "Okay. You may have noticed that I haven't been as present as I should be. I won't go into the details, but I will tell you that I'm coming to terms with a relationship that ended. It was my first relationship, and I made the mistake of falling in love." She spoke matter-of-factly and nodded to commute the conversation to Luke.

"Wait. You didn't talk about regret," Martine said.

"Oh. Well, I regret not being able to have that relationship in my life going forward."

"You don't regret letting yourself fall in love with a civilian?" Carlos asked.

"As you may imagine, I didn't exactly plan on it. And no," she said pointedly. "I don't regret falling in love." She wasn't sure where Carlos's attitude was coming from, but she hoped that would shut it down.

To her annoyance, he continued. "I can't imagine a scenario where it doesn't affect the mission. How will you move past this? I do not think it is fair to the rest of us to be distracted. How will you be able to focus on your job in a few weeks when any distraction could cost us our lives?"

Ana cleared her throat. She didn't know what to say. Carlos wasn't wrong. Her main focus should be on making sure they all landed safely on Mars. "I can't really answer that, because I don't know. But I give you my word that I'll put the safety of this group before myself. I always have, and I'll continue to." Except when you got yourself a roommate. Except when you kissed her and then fell in love with her, she thought. She felt her temperature rising and quickly asked Luke to continue. As he discussed leaving his family behind, she avoided looking directly at Carlos's cold, hard stare from across the circle.

"I am proud of you, owning up to your feelings," Martine said later, as they retired for the night. She reclined on Ana's small bed and closed her eyes. She wore the standard-issue white antibacterial suit that would comprise her entire wardrobe on Mars. From her chair, Ana could see the outline of her breasts as the fabric draped over them. She let the view stir her, hoping she could prove to herself that future relationships were a possibility.

"Thank you. Especially for the talk earlier. I think it's just easier to stay the course, and do my best to get over Jolie. I hope she's not home when I get there. That would make things more difficult." Ana leaned her elbows on her knees. "I know that no matter what I do, in a four-dimensional universe, I've already made those choices anyway. I just wish I could travel through time and see how I did it. Anyway, it's no use trying to imagine things being different."

"What's done is done, you are right. In the grand scheme of the universe, it's completely inconsequential. Humans are pawns. Inefficient, disgusting, crude. But we have a job to do. I can only hope that someday, something better and more evolved will come along and do it better." She paused for dramatic effect. "In the meantime though, I'm going to do my best, as a lowly human."

"When did you become so dark? I always thought of it as making a better society, a better life for humanity. And if we die trying..." Ana looked at Martine. She knew what they were both thinking.

"We destroy ourselves here, and we destroy ourselves there. So who cares? Be happy doing it."

Ana let the words sink in. Be happy doing it.

Martine watched her mull· over her happiness, and finally spoke. "Ana, come here."

She froze. She knew what Martine was suggesting, the dangerous opportunity to decide if she could be happy right here and now.

"Ana, we are all worried about you. You are not going to spend the rest of your life resisting perfectly suitable relationships because you are in love with someone on Earth. That will pass. Just give it time. I will help you." She reached her hand out and caught Ana's, pulling slightly.

Ana responded to the touch and sat on the bed. Her mind swirled with static, drowning out thoughts of Jolie. This was her future. Jolie was her past, and that past was sealed up and put away deep in her mind, to be looked upon at a much later time. Martine drew her down on top of her in a fluid, skilled motion. Her practiced fingers pulled Ana's face to hers and their lips met.

She felt a pleasantness in her body, but nothing like the all consuming hunger she had experienced with Jolie. Martine took Ana's hair down from a loose ponytail and kissed her again, their tongues pressing together. Ana's body took over, relishing the relief from pent up anxiety she'd hidden during the last few weeks. Martine undressed them both, then jockeyed to the top and pinned Ana's wrists above her head. Her mind flashed to the first time Jolie made her come, her wrists pinned helplessly to the bed. She closed her eyes and pretended Jolie was there now, her hair tickling Ana's breasts.

Ana breathed heavily, pinned under Martine's nakedness, arching her back when Martine pressed her lips to her neck. The last time Jolie had done that, her skin had smelled like the rosemary oil Ana had given her. She breathed in the ghost scent and smiled. Ana retreated into her sensitive nerve endings as Martine kissed down to her breasts and put her lips around a nipple. Ana needed to be touched now, her body reawakening to the depths it had discovered with Jolie. Imagining it was Jolie on top of her heightened her senses and drove her crazy. Martine breathed heavily as she slid back and forth on Ana's thigh, returning to kiss Ana fervently on the mouth. Ana found herself pulling Martine into her as if she couldn't be satiated with what had been offered. She needed more. She needed control. She needed Jolie's wetness on her leg.

She stopped Martine's motion and, as if punishing Martine for who she was, thrust her fingers inside of her. Martine moaned and pushed them deeper inside. Ana could feel Jolie riding her hand, and she kept her eyes shut tight to preserve the illusion. Jolie needing her, Jolie moaning louder and louder.

Time seemed to stop completely. Ana was helpless to the circling of Martine's fingers against her. She focused all of her energy on her fingers pumping in and out. She was vaguely aware of muscles clenching against her hand as Martine rode out her orgasm, settling on top of Ana, the weight holding her there, under someone who wasn't Jolie, with a hand that didn't belong to Jolie still moving against her. Ana came desperately with a release that brought a stunning clarity to her thoughts. She shut her eyes even tighter as the tears came, and Martine-who-wasn't-Jolie, who would never be, curled up against her.

"That was nice, no?" Martine murmured, her eyes dark with desire.

Ana held a sob in her throat, burning in her chest, as she willed it to go away. She prayed Martine wouldn't look at her. A deep emptiness replaced any pleasure she'd felt. She would never fall in love with Martine, or any of the other crew members. Not the way she had fallen for Jolie, with her entire body and soul, vulnerable to feelings she hadn't known she could experience. She couldn't bear the thought of never feeling them again. Finally, Martine reached over her stomach to hold her, and the flood of sadness she'd held so well escaped. Once she opened up, everything she'd felt since she signed the contract dissolved down her cheeks. Martine hugged her with all the compassion in the world, and Ana knew it was over. Eventually, when all her demons had fled, she broke away from Martine, whose eyes held a sadness she hadn't seen since the moment she'd let Jolie go. She watched helplessly while Martine's world crumbled as hers just had.

CHAPTER TWENTY-FIVE

Jolie let out a deep breath as she walked out of the admissions office and into the bright day. She folded the paper they'd given her and tucked it into her pocket. Nova waved from across the lawn. She beamed. Finally, her life was back on track. Finally, she could move on. She heard feet pounding on the sidewalk behind her, and turned around just in time to be accosted by Karlee, who flung her arms around her from behind.

"I can't believe you're going away for so long." She pouted. "We're both so sad. Will you at least hang out tonight?"

Jolie hugged Karlee's arms close to her chest. Despite their brief flirtation with hooking up, their friendship had deepened and Jolie couldn't imagine leaving her. "It's only for a couple weeks. Anyway, I don't plan to go back to the house, and I'm leaving tomorrow morning, so I'm all yours tonight." She was elated at the thought of her upcoming trip, a chance to take a break while Ana was off getting blasted into space. They hadn't spoken since the night of the meteor shower, and Jolie had blocked all incoming messages from her number. It was something she had to do to stay sane. She didn't plan to be in touch with Ana again, even after she safely arrived on Mars. It wasn't going to be easy to avoid Ana's public presence, but she'd do her best. She'd go away for a few weeks, the media storm would happen, then she'd come back in January for the art show. This morning, she'd given all of her completed pieces to Professor Anderson, who promised to help her set up. She packed most of her belongings in the sorority's attic, and the rest into the small green rental car she'd be driving home. The only trace she'd left of herself at Ana's house was a handwritten note on the counter.

Nova was opening a bottle of wine as they reached the picnic blanket. It was covered in an impressive spread of cheese, crackers, and various dips. Jolie deposited a bag of apples she'd picked earlier in the week.

"Thank you guys for doing this for me. You know I'll be back soon, but it's going to be a long few weeks without you."

"I'm glad you finally get to go back home, even if it is for a mental health break." Nova dipped a cracker in some hummus.

"If you want to crash with us when you get back, we can probably dig up an extra bed somewhere." Karlee tentatively placed her hand on Jolie's back, and when Jolie didn't shrug it off, she rubbed in small circles. Jolie leaned into it, savoring the touch, emboldened by her impending freedom from everything related to Ana.

"That might be what I'll do." She thought for a moment, and a grin spread across her face. "I'm so excited to get back to Nebraska. I didn't think I really missed it, but that might have been just a convenient excuse for not going back home."

"Bad memories?" Karlee asked.

Jolie shrugged. "Just didn't want to get stuck there. It's the kind of place where you get stuck and never leave."

Nova nodded and Karlee squeezed her shoulder. They ate in silence for a while, Jolie's gaze wandering to the students milling about campus all around them.

"How long's it going to take you?" Nova asked, her mouth full of cracker.

"A few days. Depends on how much I stop. I might have an adventure or two on the way. Haven't decided yet. Actually, I think I will stop in Chicago. I've always wanted to go."

Karlee perked up. "My dad's family is there. Just call me and I'll tell you all the good places to eat in every neighborhood."

"All the good cheap places. I've barely got enough money to make it back with fuel and the cost of the car," Jolie said.

"You'll make it there okay. If you don't, I'm happy to lend you whatever you need," said Nova. "Seriously, if I find out you're stranded halfway there and you don't call me, there's going to be hell to pay."

"All right, I got it. How about we pack this up and head inside?"

The three of them gathered the remaining food, folded up the blanket, then slowly made their way back to the sorority house. Jolie and Nova sat on the thinly carpeted steps leading upstairs while Karlee heated mugs of apple cider. Jolie leaned against her friend, grateful for the safety both Nova and Karlee afforded her.

"I couldn't have done this without your support, Nova. You know that, right? If you ever need anything at all, you just say the word."

"I do have one request. Make me some more of those drawings. You really took it to a new level since you moved to, well, you know. Since you moved. I want drawings of cornfields, sculptures of barns, anything you can create. It's all beautiful, Jo. You're an incredible artist."

"Thanks. Somehow I feel like your request is more for me than you, but I'll kindly ignore that." A slow grin spread across her face.

"Kindly do. What do you feel like doing tonight? It's your night, so you get to choose." Nova ran her fingers through Jolie's hair.

"I don't know. Maybe we can watch a movie or something. Anyway, we've got hours until then, so let's play a game and then walk around the pond."

"Sounds like a plan to me." Nova took one hot mug from Karlee and handed the other to Jolie.

As evening descended, Jolie found that her earlier enthusiasm had given way to exhaustion. Nova put on a romantic comedy and settled on a bean bag near the foot of the bed. Jolie sat next to Karlee on top of Nova's comforter, leaning against the headboard. Not long after the movie began, Karlee put her arm around Jolie's shoulders, pulling her in to whisper in her ear.

"I've got a little going away present for you," she said seductively.

Jolie gulped, too tired to think of any objections. The way that Karlee had been innocently touching her all day, a back rub, a casual hand on the knee, a leg against hers, had brought her to a place where she was pretty sure that in her right mind, she'd actively seek this out.

"Are you cold?" Karlee asked loudly so that Nova could hear it.

Jolie played along. "Um, yeah. Give me some blanket."

In the reflection of light coming from the TV screen, she could see Karlee's lips parting. She knew there would be no kissing because Nova would certainly catch on. Karlee replaced her arm around Jolie, pulling her close. Her fingers subtly brushed over her nipple, eliciting a gasp that Jolie had to stifle by biting her lip. She saw a wicked gleam in Karlee's eyes and moved her own arm to a similar position. Karlee bit the knuckles of her free hand, and Jolie breathed harder, watching her try to stay still. It was difficult to keep from moaning out loud as Karlee touched her, their restraint only intensifying the ache. She hadn't been touched like this since Ana left, and was eager for the chance to prove to herself that she didn't need her anymore.

Both women checked to make sure Nova had not heard them, and, satisfied that she was distracted with the movie, Karlee slipped her hand into Jolie's sweatpants. Jolie parted her legs to give her free access, and Karlee took it. Biting her own knuckles, she sat perfectly still as Karlee stroked her, inside and out, expertly bringing her close to orgasm, then stopping on the cusp over and over again. Each time, she grew more melancholy, but she pushed the feeling down in exchange for the exquisite physical pleasure she was receiving. Objectively, the torture was delicious, the danger of being found out, its own excitement. Finally, Karlee allowed her to come, and she did violently, shaking the bed as she shuddered in attempted restraint. When it was over, she noticed Nova's laughter at the movie and praised Karlee's good timing.

She wiped beads of sweat off of her forehead as Karlee extracted her hand and moved it under her own pants. Jolie was sure she was supposed to be enjoying this part, too, but it felt like she was outside her own body, watching someone else touch and be touched by Karlee. As hollow as she felt, she couldn't leave Karlee hanging. She touched Karlee's nipple as she stared into her eyes, her breath coming quickly. If they had been alone, Jolie might have pressed her lips to Karlee's, as she was silently begging her to do. Her orgasm came suddenly, and she lay with her head on Jolie's shoulder for a time afterward. Jolie let her because she wanted to be a person who could move on. After all, it had been a month. Wasn't it at least time for a rebound relationship? Near the end of the movie, Nova left for the bathroom.

Karlee smiled sweetly and kissed her on the cheek. "How was that?"

Jolie didn't know what to say, let alone feel, about the encounter, so she just hugged Karlee.

"Want to sleep in my bed tonight?"

"I don't think so. I do need to get some sleep." And some perspective, Jolie thought.

Karlee frowned slightly, but nodded. "I think I'll turn in now, then. Have a good night, and a good trip. Call me?"

"Yeah," Jolie said with a smile that didn't reach her eyes.

She leaned back and quickly fell asleep. Sometime in the middle of the night, she awoke to a dark room and a warm body next to her. Ana? She momentarily grasped for an explanation before she remembered the movie. Nova's bed. Nova. Easing back against the pillow and Nova's heavy body, she quickly fell back into a deep slumber.

CHAPTER TWENTY-SIX

The base was quiet except for the thrum of the compressor as it maintained optimal air temperature and humidity. Ana sat in the lab, absentmindedly sterilizing a series of petri dishes with a bleach solution. The sharpness of the fumes would normally merit a fume hood or at least a face mask, but they barely registered in her wandering mind. Sixteen hours until they'd ride the ATVs back to the pickup site and find themselves on jets heading home. At least that was the protocol. She, along with Martine and Liv, had other plans.

She hadn't mentioned her pending resignation to anyone except those two. They suggested that she lay low until they were all safely home. No use risking a scene in the middle of a desert, as the rest of the crew was bound to be angry. No doubt this would delay the launch, even with the replacement crew member coming from somewhere in California.

Truthfully, she didn't much care what happened with the launch. Her mind was now occupied full-time counting the moments until she could get in touch with Jolie and share with her the single most important decision she'd ever made. Since the moment she'd invited Jolie into her home, she'd begun to choose her own destiny, and now she finally felt free. But freedom was bittersweet if she had nobody to share it with. None of her messages had gone through and Cassiopeia wasn't giving her any useful information. She shifted uncomfortably on her chair, worried that Jolie had left the house and didn't want to be found. Or worse, that she'd moved on and Ana was too late. For the fifteenth time in the last hour, she checked her messages. Nothing new.

She was used to protocols and processes, and there had been one for every moment of her life, until now. She trembled and dropped the petri dish she was holding. It clattered off of the table, falling unbroken to the floor. "Ana, get it together," she said aloud, sure nobody could hear her. Everyone was sound asleep in their quarters or, in the case of Liv and Martine, working on their plan for her. The two of them had taken it upon themselves to play public relations department, and she'd agreed to go where they dictated, do what they said, and not argue about it. The situation was sticky. She had to face the stakeholders and give a vague reason for stepping down, simultaneously name someone else to her position, and Martine had to make it appear as though everything was part of some grand plan. There were so many questions Martine would have to answer, and she felt terrible for putting her in that position. Investors didn't like to see their investments sour. And, of course, she'd have to answer to her mother sooner or later.

As relieved as Ana felt with her decision, she dreaded facing her mother. Dr. Mitchell would be concerned with the optics, and the mission director's own daughter quitting the mission didn't exactly look great. She'd never cared much for Ana's happiness, and she probably wouldn't start now. On top of that, if the team managed to pull everything off without a hitch, in two weeks, her six closest friends and colleagues would be on a one-way journey to another planet. And she'd be left either holding Jolie, or emptier than she could imagine.

A brief knock on the door shook Ana from her thoughts. Liv opened it slowly and came in, making sure to shut it securely behind her.

"How can you stand those fumes? My God. Enough to sterilize your sinuses if you're here for five minutes." She lifted the top of her uniform over her nose.

"Can I help you?" Ana asked sarcastically. She pulled off her gloves.

"Oh, sorry. I was so oxygen deprived, I completely forgot why I came. Yes, we have the final plans drawn up. Here they are."

Ana suddenly stood and embraced Liv. "What would I do without you?"

Liv blushed deeply as Ana let her go and read the sheet of paper. Nothing new, just a plan for what they'd already discussed. Ana nodded.

"Did you get in touch with Jolie yet?"

Ana fidgeted with her bracelet. She'd considered trying Nova, but was afraid to hear that Jolie had moved on, and had done so with Karlee, the one person she'd choose to send to Mars if she could. "No. No word yet. Liv, what if she never talks to me again?" Ana inhaled sharply and covered her mouth.

Liv placed her hand on Ana's shoulder and squeezed. "You will find her if you've lost her. You have…an effect on people. She will come back."

"You know that I had to do this, right? I planned on the rest of the crew being upset, but you and Martine, I just need you to know that I don't take this decision lightly." Ana rubbed her eyes. "I have no idea what I'm going to do without this in my life."

"I couldn't understand more. If Martine were staying behind, there's no way I'd be on that ship. You made a decision that I'm glad I didn't have to."

"Thank you. I just can't believe I'm going to miss it all. Everything we've been through, half of my life, it's gone just like that," Ana said.

"Think of it another way." Liv cupped her shoulders. "Everything that happened led you to Jolie. That's worth something."

Ana smiled. "Yeah."

"And, Ana, nobody on Earth knows the ins and outs of the mission better than you. I would be shocked if they didn't hire you to manage the day-to-day operations."

Ana hugged her again. "I'm going to miss you."

"Come on, let's get you to bed."

She led Ana out of the room and to her quarters, pulling the covers back so she could crawl in. Ana relaxed once she was lying down, closing her eyes as Liv leaned in to kiss her softly on the forehead and then the lips. She let her linger for a moment, knowing this was the last time they'd be close enough to touch. Then, the lights dimmed to blackness, and she drifted off into a hopeful sleep.

CHAPTER TWENTY-SEVEN

Jolie blinked her heavy eyelids open. She saw the bright lights of Akron, Ohio, before her, harshly cutting into the darkness she'd become accustomed to. She told the car to stop at the nearest cheap hotel. Soon, it pulled into a roadside motel advertising a nightly rate cheap enough to make her reconsider, if she could have afforded to. She sluggishly made her way to the front desk and got a key from an old man who smelled of cigarettes and was half-asleep himself, his face as worn as the splintering wood siding that covered the walls.

Her room was dismal, a single overhead light bulb washing the floral bedspread in an unflattering bluish hue. She was hungry, but too tired to go back out to find food, too lazy to even order something. She carefully unmade the bed and got in, wearing the same clothing she'd been in since she'd said good-bye to Nova and Karlee. It seemed so far removed from where she was now, a distant memory of a better place. She pulled the blanket to her chin and pulled her knees to her chest. The light, the mustiness of the room, and the hum of traffic on the highway was too much. Miles from anyone she knew, she felt more alone than ever. She rolled over and reached into her bag, pulling out Ana's ISS Trainee sweatshirt that she'd taken as a memento. Even if she wouldn't ever speak to her again, at least she had this reminder of what they'd had. Curling into it, she inhaled deeply as the tears came. If only Ana were there beside her, this trip would be bearable. Of course, if Ana were there, it would be unnecessary. The darkness would be welcome, even an invitation for intimacy.

Jolie cried until she was an empty shell of herself, shuffling to the bathroom only after convincing herself that she wouldn't be able to sleep if she didn't brush her teeth. Under the bathroom fluorescents, she was an unfamiliar, sad looking woman, much older than her twenty years. She examined her face, studying the new creases that seemed to have formed overnight. Her eyes were bloodshot, cradled by dark bags. When did this unflattering version of herself surface? Was it sometime during the journey into the middle of nowhere today? Was it a month ago when Ana left? She was worn, tired, and she felt a tightness around her shoulders. This is my low, she thought. It can only get better from here. Sighing and resigned to a night of unsatisfying sleep, she got back under the covers and turned out the light.

She slept later than she meant to, letting herself fall back into slumber each time she woke during the morning. It was easier than facing the day. When she finally rose, it was well past ten, and her stomach twisted and groaned as if she hadn't eaten in days. She stopped at a coffee shop on the way out, then set the navigation to the heart of Chicago. She barely had the energy to think about walking around Chicago, but it was a trip she'd promised herself, and she had to try.

Later, after hours on the same highway, its signs warning of the upcoming apocalypse and suggesting she find Jesus, she had the car turn off the road. On the narrow street that ran along the highway, she passed a small diner with an assortment of older cars outside. She turned the car around and had it park next to a vintage Ford hybrid, its cerulean paint patchy where it had grown together to cover a large scratch.

Inside, the diner was surprisingly busy, so she took a seat at the counter. A waitress named Jan took her order, and she stared absently at the screen above her. A newscaster recounted some story about the war in Africa, a conflict that had been going on for years. It was clear that he was bored with reporting on it. Her eyes drifted away and landed on a digital clock and weather display across the room. In the corner, it showed the date, December 2nd. The day Ana was supposed to return home from Chile. Jolie's stomach sank as she imagined Ana walking in and finding her gone, her note the only indication that she'd been there in the first place. Most likely, Ana would be relieved. She'd be able to focus on what mattered, not a silly relationship that had ended a month ago. Jolie put her head in her hands and leaned heavily on the counter. It ended a whole month ago, and she still felt raw. She couldn't imagine the longing ever going away completely, but at least it had become intermittent.

Jan set her meal in front of her and lingered for a moment. "You okay, sweetie? Tough day?"

"You could say that. Tough month."

"You'll be fine. Whatever it is, can't be worse than those astronauts they're sending up there again. Talk about a life I'd give anything to avoid."

Jolie jerked to attention. "What did you say?"

"Them astronauts, hun. One of those bigwig corporations had their talking heads on the news this morning saying something about sending some more poor souls to die on Mars," Jan said as she rolled cheap silverware into paper napkins.

"What exactly did they say?" Jolie was desperate, practically leaning all the way over the counter as she waited for the precious information.

"Well, not much. You know how they are. They try to keep the suspense. They said they'll be taking off soon from somewhere. I didn't really pay much attention. One crazy story after another." Jan eyed her suspiciously. "Why so interested?"

Jolie just shook her head, still absorbing the information. "I know one of them."

"Really? Now isn't that something. You get to say your good-byes?"

"You could say that," she said, her eyes on the counter.

"They're going to be famous, if they make it there and then somehow survive." She patted Jolie's hand and gave her a sympathetic look. "I'm sure they'll make it, hun."

She shrugged, attempting to stem the new tears that had somehow refilled her reservoir since last night. "Can I get this to go, actually? I need to get moving," she said, wiping her eyes. "I'm sorry sweetie, I didn't mean to upset you. Here. Take it, on me. Good luck to your friend." Jan gave her an uncertain look as she repackaged the food in a container, patted her hand again, and walked away.

Jolie left enough to cover her meal and tip, and quickly walked out the door, desperate to get home.

"Coordinate change," she said to the vehicle. "Valparaiso, Nebraska."

"Arrival at destination, one a.m.," the navigation system said.

"Better get a move on, then," she said as the wheels crunched the gravel of the parking lot.

CHAPTER TWENTY-EIGHT

A na opened the door to her house slowly, hoping against all odds that Jolie had stayed. The main room was silent, as if a switch had been shut off, all the life drained out. She knew immediately that she was alone. She let her bag drop to the floor with a thud. After a month away, the house looked unlived in, the counters too bare and the floor too clean for her liking. She sensed that Jolie had left it like this on purpose to make it easy for her to focus on the important preparations she should be making now. But instead of feeling grateful, she was indescribably sad. The organized paperbacks and neatly folded blanket meant that Jolie had given up on her and moved on. "As she should have," Ana said. After all, what did she have to offer? She was a failure. She had failed Jolie, and done the same to her fellow astronauts.

She started toward her room, exhausted from the journey, but paused when she saw a note on the ground behind the island.

My dearest Ana. I wish you all the luck in the world (this and others) on your journey. Please know that you brought me more joy than I could have imagined ever feeling. I hope you understand why I left before you came back. I do love you, and will forever.

XO, Jolie

P.S. I don't want you to worry about me, so I blocked your messages. You have more important things to do.

"I disagree," Ana said. She clutched the note and peeked into Jolie's room. Empty as Ana felt. She walked over to the bed pod and felt the mattress. Cold. As she sat down on it, she realized how exhausted she was, and she laid her head against the pillow. Out of the corner of her eye, she saw the edge of a piece of paper sticking out of the ceiling. After pulling it down, she felt tears form and heat rush to her cheeks. It was the most beautiful drawing she'd ever seen, an image of herself reclining on the couch, every inch of her skin rendered with such care, her heart broke all over again.

Her wrist buzzed and she jerked upright. For a fleeting second, she thought it might be Jolie.

"Hi," she said to the small image of Martine.

"Hi, love, are you home? Did you find what you were looking for?"

"No. She's not here," Ana said, defeated. "She left a note and said she moved on. She blocked my calls, Martine. I have no idea where she is, and I need to find her now." Ana held the drawing tightly against her chest.

"Okay, let's think through this like the rational scientists we are."

Ana took a deep breath. "Right. Let's figure this out."

"So, she left. You do not know where?"

"No," Ana said.

"Is there anyone you can ask?"

"Not real—" She paused a moment. "Yes. Yes, there is someone I can ask. I didn't want to, but now I have no choice. Can I call you back?"

"I will be here."

She quickly hung up and cleared her throat.

"Cassiopeia, bring up a directory of Singer students."

"Who would you like to find, Ana?"

She smiled at the familiar voice of her house system. "Nova. Can you bring up the address of anyone named Nova who goes to Singer?"

"There is one result. Sixteen Barn Lane. The property is owned by Sigma Nu sorority."

Ana laughed out loud with relief. This would be easier than she thought. Jolie was probably staying with Nova. She ran to her truck, eager to close the few miles' distance between them once and for all. She imagined Jolie opening the door in a mixture of confusion and elation. Her heart pounded with excitement and the dread of uncertainty. She set the truck to go slightly above the legal speed and zoomed toward town, only allowing it to slow down as she approached the University. The midday lunch crowd crossed from the campus to the strip of restaurants, at every conceivable point along the road except the crosswalks, it seemed to Ana.

"Come on, come on." She drummed her fingers on the dashboard. Every moment that passed, Jolie slipped further away from her.

Finally, the truck turned onto Barn Lane. She shuddered, thinking of the last time she'd been here. She'd been a confused coward then, but she was back, more sure of what she wanted than ever before. The truck rolled to a stop across from the familiar white sorority house. The moment she shut the door, she noticed someone on the porch swing, and a chill ran through her. It was too late to turn around. Karlee had seen her and was staring directly at her unkempt hair and tired white training suit. Ana had no choice but to approach the house, but not before taking a deep breath and rehearsing her greeting in her head.

"Can I help you?" Karlee stood and leaned against the porch railing, crossing her arms. It was a gesture not lost on Ana.

"Hi, Karlee. Nice to see you again." Ana stood tentatively on the top two steps. "Actually, I was wondering if Jolie is here."

"Is she expecting you?"

"Not exactly."

"I don't think she wants to talk to you," Karlee said with a piercing gaze.

"I know, but I need to talk to her." Ana averted her gaze. "Do you know if she's here?" This was going much worse than it had in her head.

"No."

Ana gritted her teeth. "No, you don't know? Or no, she's not here?"

Just then, the front door opened and a familiar face peeked out from behind. "There you are, Karlee. I was trying to find—" Nova looked in Ana's direction and her eyes went wide. "Ana. What—why are you here?"

"Hi, Nova." Ana sighed. "I was hoping someone could help me find Jolie."

"I already told her that Jolie didn't want to talk to her," Karlee said.

Nova stepped out. "Karlee, let me, okay?" She turned to Ana again. "What are you doing here? Jolie left because she couldn't take seeing you again. Why are you making this more difficult than it has to be?"

"Nova, trust me. I wouldn't be here if things had gone according to plan."

To her chagrin, Karlee stepped forward and started in. "Why should we trust you? You weren't here to pick up the pieces after you left her. You know what? She was actually pretty happy when she left yesterday. Why don't you let it be?"

"What Karlee means is, tell us why you're here. If we think it's a worthy reason, then we'll tell you where she is." Nova crossed her arms.

Ana deflated. She was glad Jolie had friends so fiercely protective of her, but it certainly wasn't working in her favor. "I want to tell her that I changed my plans." She held her breath in the silence that followed. This was the make it or break it moment.

Nova eyed her, then glanced in Karlee's direction, finally settling back on Ana with a penetrating stare. "So, what? You're staying?"

"Yeah, I'm staying." Ana's voice quivered. "Nova, please tell me where she is. I will beg if I have to. I need to find out if she'll give me another chance. Please. It's the only thing that's holding me together right now." Ana realized how desperate she sounded, but she didn't have anything else to lose, not even her pride.

Nova sighed. "I believe you. I don't know where she is, exactly. I can give you the address of her parents' house, though. That's where she's going to be for the next few weeks."

Ana almost burst into tears. Instead, she ran to Nova and hugged her.

"Jesus. You're a fucking mess. What happened to you, anyway?" Nova hugged her loosely, keeping a little distance between them.

"You have no idea," Ana said, half laughing, half sobbing. She turned to see Karlee staring at the worn wooden boards of the porch. They had more in common than she'd like, if Ana had read the situation correctly, pining away for the same woman.

"Please tell me you're going to go home and get yourself together before you drive halfway across the country. I think she'll be more receptive if you look decent." Nova continued to appraise her.

Ana shrugged. "I wasn't planning on it. I guess I could, theoretically."

"You will. You look like you need to take a nap. Go home and I'll send you the address, okay?"

"Okay," Ana said, sniffing. "Thank you, Nova, really."

Nova nodded, and Ana retreated from the porch and headed home. She quickly showered and promised herself a quick nap before she headed cross-country. Sleeping in her own pod felt too lonely, so she opted for Jolie's, at least what used to be hers. The pillow still smelled like Jolie, and Ana buried her face in it, a wave of calmness washing through her. She could do this, she thought as she drifted to sleep. She was already free, besides making a few statements and facing her mother. And then all she had to do was win back the woman she loved.

Ana woke much later than she intended, in complete darkness.

"Shit. Shit." She scrambled to find the time on her bracelet. She scrolled past the messaging app, which indicated seventeen missed calls, none from Jolie. The darkness was disorienting, until she realized it was only 7 p.m. Much later than she wanted to leave, but at least it wasn't the middle of the night. Plus, she noticed that her energy level was back to normal. At this rate, she might even be able to drive all the way to Nebraska without stopping.

Ana packed a small bag and was about to head out to her truck when she heard the familiar crunch of her gravel driveway. For a split second, she was sure it had to be Jolie, who had miraculously turned around and driven straight back home to see her. When she saw the car, her face fell.

Without knocking, Dr. Mitchell stormed into the house. She took one look at Ana, who was trying not to panic, and pierced her with an icy stare. "What the hell, Ana? What are you trying to pull?"

"Um," Ana began.

"Do you realize what you've done to me? My reputation, my years with the company trying to put this all together, completely ruined. Did you even think of that? And what in the world are you going to do now? Go play house with your girlfriend? What happens when that's over?"

Ana snapped at the mention of Jolie. She balled her hands into fists and squeezed them at her sides, taking a step closer to her mother. "Yes, actually, I realize what I've done. I don't give a shit about your reputation. Is that all I am to you? A child you had to build up your reputation?" Dr. Mitchell didn't answer, and Ana continued. "I'm finally happy for the first time in my life, and I don't want to give that up. I may have put everything I have into your mission, but you never asked me if I wanted to go in the first place."

Dr. Mitchell blinked. "You want to simply throw away millions of dollars that Hammer has poured into your training, your education, even this house? You signed a binding contract."

Ana clenched her jaw. "When I was thirteen, Mother. Thirteen. I don't expect you to approve of my decision to leave the mission, but I do expect you to let me live my own life."

Dr. Mitchell looked exhausted with their conversation, and Ana realized how deeply creased her face had become. Surely, directing the mission had taken its toll, and Ana suddenly felt sorry for her.

"Look, I'm sorry this changes your plans, but we've already got my replacement on board. The mission will happen no matter what." Ana cleared her throat. "I'm willing to take the consequences for breaking the contract, but I hope you'll realize how important it will be to have me in the control room. With you."

Dr. Mitchell looked up and Ana swore she saw a flash of consideration. "We'll see. You'll have to discuss it with the Board." With a curt nod, she said, "I think we're done here. There's a meeting at 7:45 for you to make your announcement. I hope you've figured out what to say." With that, she left as abruptly as she'd come.

Ana waited a few minutes, then threw her bag into the truck and set the coordinates to take her to Nebraska. If she drove through the night, she'd probably get about halfway there by tomorrow afternoon. She cursed her older truck, which didn't have software reliable enough for her to sleep during the drive. She'd have to stay awake in order to take over manually in case something went wrong.

As she rode beyond the town line, she checked her messages, mostly from Martine, and a few from Liv. At first, Martine was just checking in. By message six, she was getting worried. This was around the time that Liv chimed in, wondering if she had blocked Martine, and begging her to call either one of them. By the last few, Martine was giving her information about the call she had set up with the stakeholders, the same one her mother mentioned.

"Roger," she recorded, and sent it to both women.

At precisely 7:45, her bracelet beamed a hologram of a screen full of small faces. The meeting included the executives from the Hammer Corporation, as well as the small team of scientists and engineers who would serve as ground mission control. Martine had managed to assemble all of the key players, who were probably on the edge of their seats for this important update so close to launch.

Martine spoke at precisely 7:45. "Thank you for being here tonight. We have an important announcement to make about our mission, and we'll need all of your resources to make sure that this does not affect our launch date. Commander Mitchell is on the line and will give the announcement."

Ana took over from Martine. "Members of the operations team, financial backers, and anyone else who is on the line, I have come to the conclusion that my presence aboard HammerOne is not only detrimental to the rest of the crew, but also to myself. I cannot in good faith fulfill the duties of astronaut and colonist on this mission, and for that reason, I have resigned. You can direct further questions to Captain Legrand." She felt a tightness in her chest and realized she'd been holding herself rigid during her short speech.

The line was silent for a brief moment before the clamor began. Everyone spoke at once, and Ana could only make out shades of alarm and anger. She tuned it out as best she could.

"Excuse me," Martine shouted. "This is the captain of HammerOne speaking." Her authoritative tone reverberated through the speaker and, Ana imagined, throughout every room containing one of the attendees. The noise quickly fell to a hum. "We plan to go on as before. We will launch in twelve days. The rest of the crew has been notified, and Commander Mitchell's replacement has been preparing. Commander Liv Skarsgaard and I will ensure that all crew is up to speed on the relevant information."

Ana saw an incoming message from her mother, and ignored it, too keyed up to get into another argument with her. When she called a second, then a third time, Ana finally relented.

"Yes?"

She heard her mother hesitate. "I've spoken to the Board, and they agree that you should be on the ground with us before launch. And after. They want you to be in charge of communicating with the crew. You'll be here at headquarters the day after tomorrow."

Ana sighed and shook her head in disbelief. "You don't get it. You can't keep controlling my life like this."

Dr. Mitchell tried to interject. "But—"

"I quit the mission and I get to decide what I do next. Offer me the job like you would anybody else."

The line was silent.

"Fine, then I can't—"

"Fine." Dr. Mitchell's tone was brusque. "On behalf of the Hammer Corporation, we'd like to have you in the control room. So?"

Ana smiled a little at her mother's relenting. "Let me get back to you. I need a few days to address some personal matters." With that, she ended the call, and instead of switching back to Martine and the stakeholders, she sank back into her seat and listened to the sound of wheels gripping the pavement, propelling her closer to the moment she'd have to face Jolie.

She sent one more message before turning off the truck screen and disconnecting her bracelet: *Wait for me, please. XO, Ana.*

CHAPTER TWENTY-NINE

When the car finally pulled off of the highway and into Valparaiso, Nebraska, the sun had been gone for hours. The vehicle navigation system did its best to avoid the potholes that riddled the cracked pavement, but Jolie and her belongings rattled along anyway. The town was even further past its prime than she remembered, the street peppered with run-down houses and dilapidated buildings. She passed through the town center and, in the dim glow of the headlights, recognized what used to be the diner. Its broken windows caught the headlights' glare unevenly. On the right was her sister's house, her husband's rusty truck in the driveway. After all these years, he still had the same one he'd had since high school. As she rolled past, a light came on upstairs. Probably Danielle waking up to feed the baby. It felt strange to be so physically close to family she hadn't seen in several years, but she couldn't knock on Danielle's door at this hour.

Two turns off the main road brought her to the outskirts of the small town. A field lay before her on either side, and ahead she recognized the greenhouse she'd helped build, her headlights glancing off the glass. Home, at long last. She parked on the dirt in front of the ranch house. Her parents still hadn't paved the driveway after all their talk of doing so, summer after summer. Time seemed to have escaped the entire town, leaving it stuck somewhere earlier in the 21st century. A current ran deep here, she knew, drawing the residents down and carrying them until they either died or managed to escape, as she had. It pulled them just beneath the surface, eluding success and prosperity, drowning them little by little in the mundane rhythm of small town life.

As the car shut off, she saw the hallway light switch on, and the outdoor flood illuminated a path to the front door. Her mother stood in the doorway, thinner and markedly older than the last time she'd seen her. She knew immediately that she should have come home sooner. She'd missed too much of their lives. Her sister had given birth twice in the last couple of years, and all she knew of her new nephews was through videos she'd viewed indifferently on her screen.

"Sweetie, I'm so glad you're home," Iris said sleepily. She wrapped her skeletal arms around Jolie and pulled her in for a long hug. "Too long, too long."

"I'm sorry, Mom, I shouldn't have waited. You look thin. What's wrong?"

"Oh, just working hard and not eating enough."

Jolie's eyes filled with tears. Things were falling apart here. She'd stay, she had to, and help them with the farm, however long it took, until they didn't need her anymore. She closed her eyes and felt her body slip into the water already, floating with all the other townspeople toward the inevitable.

"Why don't you come in and have some tea with me, sweetie. You look like you could use a little relaxing and a chat before you go to bed."

Jolie just nodded, slinking into the house. The hallway seemed to close in on her. Had the walls become narrower in her absence? She perched warily on the edge of the overstuffed brown couch as her mother boiled water. The ancient flat screen television leaned backward from its broken base and rested against the corner across from her. Danielle had run into it during one of their games of tag when she was about six or seven, and there was never enough money to buy a new one. A pair of dirt dusted work boots had been thrown next to the coffee table, and Jolie imagined her tired father kicking back on the couch with a beer after a difficult day of work. Did he have the same bedraggled look that her mother wore?

"Here you go, sweetie." Her mother placed a mug in front of her. "Chamomile, to help us sleep." Her glasses rested crookedly on her nose, a piece of duct tape holding one side of the frame together near her temple. Iris ran a hand through her honey brown hair, streaked with gray. Jolie had inherited her own freckled skin and red hair from her father's Irish ancestors.

"Thanks, Mom." She sipped the tea and it burned her tongue. "Hot."

Her mother smiled uncertainly at her, as if one wrong move would send her packing for another few years. She set down her tea. "How was your trip?"

"I stopped in Akron on the way. Almost went to Chicago for a few days, but I decided not to." Jolie couldn't bring herself to share any more details or dredge up any difficult feelings at this hour.

"Well, we're happy you're here now. Danielle and the boys will be over tomorrow. They can't wait to meet their aunt." Iris patted Jolie's hand.

Jolie turned up the corners of her mouth in what she hoped looked like a smile. "I think I'll head to bed now. I'm exhausted."

"You just come out when you're ready for breakfast, okay? We won't make too much noise."

Jolie nodded and hugged her mom briefly before lifting her mug and turning the corner to her room. The walls remained the depressing lilac that she'd painted years ago. Her twin bed stood in the corner with its pilly floral comforter. Opening the closet, she recognized the collection of work clothes that she'd left behind. They wouldn't fit her now. She'd lost too much weight in the past four weeks. It was all a reminder of something she'd left behind long ago, something that felt foreign to her now. Her leg tingled slightly, reminding her that she was a different person with new heartaches and new goals.

She closed the closet door and sat on the bed. She sat there for a long time trying to reconcile the two versions of herself that inhabited the room. The eager and fearful college bound girl who counted the days until she could make the trip out east and start her new life. And now, the broken woman who had returned, trying to find solace in a place she had never been entirely happy.

Her eyes closed as her head hit the pillow, but she forced them open again. There was one more thing to do. *Made it*, she sent to Nova and Karlee. She received a smile from Nova, and a puzzling *good luck with everything* from Karlee. Whatever its meaning, Jolie quickly forgot about it as she fell into a fitful sleep.

❖

Something wet hit Jolie in the nose, and she groaned, the sunlight way too bright for how tired she still felt.

"Annie Joey?" a small voice asked. A fist pulled a handful of her hair, and she rolled toward the wall. The bed sank as her tormenter climbed on top of it, then onto her.

"Jimmy, there you are. You leave your Aunt Jolie alone. She's sleeping." Danielle's voice broke into her foggy head.

"But I wanna see her!" The child screeched, the shrillness sending a shiver through her. She wouldn't be able to sleep now anyway, having been awakened so effectively.

Rolling over, she rubbed her eyes and squinted at her sister, who was holding her squirming nephew.

"Hey," she said.

"Welcome home, Jo. Same as when you left, only more awful, right?" Danielle put Jimmy down and leaned over to hug her. Her long brown hair tickled Jolie's cheek. She was the opposite of her sister in almost every way. Danielle took after their once stocky mother while Jolie had inherited her slight frame and pale complexion from their father.

"Good to see you, Dani. This is the Jimmy I've heard so much about?" She directed the last part to Jimmy, and truthfully she may have heard a lot about him if she'd bothered to call her sister more often. No matter, Jimmy's face lit up and he ran with chubby arms outstretched toward the bed once more. Jolie ruffled his hair and he cozied up to her.

"If you can watch Jimmy, I'll cook you up something for breakfast."

Jolie nodded. "Sure, sounds great." Then, she remembered her mother the night before. "Wait." She lowered her voice. "What's wrong with mom?"

"Oh, don't worry about her. She's been that way ever since you missed Christmas for the first time," Danielle said matter-of-factly.

Jolie was stunned. "Why didn't anyone tell me?"

Danielle sat down on the edge of the bed and pulled Jimmy onto her lap. "What would you have done? Come back out of guilt? You clearly wanted to stay at school, and trust me, Mom wanted that too. We all watched you get out, and I can't say I'm not jealous, but I am proud of you, little sis."

Jolie lay back against her pillow. "Jesus," she whispered.

"Don't beat yourself up. Mom's already done that enough for everyone in this family. Okay? I'm getting you some breakfast."

Jolie sat up again and corralled her nephew. She checked her messages while she waited. Nothing new had come in since nine hours earlier. Unable to contain her curiosity, she checked a news feed, searching for a story about Ana's mission. It didn't take long to find one. It seemed the entire world was now abuzz over the secretive plans to launch a new crew to Mars in the next few weeks. The story was rife with speculation. Nobody knew much of anything, it seemed. Just that a ship would be launching soon from Texas. Even she knew more than that.

A wicked idea crossed in her mind. She could sell her story for a lot of money. Details were what people wanted, and she had them. Intimate details about one of their astronauts. She knew she couldn't bring herself to do it, despite how tempting it seemed. But she took comfort in knowing that she had stories Ana wouldn't want the world to know, ones that would bring Jolie's family a lot of money. After all, Ana was going to be famous, with stories about the mission, about Ana choosing a suitable partner, even having children with someone, written in the public record.

The more she read, the further she felt from Ana's life. The millions of people following the story seemed to insert themselves between them, and she could no longer see Ana beyond the crowd. She quickly put the screen away. She would just have to be careful to avoid any news at all for the next few months. After that, maybe the noise would die down.

Jimmy squirmed in her lap and she helped him down to the floor as Danielle returned with a plate of mouthwatering food. She eyed the scrambled eggs and toast hungrily.

"Dani, this looks amazing. Thanks for making it."

"Anything for you, sis." Danielle sat on the bed again as Jolie ate. "Do you want to tell me what prompted this little family reunion?"

Jolie swallowed a half-chewed bite of eggs. "It's complicated."

"Oh, good. I love a juicy story. And I've got all day."

"James is working?"

"You bet. And mom's got the other rascals in the living room. Jimmy likes to stay with me, though. Anyway, get to it. Tell me everything."

Jolie spoke through forkfuls of eggs and bites of toast. "Did you know that I moved off campus?"

Danielle nodded. "You did call me once in the past few months, so yeah, I heard that part."

Jolie ignored her jab. "I moved in with a woman named Ana. Gorgeous. Brilliant scientist. Of course, I can't pick a normal person to fall in love with. I have to pick the one who's going to Mars in a few days."

"I'm sorry. Can you repeat that? You lived with someone who's part of that Mars mission that's all over the news?" Danielle stared in disbelief. "How did they even let that happen? I thought they'd all be living together or something."

"Nope. Little old me lived with a secret astronaut. She never did tell me she was going to Mars. I had to figure it out."

"Christ," Danielle muttered. "So what happened?"

Jolie found it easier than she expected to recount her feelings. Maybe a part of her was really getting over Ana. "We were dating. I was in love with her, and I know she felt the same. But I can't compete with a one-way trip to Mars."

"So you were upset about the breakup and thought spending time in this shithole would make you feel better?"

Jolie smirked and play punched her sister in the arm. "More like, if I'd stayed in the house, I'd probably see her again, and I couldn't handle that. I had to hide until she's long gone. For good." Her face fell and she put her plate on her lap.

"You've got it bad for her, don't you. I can see it in your eyes."

Jolie sighed. "You have no idea. I just can't imagine finding someone else like her, ever."

"You will, honey."

"I don't know. It just sucks that she had other obligations."

"Like going to Mars," said Danielle.

"Like going to Mars."

"Well, I suppose if you have to have another obligation, that's a pretty good one to have."

"Yeah, for her." Jolie pushed the plate away. She wasn't hungry anymore. "Is Dad around?"

"Out in the fields, as usual. He's harvesting tomorrow, I think, so it looks like you're in for a little work."

"A little?" She chuckled. If she remembered anything from living here, it was the long hours she'd put in on the farm every spare moment she had. Between that and her schoolwork, she'd had little time for anything besides sleep. That was why, even with all the upkeep she had to help with at Ana's, she was grateful for the time she could spend sitting by the river, staying late in the art studio, or lazing about with Ana after a particularly sleepless night. That was over now. She'd have to get used to her old schedule again.

"I think he's cleaning the silos today. I saw him walking that way when we got here."

"Thanks. I think I'll go help."

Danielle got up and placed Jimmy on her hip. "You're going to regret coming back here before you know it. Oh, and Dad already brought in all your boxes. They're in the living room."

Jolie pulled on a flannel shirt and a pair of old jeans that were a little too big. She slipped into her boots and rushed out the door, barely giving her mom more than a brief hug. She found her dad sweeping inside one of the large structures.

"Hey, Dad. I'm back."

He turned at the sound of her voice. "Hey, there. Good to have you home." He embraced her for a long time, then held her at arm's length, looking into her eyes. He must have sensed her deep heartache because he didn't ask questions. "Grab a broom," he said.

She took one from the rack of tools and began sweeping next to him. Having something to do was cathartic, and they worked side by side in an easy silence. When they were done, he motioned her over to sit on a bench while he drank water from a gallon jug.

"Your mom didn't tell me much about why you came home, but you wouldn't have done it unless something threw you off. What happened out there?" Her dad spoke in his slow Midwestern rhythm, and Jolie remembered how much she missed talking to him face to face.

Jolie took a swig from the jug, passing it back to her dad like they used to do. "I fell in love with someone who was in love with something else."

He nodded. "You were never one to do something half-hearted. Just like your dad."

Jolie looked at her boots and knocked them against the bench.

"Whatever she had going for her, it's not as special as you," he said.

She chuckled. "What if I told you she's on that mission to Mars? The one that's all over the news."

Her dad put his arm around her and squeezed her shoulder. "My baby girl, in love with an astronaut. Good thing we sent you to school all the way out East where they have fancy astronauts and whatnot."

"It's not as fancy as you think out there. Actually, I might take next semester off. I think I'll stay here and help you with the farm. I know you need it."

Her father shook his head. "Absolutely not. Honey, your mom and I want you to have the choices we didn't. You can't stay here and waste away like this piece of land. Hardly get anything from it anymore. You've got to do something for yourself."

"I want to be able to help. I hate seeing you like this."

He looked Jolie right in the eye, holding her gaze for a moment. "The way you can help is by being happy. When we know you're happy, your mother and I are happy. And when you become a famous artist, you can fly us out to see your shows. Okay?"

Jolie leaned into his shoulder. "Okay. I love you, Dad."

"I love you too, sweetie. Now let's get the rest of this floor swept up." Her dad rose from the bench and made his way to the other side of the silo.

After a late lunch, Jolie was given leave of her farm duties for a few hours. "As long as you're with me all day tomorrow. Five-thirty, we start," her dad said.

She'd agreed reluctantly. At least she'd be helping put food on the table while she could. A quick peek inside the cupboards and refrigerator revealed little to eat, and certainly nothing close to the variety she was used to. If she was going to be living at home for a little while, she couldn't be a burden to the already tight budget. Between catching up on schoolwork tonight and the early morning tomorrow, there wouldn't be time for much sleep, and she couldn't afford much anyway. If she couldn't help out long-term, she could at least sacrifice a little rest to make it easier on her parents.

"I'm going out for a bit," she said to her mother as she passed through the living room. A flash of desperation clouded Iris's features for a moment, and Jolie instantly felt guilty for leaving, yet again. "I'll be back, Mom. I promise." She shut the door carefully behind her and avoided looking at her mom again.

She had the car wander aimlessly through town before directing it down a familiar road. The last time she'd been to the old reservoir, it had been a late summer evening. Somehow, she and her two best friends had known it would be the last time they'd all be in one place. They'd set off some celebratory fireworks and drank from a bottle of cheap vodka. Then, she'd left for school and, in an attempt to make a clean break into her new life, had lost contact with them. She wondered where they were now, but not enough to find out.

She ambled along the dusty reservoir lake bed. Here and there, a skeleton of one unfortunate amphibious creature or another lay half uncovered in the dried mud. Cigarette butts rested in piles along the edge, and a gust of wind sent an empty can clattering across the basin in front of her.

Jolie shivered and pulled her fleece more tightly around her shoulders. The place was eerily deserted, the few trees that lined the edges doing nothing to block her view of the fields that surrounded the former lake. She was exposed, vulnerable to the wind whipping across the cracked ground, desperate to fill the void that had begun to close during the last month, only to expand in each moment that brought Ana closer to launch time. Jolie realized that she had held onto a small hope that Ana would somehow find her way back, but now she knew for certain that she wouldn't. The launch would be final. And compared to that future, Jolie was nothing. She couldn't provide the life Ana wanted, full of adventure and importance. The finality hit her like a truck and she fought to wipe away tears mixed with wind-whipped grit. Her lungs constricted, panic washing over her in waves.

Sinking to her knees, she struggled to breathe. In a swift motion, she took off her fleece and the ISS sweatshirt she wore underneath. It was the one she'd taken from Ana, and she'd only parted with it when she was working with her father. She folded it and placed it on the ground, willing all of her pain into the garment as she slowly stepped away. Here lies our relationship. It was really and truly over. Jolie broke into a run, dust rising behind her as she put every ounce of power into running from the sweatshirt, from Ana. She was good at running, as good as Ana was, and she bolted to the car, set the coordinates to home, and traded one desolate landscape for another.

CHAPTER THIRTY

A na rubbed her eyes. She'd been in the truck for hours, and had finally just crossed into the tiny town of Valparaiso, population 208, as the sun rose behind her. Her erratic sleep schedule the last few days had left her ravenous at inopportune times, like a few hours ago when she passed through the heart of Iowa, a packet of peanuts and a gas station hog dog the only food she could find in the middle of the night. It was a little after seven in the morning now, and though she was excited to see Jolie for the first time in a month, she needed to be careful. Showing up so early indicated desperation, and she didn't want that to be the first impression Jolie's family had of her. She was, after all, someone that many, many people would have looked up to if she hadn't resigned her position. She could still stand to be respectable.

The truck slowed at a four-way stop. A closed up diner was up ahead, its parking lot riddled with streaks of grass and other weeds that had crept into the cracked asphalt. If this was the center of town, Ana didn't know how it ever sustained itself. There wasn't a single house on the street that looked like it had been built or updated in the past fifty years. Shutters hung lopsided on single hinges, paint peeled, cars rusted in front yards. A few vehicles had passed hers on the way, headed down the road toward Lincoln, but there was little other activity or movement. The town seemed to be a still life of the remnants of rural America.

Ana couldn't spend much more time driving around before someone inevitably got suspicious, so she directed her truck left at the instruction of an arrow on a sign pointing the way to a reservoir. A few miles down the road, she approached a dry lake basin. The wind on the plains was something she'd heard about, like the drought, but she'd never seen the impact of either. It was as empty as the desert she'd just come from, a melancholy, dusty haze covering the landscape. She sat in the truck as the dust from the lake bottom swirled close to the ground, sometimes flying up into a short-lived funnel. It was mesmerizing, watching it from here, and she felt the urge to walk across the fractured landscape. The lip of the former lake sloped quickly down to a wide swath of cracked mud that stretched far in one direction.

She took a deep breath of dusty air, coughing as it hit her throat. Jolie was nearby, somewhere, breathing the same air. She walked the length of the basin slowly, the sun filtering through the grit, bathing her in the ghost of an entire ecosystem that was long dead. She stepped on a fish skeleton, which made a sickening crunch under her foot. Ahead, she saw something on the ground. The closer she got, the more it resembled a torso, tossed carelessly into this lonely place. She quickened her step until she was twenty feet away, and then she saw what it was. A sweatshirt. She blew out a breath in relief, but something caught her eye. She picked the garment up and turned it over, her eyes widening. It had to be a coincidence. The front of the sweatshirt read ISS Trainee. It couldn't be, could it? She noticed a hair trapped inside, its tail flying in the wind. Its color was unmistakable. There was no question in her exhausted mind as it connected the dots. Jolie had been here. Her impatience got the best of her and she ran back to her truck. She had to find Jolie now, before another moment went by not knowing whether she'd take her back.

The truck pulled in front of the small ranch house and Ana jumped out, rushing to the door. She rang the doorbell once, and waited. She heard movement in the house, but nobody came. As she lifted her finger to ring it again, an older woman opened the door a crack. She knew instinctively that this was Jolie's mother, and Ana felt a deep ache in her chest. She was close, so close.

"Can I help you?" The woman asked, a look of annoyance crossing her face momentarily.

"Is Jolie here?" Ana asked, voice cracking.

"No." The woman sighed. "She's not here."

Ana's lip trembled.

"She's been out in the fields all morning. They'll be back for lunch in a couple hours. Can I help you in the meantime? It's quite early, you know. Are you one of her high school friends?"

Ana froze, not knowing how to answer her. "I'm—No, I'm Ana."

The woman looked surprised, then confused. "Honey, why don't you come in and I'll make you a cup of tea. I'm Iris, Jolie's mother."

Ana followed Iris into the small house, down the beige hallway and into a tidy but dismal living room. As she waited for the tea, Ana glanced around the room looking for signs of Jolie. The house felt so unlike her, everything compacted into a small space, confining to a free spirit like Jolie. Ana recognized a few boxes leaning against the far wall, ones she'd packed herself only months ago. Articles of clothing peeked from the half open lids and Ana smiled to herself at Jolie's poor packing skills.

She heard the thud of a mug placed in front of her, and looked up. Iris stared at her for a moment, concerned, then took a chair across from the couch.

"Thank you," Ana said.

"Why don't you tell me why you're here. My daughter's been very upset lately," Iris said.

Ana nodded and looked down at her hands. "Should I assume you know some of the back story?"

"Of course. Jolie said there were some secret parts, but she told me the basics."

Ana nodded and took a good look at Iris. She looked tired, in the same way her own mother did, but there was a humanity behind her exhaustion. If anything, Iris loved too hard and worried too much. "I need to see Jolie because I can't imagine my life without her. And now that I've resigned my position, I just hope she'll take me back."

Iris considered her for a long moment. Finally, she stood and crossed the room to sit on the couch. Ana scooted over a few inches to make room.

"I can't speak for my daughter, but I think she'll be happy to see you. It'll be a couple of hours yet until they come back. I think you should let them alone until then," she said, reading Ana's thoughts. She wanted to run to her now, find her in the fields, and tell her everything. Jolie was so close, but may as well have been miles from her.

It took every ounce of willpower for Ana to consider waiting, but she agreed. "Okay, I'll wait. Thank you for the tea. Jolie was always talking about how much she wanted to come back and visit."

"So she talked about us? I thought she'd near forgotten she had family at all."

Ana nodded. "She was scared to come back. I think she was afraid she'd never leave again."

Iris sighed. "Can't say I blame her." She pulled an album from under the coffee table and handed it to Ana. "Why don't you look at this and I'll fix us some breakfast."

Ana chuckled as she opened the book to a screen displaying baby pictures of Jolie. As Iris clattered around in the kitchen, she felt as close to home as she'd ever been. There was just one thing missing. She still didn't have Jolie.

CHAPTER THIRTY-ONE

Jolie wiped her hands on her jeans and jumped into her dad's truck, not bothering to buckle up for the short ride back to the house. They'd finished the morning harvest and her stomach was rumbling. A nice big lunch before heading back out to the fields was the only thing on her mind. She loved the way hard work cleared her thoughts, especially when those thoughts were about Ana.

"Whose truck is that?" Her dad asked as they pulled onto the front yard.

Jolie looked up from cleaning the dirt out of her fingernails to see a familiar blue truck parked next to her rental car. She drew in a quick breath and froze. What the hell was Ana doing here? Didn't she realize Jolie had left the house on purpose, so she wouldn't have to see her again?

Her dad looked at her. "Is that one of your friends?"

Jolie's heart raced to understand, but nothing about this made sense. She pushed open the door without thinking and stormed up to the front door, dreading the moment she'd lay eyes on her very much ex-girlfriend. As she threw the door open, she heard laughing from the living room.

"Honey, is that you?" Iris called out, much too cheerfully. "You have a guest."

She steeled her emotions and entered the room to a scene she couldn't have made up. Her mother and Ana, sitting side by side on the couch, looking through old pictures. Two empty plates and some mugs littered the coffee table. A fork had even fallen on the floor. This was not the house she left this morning, and it wasn't the mother she remembered. Ana had somehow charmed her way back into her life, and she couldn't handle that again.

Ana's hair was down and she raked it over one shoulder in a motion Jolie used to find appealing. Now, it annoyed her that Ana could sit in her living room and be so sexy when Jolie wasn't supposed to want to run over and kiss her.

Jolie caught her breath and said, "Ana."

"Hi," Ana said, meekly.

Jolie hardly noticed when her parents slipped out of the room.

"Why are you here?" She had meant for it to sound demanding, so she was surprised to hear her voice crack with sadness.

Ana stood and walked toward her, wringing her hands. Jolie's throat constricted as she recalled the last time she'd seen Ana in person, the heartbreak in the truck and the moment she walked away and heard Ana cry.

She felt tears forming and swiped at them with her palms. "Fuck. I was doing so well getting over you, and then you have to show up at my fucking house." Jolie shook her head. "Don't you get that I left so I wouldn't have to see you again?" Tears ran down Jolie's face as she tried to get a handle on her wildly shifting emotions.

"I'm sorry. I tried to call, message you, I tried everything."

Jolie barely heard what Ana was saying. "You wanted to see me one more time before you leave me again? That's fucking selfish."

"Jo, please listen."

"How can you just do that to someone?"

"Stop." Ana caught her hands and held them, looking into her stinging eyes. "I'm not going anywhere. I resigned."

"I don't understand."

"I'm not going to Mars anymore. You helped me realize that it's not what I wanted," Ana said.

"I don't understand."

"I love you, more than anything. I couldn't imagine living millions of miles away from you and being happy, so I had to resign.

I let a lot of people down, but it was still nothing compared to when I let you walk away in the first place. I don't ever want to feel that way again." Ana had subtly slipped her hands around Jolie's waist as she spoke.

Jolie couldn't believe she was hearing these words, and she was too jaded to take them at face value. Ana couldn't possibly mean what she was saying. "But how can you just walk away from your whole life? I can't give you what you want, Ana. I can't give you anything like that. I'm just one person and I'm not exciting or far away." Jolie wiped tears from her face. She found Ana's hands and squeezed them. "I don't want you to make a mistake. What if it doesn't work out between us and then you lost your chance to do something extraordinary?"

"It's not a mistake. I did it because there was no chance I'd be happy up there. Here, at least, I have a chance. Will you take it with me? Please?" Ana plead with her eyes, silently begging Jolie to jump back in. Ana pulled her closer. "Do you still love me?"

Jolie swallowed, her lips parting. Despite her reservations, the truth tumbled out. "I never stopped," she whispered.

CHAPTER THIRTY-TWO

Jolie paced the student art gallery, checking obsessively to make sure her sculptures were perfectly aligned and her drawings were in the correct order.

Nova appeared from behind a curtain and offered her a glass. "Here. Have some wine."

"You know I shouldn't drink this if I'm supposed to talk to people," Jolie said in a harsh whisper, hoping Professor Anderson wasn't within earshot.

"Look, hun. You've got thirty minutes before showtime, and you're never going to make it without a sip of this." Nova held the glass out.

Jolie took a deep breath and let it out with a sigh. "Fine. One sip."

"You look hot, by the way. Great dress."

Jolie rolled her eyes. "We all know you picked it out for me. Stop congratulating yourself." She smirked and took the wineglass from Nova.

As she was lifting it to her lips, she heard fast footsteps approaching.

"Eee! This is it! I'm so excited for you." Karlee screeched as she hugged her from behind.

"Thanks. Now, you two go do a final walk-through and see if everything looks okay." Jolie needed a moment alone to gather her thoughts before the gallery opened. Professor Anderson had confirmed the arrival of her friend who owned the gallery in Boston, and Jolie was certain she saw a local art critic milling around outside.

The chime of her bracelet signaling a new message caught her attention. *I have a surprise for you*, it said. A smile spread across her face and she bit her lip. The gallery doors opened and in walked her parents, looking completely overwhelmed and out of place. Jolie ran to them and hugged them both tightly.

"I can't believe you guys are here," she said, choking back tears. "How did you get here?"

They all turned toward the door and Ana sauntered in, wearing a simple black cocktail dress and an enormous smile.

"Can I steal her for a moment?" Ana asked, not waiting for an answer as she grabbed Jolie's hand and led her behind the curtain.

As soon as they were out of view, Jolie snaked her arms around Ana's neck and pulled her in for a long kiss that took her breath away. She was still getting used to Ana being here, especially when she saw an update from the Mars crew, currently hurtling through the darkness of space at thousands of miles per hour. She pressed her face to Ana's neck, breathing her in. She was here. She was real.

"Thank you, thank you, thank you. That was the second best surprise ever." Jolie ran her fingers along Ana's exposed upper back.

"Mmm, yeah? What was the first?"

"You know what it was. When you showed up at my house. You're good at surprises. I love you for that."

Ana slid her hands below the hem of Jolie's lacy red dress, grabbing her butt and pulling her closer. "I am good at surprises. But who said that was the surprise?"

Jolie moaned and pressed her mouth to Ana's, their tongues entwining.

"Ahem," she heard faintly. "Ahem." Louder this time, almost giving her pause. "Jolie. Ana," Nova's voice boomed. "Get your asses out here before I have to come back there, which I do not want to do."

Jolie heard some snickering on the other side of the curtain and pulled away from Ana. "I guess we should continue this later."

"Yeah." Ana gathered her into one final hug. "We have all the time in the world."

About the Author

Jane C. Esther is a librarian by day and a writer by night. Her idea of a good time involves a microscope, binoculars, trashy TV about the British royal family, or randomly singing Broadway show tunes. You can find her recounting the results of the latest scientific studies to whoever will listen, and secretly transforming her house into an indoor vegetable farm. She lives in New England with her wife and dog, and can be reached at www.janecesther.com. *The Universe Between Us* is her first novel.

Books Available from Bold Strokes Books

Between Sand and Stardust by Tina Michele. Are the lifelong bonds of love strong enough to conquer time, distance, and heartache when Haven Thorne and Willa Bennette are given another chance at forever? (978-1-62639-940-2)

Charming the Vicar by Jenny Frame. When magician and atheist Finn Kane seeks refuge in an English village after a spiritual crisis, can local vicar Bridget Claremont restore her faith in life and love? (978-1-63555-029-0)

Data Capture by Jesse J. Thoma. Lola Walker is undercover on the hunt for cybercriminals while trying not to notice the woman who might be perfectly wrong for her for all the right reasons. (978-1-62639-985-3)

Epicurean Delights by Renee Roman. Ariana Marks had no idea a leisure swim would lead to being rescued, in more ways than one, by the charismatic Hudson Frost. (978-1-63555-100-6)

Heart of the Devil by Ali Vali. We know most of Cain and Emma Casey's story, but *Heart of the Devil* will take you back to where it began one fateful night with a tray loaded with beer. (978-1-63555-045-0)

Known Threat by Kara A. McLeod. When Special Agent Ryan O'Connor reluctantly questions who protects the Secret Service, she learns courage truly is found in unlikely places. Agent O'Connor Series #3. (978-1-63555-132-7)

Seer and the Shield by D. Jackson Leigh. Time is running out for the Dragon Horse Army while two unlikely heroines struggle to put aside their attraction and find a way to stop a deadly cult. Dragon Horse War, Book Three. (978-1-63555-170-9)

Sinister Justice by Steve Pickens. When a vigilante targets citizens of Jake Finnigan's hometown, Jake and his partner Sam fall under suspicion themselves as they investigate the murders. (978-1-63555-094-8)

The Universe Between Us by Jane C. Esther. Ana Mitchell must make the hardest choice of her life: the promise of new love Jolie Dann on Earth, or a humanity-saving mission to colonize Mars. (978-1-63555-106-8)

Touch by Kris Bryant. Can one touch heal a heart? (978-1-63555-084-9)

Change in Time by Robyn Nyx. Working in the past is hell on your future. The Extractor series: Book Two. (978-1-62639-880-1)

Love After Hours by Radclyffe. When Gina Antonelli agrees to renovate Carrie Longmire's new house, she doesn't welcome Carrie's overtures at friendship or her own unexpected attraction. A Rivers Community Novel. (978-1-63555-090-0)

Nantucket Rose by CF Frizzell. Maggie Jordan can't wait to convert an historic Nantucket home into a B&B, but doesn't expect to fall for mariner Ellis Chilton, who has more claim to the house than Maggie realizes. (978-1-63555-056-6)

Picture Perfect by Lisa Moreau. Falling in love wasn't supposed to be part of the stakes for Olive and Gabby, rival photographers in the competition of a lifetime. (978-1-62639-975-4)

Set the Stage by Karis Walsh. Actress Emilie Danvers takes the stage again in Ashland, Oregon, little realizing that landscaper Arden Philips is about to offer her a very personal romantic lead role. (978-1-63555-087-0)

Strike a Match by Fiona Riley. When their attempts at matchmaking fizzle out, firefighter Sasha and reluctant millionairess Abby find themselves turning to each other to strike a perfect match. (978-1-62639-999-0)

The Price of Cash by Ashley Bartlett. Cash Braddock is doing her best to keep her business afloat, stay out of jail, and avoid Detective Kallen. It's not working. (978-1-62639-708-8)

Under Her Wing by Ronica Black. At Angel's Wings Rescue, dogs are usually the ones saved, but when quiet Kassandra Haden meets outspoken owner Jayden Beaumont, the two stubborn women just might end up saving each other. (978-1-63555-077-1)

Underwater Vibes by Mickey Brent. When Hélène, a translator in Brussels, Belgium, meets Sylvie, a young Greek photographer and swim coach, unsettling feelings hijack Hélène's mind and body—even her poems. (978-1-63555-002-3)

A More Perfect Union by Carsen Taite. Major Zoey Granger and DC fixer Rook Daniels risk their reputations for a chance at true love while dealing with a scandal that threatens to rock the military. (978-1-62639-754-5)

Arrival by Gun Brooke. The spaceship *Pathfinder* reaches its passengers' new homeworld where danger lurks in the shadows while Pamas Seclan disembarks and finds unexpected love in young science genius Darmiya Do Voy. (978-1-62639-859-7)

Captain's Choice by VK Powell. Architect Kerstin Anthony's life is going to plan until Bennett Carlyle, the first girl she ever kissed, is assigned to her latest and most important project, a police district substation. (978-1-62639-997-6)

Falling Into Her by Erin Zak. Pam Phillips, widow at the age of forty, meets Kathryn Hawthorne, local Chicago celebrity, and it changes her life forever—in ways she hadn't even considered possible. (978-1-63555-092-4)

Hookin' Up by MJ Williamz. Will Leah get what she needs from casual hookups or will she see the love she desires right in front of her? (978-1-63555-051-1)

King of Thieves by Shea Godfrey. When art thief Casey Marinos meets bounty hunter Finnegan Starkweather, the crimes of the past just might set the stage for a payoff worth more than she ever dreamed possible. (978-1-63555-007-8)

Lucy's Chance by Jackie D. As a serial killer haunts the streets, Lucy tries to stitch up old wounds with her first love in the wake of a small town's rapid descent into chaos. (978-1-63555-027-6)

Right Here, Right Now by Georgia Beers. When Alicia Wright moves into the office next door to Lacey Chamberlain's accounting firm, Lacey is about to find out that sometimes the last person you want is exactly the person you need. (978-1-63555-154-9)

Strictly Need to Know by MB Austin. Covert operator Maji Rios will do whatever she must to complete her mission, but saving a gorgeous stranger from Russian mobsters was not in her plans. (978-1-63555-114-3)

Tailor-Made by Yolanda Wallace. Tailor Grace Henderson doesn't date clients, but when she meets gender-bending model Dakota Lane, she's tempted to throw all the rules out the window. (978-1-63555-081-8)

Time Will Tell by M. Ullrich. With the ability to time travel, Eva Caldwell will have to decide between having it all and erasing it all. (978-1-63555-088-7)

A Date to Die by Anne Laughlin. Someone is killing people close to Detective Kay Adler, who must look to her own troubled past for a suspect. There she finds more than one person seeking revenge against her. (978-1-63555-023-8)

Captured Soul by Laydin Michaels. Can Kadence Munroe save the woman she loves from a twisted killer, or will she lose her to a collector of souls? (978-1-62639-915-0)

Dawn's New Day by TJ Thomas. Can Dawn Oliver and Cam Cooper, two women who have loved and lost, open their hearts to love again? (978-1-63555-072-6)

Definite Possibility by Maggie Cummings. Sam Miller is just out for good times, but Lucy Weston makes her realize happily ever after is a definite possibility. (978-1-62639-909-9)

Eyes Like Those by Melissa Brayden. Isabel Chase and Taylor Andrews struggle between love and ambition from the writers' room on one of Hollywood's hottest TV shows. (978-1-63555-012-2)

Heart's Orders by Jaycie Morrison. Helen Tucker and Tee Owens escape hardscrabble lives to careers in the Women's Army Corps, but more than their hearts are at risk as friendship blossoms into love. (978-1-63555-073-3)

Hiding Out by Kay Bigelow. Treat Dandridge is unaware that her life is in danger from the murderer who is hunting the woman she's falling in love with, Mickey Heiden. (978-1-62639-983-9)

Omnipotence Enough by Sophia Kell Hagin. Can the tiny tool that abducted war veteran Jamie Gwynmorgan accidentally acquires help her escape an unknown enemy to reclaim her stolen life and the woman she deeply loves? (978-1-63555-037-5)

Summer's Cove by Aurora Rey. Emerson Lange moved to Provincetown to live in the moment, but when she meets Darcy Belo and her son Liam, her quest for summer romance becomes a family affair. (978-1-62639-971-6)

The Road to Wings by Julie Tizard. Lieutenant Casey Tompkins, Air Force student pilot, has to fly with the toughest instructor, Captain Kathryn "Hard Ass" Hardesty, fly a supersonic jet, and deal with a growing forbidden attraction. (978-1-62639-988-4)

Beauty and the Boss by Ali Vali. Ellis Renois is at the top of the fashion world, but she never expects her summer assistant Charlotte Hamner to tear her heart and her business apart like sharp scissors through cheap material. (978-1-62639-919-8)

Fury's Choice by Brey Willows. When gods walk amongst humans, can two women find a balance between love and faith? (978-1-62639-869-6)

Lessons in Desire by MJ Williamz. Can a summer love stand a four-month hiatus and still burn hot? (978-1-63555-019-1)

Lightning Chasers by Cass Sellars. For Sydney and Parker, being a couple was never what they had planned. Now they have to fight corruption, murder, and enemies hiding in plain sight just to hold on to each other. Lightning Series, Book Two. (978-1-62639-965-5)

Summer Fling by Jean Copeland. Still jaded from a breakup years earlier, Kate struggles to trust falling in love again when a summer fling with sexy young singer Jordan rocks her off her feet. (978-1-62639-981-5)

Take Me There by Julie Cannon. Adrienne and Sloan know it would be career suicide to mix business with pleasure, however tempting it is. But what's the harm? They're both consenting adults. Who would know? (978-1-62639-917-4)

The Girl Who Wasn't Dead by Samantha Boyette. A year ago, someone tried to kill Jenny Lewis. Tonight she's ready to find out who it was. (978-1-62639-950-1)

Unchained Memories by Dena Blake. Can a woman give herself completely when she's left a piece of herself behind? (978-1-62639-993-8)

Walking Through Shadows by Sheri Lewis Wohl. All Molly wanted to do was go backpacking…in her own century. (978-1-62639-968-6)